FROM RUST

THE FORGE

FROM RUST
THE FORGE

DANIEL JAMES CLARK

Published by Vulpine Press in the United Kingdom in 2023

ISBN: 978-1-83919-513-6

www.vulpine-press.com

To Deanna, James, and Carlene. Because without you, this doesn't happen.

The Armored Soldier's Creed

Sergeant Major John Phillips, UEMAC

I am a Soldier of the United Entities Mechanized Armor Corps.

I will fight the enemy of Stability, even if it should cost me my life.

My armor is my shield, as it shields that which I love.

My armor is my weapon against the forces that would seek to destroy us.

I will fight the enemy of stability, even if it should cost me my life.

My armor is a tool in a greater machine working to defend Stability.

I am a tool in a greater machine working to defend Stability.

I will fight the enemy of Stability, even if it should cost me my life.

Stability before self.

I am a soldier of the United Entities Mechanized Armor Corps.

CHAPTER 1

Her hair. That's what had first caught his attention. The way it moved, and smelled, like wildflowers deep in an overgrown forest. Mark smiled, wholly distracted, and crashed into a ravine.

His mechanized combat armor unit tumbled down the sandy slope. The weight of the machine brought it to a halt before reaching the bottom, and the damage was minimal. He checked the displays in front of him quickly, noting a twelve percent loss of structural integrity in the right extremity, and fifteen in the right leg. His mech, an Avian class Raptor, stood thirty feet above the desert sand when it wasn't collapsed on the side of a ravine. With a high-carbon steel hull and reactive ceramic tiles, it was built to withstand a lot of punishment. That wouldn't be any kind of solace, however, if he couldn't right the thing before rounds from an enemy unit got to him. A swift movement of his hands on the holographic display positioned the rear jump jets against the ground. He engaged them, and the jets propelled the hundred-ton unit up and out of the ravine with a heavy lurch. Coming back down to the ground was a bit shakier than when operating at full efficiency, but manual compensation for the damage in the right leg was working well.

1

From behind him, a dull metallic thud echoed through his cockpit. He swung the unit around, scanning the horizon for movement. His sensor array had been hit, and his information overlay was gone. All he had now were manual controls and what he could see through the windscreen.

"Shit, where are you?" Mark murmured as he continued his frantic search for the enemy mech. His mechanized unit had been hit hard. Noise dampeners screened out most small arms fire, so anything audible was never good news. Another hit like the first one, and his mech wouldn't survive. He pulled up the last scan he'd managed to get before his senor array had gone offline and saw the faint heat signature of the enemy mech only a few hundred yards out. Another thud echoed through his small cockpit, louder this time, and the displays and controls in front of him suddenly went black, leaving him in complete darkness.

"Oh dammit, Zak!" Mark yelled as he began taking off a complicated series of cords that allowed him to pilot the mech.

Mark Alder was a tall black man in his mid-twenties with none of the awkward clumsiness that could sometimes accompany height. He ran his hand along his close-cropped black hair and pulled his headset off. He tossed it onto the darkened display in front of him and stepped out of his simulator. It was one of twelve identical egg-shaped units that lined an elevated steel catwalk along one wall of a massive garage.

Below him was the main garage of Taycher Mechanized Armor Base. The base operated as a sort of factory, training cadets on the east side in the United Entities Mechanized Warfare Academy, and manufacturing mechs on the west side. The aim

2

was to unite the two when they were complete, then deploy them wherever they were needed.

Mark looked out over the vast garage space, admiring the dozens of hulking mechanized combat armor units of various types below. Some resembled the unit he'd been piloting in the simulator. These were tall, bipedal, and equipped with a range of large-caliber weapons. As impressive as these units were, there were much larger mechs in the garage as well. These included four-legged Lupine and Ursidae class units modeled after wolves and bears respectively. A Neith class command unit, a truly colossal eight-legged metal giant that could carry vehicles and a sizeable crew, loomed above them all near the hangar doors. There were others as well, but Mark turned away as another man of about the same age exited another simulator on the catwalk.

Zakary Lockwood was wearing the same dull grey uniform as Mark, but two sizes smaller. Even this size didn't fit him perfectly. The bottoms of his pants were folded up so that they didn't drag at the heel. In contrast to Mark's broad and gregarious nature, the way Zak carried himself was calm and reserved. If he didn't want to be noticed, he had a way of slipping into the background when he needed to. His complexion was naturally pale, but the hours spent in the parade yard during formation drills had forced a tan on his skin that often threatened to bloom as a sunburn on longer days. Straight dark hair, always kept just below regulation length, accented his already sharp features.

"I don't even know what to say," Zak said, shaking his head. "You can't leave yourself open like that. What the hell even happened?"

3

"I don't know." Mark laced his fingers behind his head and looked up at the ceiling. "I was thinking about Brooke, and my mech walked into a ravine."

"Your mech can't just walk into a ravine by itself unless you point it that way to begin with." Zak shook his head in amusement as he closed the door of his simulation pod. "You should seriously engage some amount of autopilot background correction when you boot up. It's common practice these days."

"Fuck ABC. When I'm in one of these things for real, I want to know exactly what they're doing at all times." Mark gestured down to the mechs on the ground floor. He looked for Brooke down there for a moment and then back at Zak. "I don't want my unit making decisions for me."

"Sure thing, I guess we'll make sure to take deployments to massive flat pieces of land. Maybe a glacier or something." Zak laughed and shifted his gaze toward the elevators at the far end of the catwalk. "I'm going up to Rec. Five. Some of the others are headed there to celebrate before Live Piloting starts tomorrow. Maybe Turner will clue us in on what's even going to happen. Are you coming? I'm sure Brooke will show up at some point, whenever she finishes up down there." He gestured toward the mechs below.

"Maybe later. I've got some drills I still need to log before tomorrow." Mark knocked on his simulator with a closed fist and a metallic tone rang out.

"Cutting it close, aren't you?" Zak cast a stern look at Mark, then smiled as he turned to go. "Just stop by for a drink after you're done. I suck at social stuff without you, you know that."

Mark nodded and leaned onto the railing between the simulators as Zak headed for the elevator. Below him, sparks rained off the armored shells of mechanized combat armor units as technicians worked on repairing and fitting them for deployment. The sounds of hydraulic impact wrenches and welding torches echoed and faded intermittently in the cavernous space. The positioning of the simulators along this wall gave cadets at the United Entities Mechanized Warfare Academy the chance to see what they were working toward. Maybe that was the point, but sometimes Mark thought it was more like hazing, letting them get so close. After a few minutes, he straightened up and walked back to his simulator.

"Fifty bucks says you don't do it," Turner said. He was a blocky cadet with a square jaw, black hair, and dark brown eyes. He crossed his arms and raised one eyebrow, clearly thinking he'd called a bluff.

"I'll take that bet," Mark said, giving Zak a supportive smirk. "My man's got this."

Six cadets, obviously mildly intoxicated, were standing at the far end of the simulator catwalk. It was late. The evening work shift downstairs in the garage had just ended and the techs had all left early. The first of the night shift wasn't due to arrive for another hour. Lights shone from the high ceiling on each unit downstairs, looking so much like a field of slumbering giants waiting for the call to battle.

Mark and the others were all wearing the regulation grey uniforms of pre-pilot cadets. Because of the dull nature of the uniforms, personal affectations or minor modifications were exaggerated to assert an identity. Zak could often be identified by his reserved and careful movements, along with the slightly ill-fitting size of his uniform. There was a quiet intelligence in the way he presented himself, often lifting a hand slightly before he spoke to assert an almost scholastic correctness. Now, however, drink had given him a confident swagger that bordered on a stumble. Instead of his customary slight hand raise, his arm swung up like a pendulum before he spoke.

"Okay, yeah," Zak said, as he scanned the faces of the group around him. "I've got it. I do, I swear. Turn it on, boot it up, and that's it right? Yes, all right then, let's do it."

He hoisted himself over the railing and reached out for an air hose hanging from the ceiling. The cadets watching held their breath and laughter. Grasping the hose with one hand, he made a leap for the garage floor. He had hoped the hose would work like a rope for a controlled descent. It didn't. The hose wasn't locked in and began to unroll from the spool above. With a crash and a sharp inhalation of breath, Zak landed awkwardly on the garage floor. Above him, the rest of the group failed to contain their amusement, and their laughter echoed through the garage.

"Holy shit," Mark said in an emphatic whisper to the group. "Are you serious? He did it! I told you he's got this." He held out one hand expectantly toward Turner. "Pay up."

"Hell no, he's still got to boot one of those things," Turner said. "Good luck, asshole." He directed his last remark down toward the garage floor, a confident smirk returning to his face.

6

Zak limped across the garage to the closest mech while wildly checking his surroundings for mechanics, guards, or a stray instructor. He climbed up onto an older Jotun class mech using the worn metal handholds and opened the rear hatch. The sound was like a groaning metal beast in the empty garage. He cast a paranoid look around before ducking inside.

There were a few moments of uninterrupted silence, and then the cadets upstairs stared down in amazement as the external lights came to life and the engine started.

"Pay up, dickface," Mark said, turning a manic grin and the same expectant hand toward Turner.

Down in the garage, the mech powered back down and Zak stepped out, arms raised triumphantly.

"How the hell did he even do that?" Turner asked. "They're supposed to be pilot-coded,"

He fished out a crumpled wad of bills and handed them over, stunned. Mark did a short dance to seal his victory and then counted his winnings.

"Guys," Zak called from below. "Get me back up there."

Together the group used the same hose to hoist him back onto the training deck and then let it swing back into its position. Once he was up, they congratulated Zak with a barrage of back slaps and profanity before heading back to the bar on Rec. Five.

CHAPTER 2

Recreation Level Five, known simply as Rec. Five to the cadets that frequented the establishment, was dimly lit like any bar. There was a space near the center of the room where tables were routinely pushed aside to make room for the complex social rituals of youth, namely dancing and practiced looks. Mark and Zak sat at one end of the long bar talking over the constant beat of the music.

"I didn't think you'd do it, you know," Mark said after finishing a victory glass of the cheapest beer on tap. "But I sure as hell loved the look on Turner's face though. When you got it started, I looked right at him and was all, 'Pay up dickface.'"

"Hold on." Zak put his glass down on the bar with a thud. "I jump down how many feet, do something that's supposed to be impossible, and the best you come up with is 'Pay up dickface.' Are you serious?"

"I did do a little dance afterward." Mark raised his empty glass and met eyes with the bartender. "How'd you do it anyway? Not the jump. I saw that failure. I mean, mechs are supposed to be coded for the assigned pilot and crew. Only the guys with clearance can even get to the login screens."

Zak looked down at the drink in his hands. He turned it around a couple of times on the bar and then took a long gulp. He cleared his throat for dramatic effect.

"That was an early model Jotun class Aegir." He raised his hand in his scholastic way and smirked. "Those don't require anything to turn on the air conditioner and headlights, and the AC units in those things could wake the dead."

"You motherfucker," Mark said. "I knew there was a reason I liked you." When the bartender arrived with his refill, he turned to her. "Two shots of your second cheapest whiskey, please. We just hustled somebody."

~

The barracks were silent. Pale blue light flickered onto the floor out from the rows of bunks that ran the length of the room. About half the cadets were studying feverishly for their first Live Piloting session in the morning. Many others stared sleeplessly into the relative darkness.

Mark was studying using his optical display on one of the top bunks. Information projected from lenses implanted in his eyes floated by in front of him. The optics could also display directly onto the retina if desired, but having the images projected out in front of him had the added benefit of creating some light in the space around him, giving the display more depth. Occasionally he would sweep a piece of information aside with a wave of his hand or pull another in for closer inspection. Every time he blinked; the image blinked out with him. Audio was also transmitted by the implant via the optic nerve through some process

9

Mark didn't quite understand. Diagrams of control panels, graphs of power drain, short clips showing different procedures, and various other bits of information washed in and out in front of him.

In the pale light, a disorganized pile of tattered blue packets could be seen on a makeshift shelf next to him. These were his now obsolete course materials from the previous semester. When he attended his new slate of courses starting in the morning, he would need to replace these. The shelf was constructed of a cardboard box that had been stapled directly to the wall. Next to the packets were two unframed photographs.

One was of a mother, father, and three distracted children standing in front of a grey government housing unit. The home wasn't exactly a mansion, but units like it were typically afforded to low level officials. The tallest child was Mark, and in the photo, he was almost as tall as his father, though not yet as filled out. The second photograph was of a woman with long brown hair and stern green eyes. She looked like she had been asking the person not to take a picture right as it was taken.

Filling the rest of the space were several loose pieces of chalk and innumerable small paper notes. These were written in what looked like code but was just bad handwriting. One note, circled and written in red marker, read "Graduation gift!"

One of his uniforms was crumpled near the foot of his bed. He should have folded it and returned it to the locker next to his bunk, but when the call for lights out had come, he hadn't had time. He was on laundry detail that week anyway and could press it tomorrow while he did the rest.

Zak also lay awake, using his optics while facing up at the bottom of Mark's bunk. His eyes moved around in the semidarkness tracking many of the same images flitting by on the other cadet's optics. He seemed to be working faster, however. At times the images and diagrams that went by were scarcely there a moment before he swiped them away.

His bunk was sparse by comparison to Mark's. His dog tags hung on a nail near the head of the bed. They glittered blue in the low light cast by his optics. His name, Zakary Lockwood, stood out in relief letters along with other information about him. Inside another improvised cardboard box shelf, a neat stack of blue packets that looked nearly pristine was in one corner. A single wooden pencil and a pad of paper were the only other personal effects.

As the night went on, the blue lights turned off as cadets either decided to sleep or were taken there involuntarily. The myth that no one slept before their first Live Piloting session was apparently false.

A screaming, fiery explosion sent twisted metal raking into the sky. Using one of the mech's arms to protect himself from the debris, Mark blindly fired the rifle mounted on the other arm. His remaining ammunition was counted down on the display. Three. Two. One. Click. A frantic expression bloomed across Mark's face, and his masculine façade was replaced with one of

11

childlike terror. Rounds began to cut the air nearby, one after another. One struck the glass in front of him with surprising force and sent cracks radiating outward like a spider web. He turned his head around, looking for a reassuring sign that this was just a simulation, and found none. Another round sheared one arm from his unit completely at the shoulder. Alarms inside the cockpit reached a crescendo. The lights on his display became a twisted smear of color as tears obscured his vision.

Mark opened his eyes in a flash, startled to find a vivid projection of live combat still playing on his optics from the night before. He let out a cry of panic as he was treated to a few more educational moments. Struggling with his sheets, he managed to turn off the video with the correct hand movement.

"Good morning," he said to no one in particular.

Cadets had begun stirring just before dawn either from excitement or their private alarms. All but a few were awake as the station-wide morning alert sounded. A single unpleasant tone stretched on longer than it seemed it should, and Mark put his hands over his ears while he waited for it to stop. Since he first entered the Academy, he often had trouble getting out of his bunk on time. It had even been a major point of tension between Mark and Zak early on.

They had met on Reception Day, the day when they underwent the first formative steps that would mold them into pilots in the United Entities Mechanized Armor Corps. Pre-selection school had already prepared them for the rank structure, but nothing could have prepared them for the sheer physical toll of the first few weeks of training.

One particular morning had caused the initial strife between them. Their barracks group had been up late the night before performing drills out on the parade yard. The instructor, an upper-level cadet who already acted like a high-ranking officer, had them running the same repetitive marching sequences until they all got the steps of the formation right. Mark had grown tired of it and he'd said something crude under his breath. Their instructor hadn't taken it very well and they had all been instructed to continue the drills for another two hours.

When they were eventually allowed to return to their barracks, many of the cadets gave Mark sly grins of support. While many of them were frustrated at the additional drills they had run, it seemed that being the one who had mouthed off to a superior had earned him some notoriety. Zak, by contrast, had climbed into his bunk without a word and gone to bed.

When the morning alert had sounded the next morning, Mark was slow to get out of his bunk. Zak had attempted to get Mark up and ready. As a result, neither of them were completely dressed by the time a routine company inspection began. Mark and Zak were both reprimanded and ordered to spend their recreation time cleaning the mess hall that evening.

"You missed a table over there," were the first words Zak said during their cleaning shift.

"Sorry sir, I didn't realize you were my commanding officer." Mark wet his rag and then snapped it in the air, sending droplets of water toward Zak.

"If you're not going to take this seriously, get out," Zak said. "Some of us are here for a reason. Some of us actually worked to get here."

That had stung, partly because it was true.

"Hey, fuck off," Mark said. "I work just as hard as anyone else. At least I'm not some goddamn charity case."

As soon as he said it, Mark had regretted it. Zak hadn't responded, just calmly walked to the table Mark had missed and cleaned it himself. Before Mark had time to formulate an apology, Zak finished cleaning the last table and left.

Mark stood in the empty mess hall for a while, not wanting to run into Zak before he had a chance to get into bed. While he waited, he considered Zak's words.

It was true. He wasn't sure if he deserved or even wanted to be at the Academy. His parents did though, and that was what mattered. He'd been basically average when it came to academics in preselection school. His mother was a mid-level government official, however, and had leveraged some contacts to get him accepted to the Academy based on his "Outstanding Leadership Potential".

He'd led the football team on a championship run as the quarterback, sure. Mark wasn't sure that translated to the ability to lead soldiers in battle. Mark seriously considered not even returning to his barracks that night. He could have just reported to the administration building and resigned from his posting. Someone else would have been called in to fill his spot before sunrise. Eventually, even that option had felt too daunting, and he'd returned to his barracks as quietly as possible and climbed into his bunk.

The next morning Mark made sure he was ready in time for inspection. Zak didn't bother to even glance at him all day. During recreation time in the evening before lights out, Zak sat at one of the terminals at the back of their barracks room, studying whatever lesson they'd learned in tactics that day. They all shared six terminals back then, because they hadn't been fitted with their optical implants yet. All six terminals were in use, but Mark tapped another cadet named Kalen on the back.

"Hey, let me use the terminal," Mark whispered. "Or I'll tell command you're engaged in an inappropriate leader-subordinate relationship."

Kalen rolled his eyes and smirked. "You do that, and I'll list the half dozen infractions you've piled up just today."

"Okay fair," Mark said. "Really though, can I use the terminal for a minute?"

"Sure," Kalen said as he stood up. "But only because I've got a date with my inappropriate leader-subordinate relationship in Rec. Six."

Mark sat down and looked at the login screen. He took a deep breath and turned to Zak.

"Hey, Lockwood," Mark said. "I'm sorry, about what I said. I know you probably worked harder than anyone else to get here."

Zak didn't respond, simply went on studying a projected battle scene and taking notes with his pad of paper.

"You were right too. I think my parents worked some kind of deal to get me here," Mark said in a whisper. Though it wasn't uncommon, he still didn't want people to know he hadn't exactly earned his place at the Academy. "But I'm here because I

15

want to be. I thought about scrubbing out after what you said last night. I really spent some time thinking it through, and I have you to thank for it."

When Zak still didn't respond, Mark got frustrated and waved his hand in front of Zak's face.

"Hello, come in Lockwood. We've got some communication interference here. Please respond." Mark had imitated talking through radio interference.

Zak looked over at Mark and smiled briefly. "I read you, over and out."

"Let's go grab a drink on Rec. Five," Mark stood up and patted Zak on the shoulder. "It's on me, call it an asshole tax."

Mark and Zak had been nearly inseparable since that day. He liked to think that they'd both grown as a result of their friendship. Mark had committed to his studies. While he would never be at the top of the class, he took pride in being competent at something more than athletics. Zak had become less secluded and had even begun to engage in social situations unprompted.

Mark swung his legs over the edge of his bunk and hopped to the floor. Zak was already dressed and was laying on his bunk calmly staring up with the same distant gaze he'd had the night before.

"Hey, I'll be ready in just a minute," Mark said defensively.

"I didn't say anything," Zak laughed.

Much of the group was already dressed and congregating near a bunk in the middle of the long room. In hushed tones, they talked about what they hoped the first day of Live Piloting would be like. The event was largely shrouded in secrecy, and all that cadets knew before they went through it themselves were rumors and wild speculation. Turner, eager for the attention, was sitting at the center of the group. His older brother had recently graduated with high marks from the Academy and was moved immediately into combat somewhere. Because of this, the other students saw Turner as a reliable source of knowledge. After he described the grueling, but also quite exhilarating drills his brother went through on his first day, there was an extended silence.

"I heard they let you blow up all kinds of stuff," said Hogan, a lanky red-haired cadet with a habit of speaking at the wrong moment.

"Bullshit, they won't let us use live ammo on our first day," Turner said looking up at him for a moment.

"Well, why not? Part of piloting is tracking and pursuit," Hogan said without much conviction.

"They will show us all kinds of stuff though," Turner said, returning his attention to his audience. "Karl did say they let them use thrusters for a jump or two. And they got to run the agility course for time in one of the new Aves class Raptors at the end of the day."

Some of the cadets grew visibly anxious at the prospect of being expected to perform these things on the first day.

"You believe any of that?" Mark asked Zak in a hushed tone. He nodded toward Turner and the other cadets as he finished buttoning his pants.

"Not a word of it," Zak said. "But who knows, I guess."

17

Mark and Zak stood with the rest of their barracks group talking in whispers inside an empty hangar as an upper-level cadet arrived with parcels for each of them. Inside, they would each find several items. The main prize was a sleek black pilot suit. It would have a connection array integrated into it, eliminating the messy wires they'd been using in the simulators. Additionally, each bundle contained three pairs of gloves and seven standard-use daily uniforms. These were a deep crimson with black trim, a major upgrade from the dull grey ones they'd worn up to that point. On each shirt their last name and their identification numbers were printed in crisp block lettering. Also included in their parcel was another important piece, a small slip of paper with five neatly printed three-letter codes.

The younger cadets lined up in order based on their identification numbers and waited for their names to be called. Ever since they filled out course request forms a month ago, they'd been impatiently awaiting these parcels and the code assignments that came with them.

"Mark Alder," the older cadet called out.

Mark took a long, exaggerated step from the line, giving Zak a wink as he walked toward the table. When he reached the table, he pressed his thumb to a pad offered by the older cadet and took his parcel. He was directed to a locker room where he would fold and leave his old uniform and change into his new pilot suit.

Zak waited as other cadets were called before him. By the time they approached his name, Mark had already exited the locker room staring down at his assignment sheet.

"Hiroki Turner." Turner stepped out of line, took his parcel, and disappeared quickly into the locker room to change.

"Zakary Lockwood," the older cadet called.

Zak walked to the table, got his uniforms, and headed to the locker room. Before he changed, he looked eagerly at the codes on the sheet of paper. Everyone received the same two codes, P1 and T2, at the bottom of their lists. These referred to the introductory Piloting and Tactics courses respectively. The only one he was truly concerned about was the first one on the list. This was the primary armor class designation, which would determine what type of mech he would be training to use for the remainder of his time at the academy.

Zak had received the code AVI, which corresponded to the Avian class mech track. These units, modeled after the form of a bird, reflected an agility and lightness that made them ideal for advance frontline work and reconnaissance. With a cockpit shaped vaguely like an attack helicopter, two to three people could fit inside the units to maintain the various systems. The units could, and often were, piloted by a single person, however.

He took off the faded grey uniform he'd worn to class and folded it neatly. The other cadets had thrown their old uniforms in a heap near the door of the locker room. Zak held the folded uniform, unsure of what to do with it. He put it down on the floor next to the pile and returned to his parcel.

He put on the crisp pilot suit. It fit him well. Unlike every previous piece of clothing he had ever worn, the pilot suit had been made specifically for him. The feeling was somehow both empowering and unnerving. Having clothing that was made just for him made him feel like he didn't deserve them. He also felt the weight of expectation that the suit brought with it. When he'd been just another face in a grey uniform, he'd been able to disappear. Now that he would be wearing his crimson uniform daily and the black pilot suit on piloting days, he could be immediately identified as an upper-level cadet.

Zak took one last look at the tattered grey uniform on the floor and walked back out into the hangar. The older cadet had finished handing out the uniforms and stood at the back of the room with a grin on his face. Some of his classmates were elated to have been slotted for their first-choice coursework. Others were disappointed, having been assigned their second or third choices. Some even received surprise assignments they had actively feared.

"Hey, Mark!" Zak called. "What did you get for your mech designation? I'm on an Avian class track. I'd rather take a standard Jotun course, that's where all the classic models are, but this is fine."

"They put me in a Neith course." Mark stared down at his paper in disbelief. "I can't believe this. That's eight legs to deal with, and I'm still having trouble with two."

"You'll be fine." Zak laughed. "Just start training with background correction from now on. I told you you'd have to use it eventually. They must really be watching our sim logs. Hey, at least it means they see some command potential."

A large door at the far end of the hangar opened slowly from the ground up, letting in a rush of crisp morning air and a blinding amount of sunlight. The cadets quickly lined back up and stood at attention, facing the door. Outside, through the glaring morning sunlight, they could see a mech positioned on cracked asphalt. Facing this class of thirty was their first mech. In the harsh light, it appeared to them as a gleaming and agile piece of equipment. They imagined it, two stories tall, laden with lethal power, and ready for them to take control. As their eyes adjusted to the light, however, reality came into focus.

The thick armor plates, those that were still attached, were corroded and looked to be held on primarily by grime and rust. The glass around the cockpit was cracked and scratched, but intact. One arm was completely stripped of everything but the frame, and the other arm ended in a useless knot of wires. On the lower half, a significant amount of green moss had grown on one side, presumably whatever side was facing north.

Their eyes then focused on a figure standing beside it. An older man who looked a year or two past retirement limped toward them. He appeared disheveled and unshaven, with his grey hair poking wildly from underneath a faded hat. As he got closer, the eyes hiding in the shadow of the brim became clearer. They were a piercing but milky blue and darted around with determined, searching intent. His eyes landed on each of the new cadets as he approached.

"I'm not going to bother taking roll," he said as he reached them. "It's safe to assume that every last one of you is here. Is that right?"

"Sir! Yes sir!" An awkward, but loud eruption of sound came from the group of cadets.

"Quiet down!" he yelled, rubbing his head beneath his cap. "I've got a hangover and I don't need any of that."

There were some quick glances to the side from many of the cadets, but training held firm, and no one said a thing.

"Now that we have that rule out of the way, I'll go on. You will call me Sergeant Major Phillips or Sir. Either that or Screwdriver if I become drunk enough in rec time."

Phillips looked out at the cadets, lingering on Zak for a moment, and then moved on.

"This mech is a piece of shit. I know that." Phillips waved toward the mech behind him. "Whatever it can do, you're allowed to do with it. If it walks you can walk it. If it jumps, you can jump. What you ultimately get to do with it will be as a direct result of your ability to make it work."

The older cadet at the back of the room let out a small laugh, and Zak realized why he'd been smiling before. He must have known that the class was getting this disappointing mech.

"You, the short one," Phillips pointed at Zak. "What were you expecting from today?"

"Just what I've been told sir," Zak said after a moment of hesitation. Earlier in his life he would have shut down even at this mild joke at his expense, but now he continued on. "That we would be piloting a mid-to-high-level mech with the most advanced controls and abilities, Sir. To prepare us for the units we'll eventually pilot in the field."

"Thank you, Lockwood," Phillips said, apparently reading the roster from his internal optics. "Now, I'm pleased to be the first to tell you that everything you've been told about Live

Piloting is bullshit. It's a little joke you get to be in on now. Yes, it's a scrap heap. But now it's yours."

The class was introduced to their mech, a very early model Jotun class Orion. Designed to roughly emulate the human form, it was meant to lumber along the battlefield while firing, occupying a similar role as a traditional tank. These units were the workhorses of the Mechanized Armor Corps. This one had, according to Phillips, been pulled from a swamp during a major conflict on the southern border after the Decline. He asked that they note the line on the hull which showed how far it had been submerged. It was then reconditioned and briefly brought back into service for a few months. But, when a similar mech of more recent casting needed a replacement set of armor for its right arm, this one had given an offering. The mech had been slowly pieced out. What remained had been left in a lot somewhere where it had baked under sunlight and soaked in rain until its recent assignment to Educational Service.

Mark chanced a glance at Zak and whispered. "Looks like you'll get to practice with a classic model after all."

Zak shushed him quietly and kept his eyes on Phillips, who was still sizing up each of them as his eyes darted around the group. A long history of first impressions had taught Zak that not attracting attention offered him the best opportunity to remain in control of situations.

"Eventually you'll name the goddamn thing," Phillips said, turning to look up at the rusted ancient machine. "Just don't call it the Phoenix. It's not original.

"You'll each go, one by one, into the cockpit and attempt to boot the mech yourselves. While each cadet cycles through,

23

everyone else will walk around the unit creating a log of whatever you think is important. A loose bolt, rodent damage, rust, missing pieces, whatever. Lockwood, you're up first. I hope you were paying attention."

Zak stepped out of line, uncomfortable at being the first to enter the mech, and walked out of the hangar to the mech outside. The rest of the class fell in behind him. He climbed up around the back of the unit and opened the rear hatch with some difficulty, making a mental note to add 'stiff door hinges' to his own log. Once inside, he noted that at least the airtight seal hadn't been compromised. The air was stale, but not unpleasant, like entering an attic that hadn't been visited in a while. The controls and the seat all looked to be in good condition. The cockpit was not very large. It reminded Zak of being stuffed inside a small pantry by older children in one of the homes he'd lived in when he was little. As he examined the cockpit in silence, he heard someone else mount the ladder behind him. Phillips' silhouette was framed in the tiny doorway.

"Good luck, Lockwood," he said, and then slammed the hatch.

The sudden darkness was temporarily all-encompassing, and Zak felt a twinge of panic before he saw a faintly glowing outline around the power panel just inside the door. He flipped the three switches and then pressed the button below them. This should have turned on the battery power. As confirmation, a second panel lit up at the front of the mech. He moved around to the front of the seat and sat down, sinking into the worn padding. The controls in front of him were minimal, as the startup procedure hadn't been initiated yet. Zak pressed the button to raise the blast shielding, hoping to get some more light in the cockpit, but only a loud whirring answered his commands. He added this to the growing list of concerns he had about their new mech.

If he were booting this unit for an actual mission, there would have been another person sitting at the impossibly small sensor and communications console near the rear hatch of the mech. He didn't bother strapping himself into the chair harness for now, as he didn't expect to be moving the mech much. The panel asked him for his pilot number and to remain still while the connection array in his suit was identified.

Zak swore under his breath as he remembered he hadn't even activated his connection array. He pressed a thumb to his right temple to turn on his optics, and then placed his gloved hands on the terminal in front of him. This brought up a screen that allowed him to key in his Pilot Number, 127-546-DNJ. Nothing happened.

The moment stretched on. Zak began to wonder if the startup systems even worked when the displays suddenly came to life. The interfaces keyed into his optical implants, displaying information directly onto his retinas. A curved flat panel in front of him lit up, and the cracked windshield gained more numbers and readings than Zak knew what to do with. Most of these were displaying readings that were red, flashing, or both red and flashing. These warnings alerted him to what the mech seemed to perceive as catastrophic damage. The blast shielding inside the mech finally retracted, allowing Zak to see out the cracked front glass for the first time.

Outside, Mark examined an exterior floodlight as it flickered and faded in like a candle catching a flame. The engine inside the main body of the unit rumbled and sounded vaguely ill, but the metal hulk seemed to have new life. The unit itself assumed a more aggressive stance as the innumerable shocks and pistons were brought out of retirement. The legs equalized and flexed at the joints slightly.

The cadets surrounding the mech took a few steps back and looked on in awe. For many, this was the first time they had ever been this close to active mechanized combat armor. Dust, caked on from years of dormancy, cracked and fell to the ground. The resulting scene was reminiscent of an ancient rock beast animating itself.

"Some life in her yet," Phillips said. "Who's next?"

At the end of their class, Mark was given the honor of walking the mech to a large hangar out in the practice fields. It moved in spastic jerks that released more trapped grit and rust as the rest of the cadets followed it. Mark was disappointed that they hadn't been given a new mech, but with every lurching, unsteady step forward, he became more attached to their assigned unit. It was their first mech. It didn't need to be perfect. They would work on it and turn it into something special.

Once it was inside the hangar, the cadets headed back toward the base, walking across the expansive desert field they would eventually use for live drills when Phillips got to that part of their coursework.

Turner, already sore from harassment, was not in a good mood and walked alone behind Mark and Zak. He'd made a fool of himself for weeks relaying the lies his brother had told him. Mark fell back into step with him and nudged his arm.

"Lighten up, they got all of us," Mark said. "Don't get me wrong, I think it's hilarious. And I'll probably still give you crap, but we all believed it, man."

"Sure," Turner ran a hand through his short black hair, turning a rare smile toward Mark. "Now we get to mess with the younger cadets. Keep the tradition alive." Turner broke off, and walked briskly back into the main group, waiting for a way back into the conversation.

"Why do you placate him?" Zimmer, a broad chested man with a dark beard and darker eyes asked.

"Because…" Mark thought for a minute and laughed. "I honestly don't know. He'd probably kill me in my sleep for my position if he could."

Jakob Zimmer was their barracks leader. They had elected him in their first week at the Academy, and Mark had made the mistake of running for second in command. Turner had also run for the position.

"He's not that desperate," Zimmer said. "You'll probably kill yourself first doing something stupid. Got time to meet the rest of us on Rec. Five tonight? We're celebrating inheriting that piece of shit back there." He jerked his thumb back toward the training hangar, a lone building out in an expanse of desert.

"Can't," Mark said. "I've got a date one level up."

"Want me and Kalen to join you guys?" Zimmer asked. "He's been bugging me for a date night too."

"Maybe next time," Mark said. "She sounded all serious, said we needed to talk."

Zimmer had made a face like he'd stepped on a live wire and put up both of his hands.

"Never mind, forget I asked," he said, and patted Mark on the back. "Good luck with whatever that's about."

CHAPTER 3

Mark was sitting with Brooke Parvata at a table in Rec. Six. The lighting was brighter than the bar on Rec. Five and the music was almost inaudible. Here it was merely background noise to guard against complete silence. The room was what amounted to a combination lounge and mess hall used for a wide range of purposes. The tables were of varying sizes, ranging from large ten-person rounds down to two-person tables lining a large window that served as one wall. The view was either spectacular or mundane, depending on the viewers' concept of beauty. At ground level, far below, the grey paved grounds ran for a half-mile to the high walls of the base. These walls rose as high as five stories in some places and were made of the same dull grey concrete as the rest of the base infrastructure. Beyond the walls was a vast ocean of desert sagebrush currently blooming with innumerable golden flowers. This ended at a jagged shock of muted red, purple, and orange mountains on the horizon. These mountains, somehow, amounted to a rich brown when taken in collectively.

Brooke, a thin woman with olive skin and dark brown hair, sat with Mark quietly at one of the tables against the window. Her uniform was a deep green, indicating a technical education track. It was made darker by the countless oil and grease stains she'd collected during her work on the mechs in the main garage. Mark had his optics on and was paging through correspondence, waving his hand as soon as a message panned in.

"I never get tired of the mountains here," Brooke said. "I mean, just look at them."

Mark put his palm down on the table and then swiped across the surface. This gesture closed his mail application, and he looked out over the landscape. "Beautiful, sure."

"I'm serious Mark. I spend all day with a welding helmet over my head." She made the rough shape of the tiny glass window in her hood with her fingers for emphasis. "This is a great relief from that."

"They're big piles of brown rock. Like shit, but bigger." He laughed at his joke.

Brooke didn't. Instead, she looked at him fiercely, the same face captured in the photo Mark had in his bunk. "Fuck off. I think they're pretty." Her face softened with a smile, and that was the end of the argument. "You know I'm headed for deployment after graduation. I got my preliminary orders today. Avian tactical unit in the north. Something about a rumored encampment of radicals. Gets me closer to home too."

"Not my favorite topic of conversation," Mark said. "Let's talk more about mountains."

"You can't ignore it forever Mark," Brooke took one of his hands and sighed theatrically. "We're star-crossed lovers doomed to be torn apart by forces greater than ourselves."

"Don't be dramatic," Mark smiled and squeezed her hand. "I'll ignore it until I can't anymore."

"Seems healthy." She laughed but gave Mark a look of concern.

Mark avoided her gaze and instead looked out the window. He thought about the first time they'd met. She had been one of his barracks chaperones when he had first arrived at the Academy three years ago.

One morning before they all headed out to their courses, they'd been called into an empty classroom. When they all lined up for a uniform inspection, Brooke had looked over the group and stopped when she saw Mark. She stepped forward and immediately began adjusting various aspects of his uniform.

"Did you even read the uniform regs?" Brooke had asked. She was a year ahead of his class and had been tasked with keeping them in line while they got settled into the routines of the Academy.

"I skimmed them." He looked down at her briefly and then thought better of it, returning his eyes to the front of the room. "I mean I read some of it, sir."

"I'm surprised your pants aren't on backward." She pulled one of his lapels to straighten it and adjusted his cap to make it sit flat on top of his head. Then she lifted his dog tags, which had been dangling in front of his dull grey jacket.

"Cadet Alder," she read his name from the dog tags. "These are to be worn inside the uniform at all times." She used a finger to pull his collar out and dropped the tags to hang inside.

She stood back, looked him over briefly, and frowned. Then she turned away and headed back toward the front of the line of cadets. As she did, her long hair had whipped up momentarily, nearly brushing across his face.

She smelled like the Earth, a deep floral scent that had taken him out of the room and to someplace far away. Immediately, he wanted to know more about her, and his eyes became more alert than they'd been before.

"For a first-time uniform inspection, this wasn't too bad," she had said. "But you should all know that failing one of these for real could mean real trouble for you in the future. Study up and soon it'll be something you could do in your sleep."

She'd dismissed them to head on to their coursework, and they'd all left the room quietly.

The look she'd given him during that inspection was the same one she had on her face now. It said, "There is more to discuss here, but I suppose it can wait."

He smiled and changed the subject. He knew she was headed for graduation at the end of the semester, but he wasn't ready to address what that would mean for them. Besides, they had the rest of the semester to figure it out.

"Did you know they give pilot cadets a piece of junk mech for Live Piloting?" Mark asked.

"Yeah," Brooke laughed again, this time more genuinely. "I didn't want to ruin the surprise. I hear yours is a real piece of work too. Let me know if I can do anything to help you guys get it done in time."

"I'll let the others know," Mark said. "You could have given me a hint, you know?"

"What? And rob you of this rich tradition of disappointment?" she said. "You'll get it working soon enough. And you've got the rest of the training fleet out in the hangar to train with until you've got yours up and running anyway. Chess?"

"Sure," Mark said. Brooke had beaten him every time they played. Once, he'd asked her why she didn't let him win once in a while. She had said that would rob him of the joy he would feel when he did beat her someday. Mark had said that that argument only worked if he was able to beat her someday. "I should practice my tactics before I head to that class tomorrow anyway. Anything I should know about that one? Are they going to drop a bucket of oil on us to continue another rich tradition?"

"Not that I know of," she said. "But even if they were, why would I tell you?"

They keyed their optics together and projected a chessboard onto the table between them. Together, with occasional laughter, they played game after game as the sun set brilliant fire to the horizon.

It was around lunchtime, and the barracks was mostly empty. A few cadets were in their bunks catching up on coursework or rest. Mark was laying in his top bunk and Zak sat up in his below.

"She likes mountains," Mark called down. He was staring up at the low ceiling with a distant grin. "She thinks they're pretty."

"You hate mountains," Zak said from below, smiling but never taking his eyes off a form he was filling out with his optics.

"I know, but she likes them. And she's already pre-slotted for an Avian class technical assignment," Mark said with an airy sense of awe in his voice.

"You *also* hate tech work," Zak spared a glance up toward his friend, imagining his look of frustration.

"That's not the point," Mark said. "What are you doing down there anyway?" He leaned over his bunk and glanced down at Zak's projected optical display.

"The update forms. I figure I'll get them out of the way now before we get really involved with classes." He checked off a box indicating that there were no changes to his religious orientation, then confirmed his lack of affiliation on the next screen.

"Those always freak me out," Mark said. "Next of kin, where to send personal effects, all that crap. Like they expect it to be useful while we're in school or something."

Zak grunted his agreement as he swiped past those fields, leaving them blank. He wondered what might happen to his personal effects if something did happen to him at the academy. Presumably, some lower-level cadet would come and clean out his locker. But where would they go with them next? The most logical place to go with them would be the administration building. After that, they might sit in a box for a while.

After some amount of time, maybe the box would be opened. The uniforms, with no one to deliver them to, might be cycled

34

back into circulation. Or perhaps the entire box would be thrown away immediately.

"What do you have planned for tonight?" Mark asked. "Anything boring or tedious you need me to rescue you from?"

"I was going to come back after I finished my classes and archive my files from last semester. Then make new ones for the new classes. Maybe get a head start on some of the readings for tactics."

"Absolutely not," Mark said. "I hereby forbid you from doing any of that boring shit. It's the first week of class. Nobody expects us to get anything important done. Let's go to Rec. Five and see if we can piss Turner off or something."

"Sure," Zak smiled and went back to the next of kin form. He filled in Mark's information for who they should give his personal effects to. He didn't have very much, but if anyone should have the option to keep any of it, it should be Mark.

After lunch, Zak walked into a round auditorium with about forty desks facing a wall-sized display panel behind it. Cadets were checking in at a small lecturer's desk down at the front of the room and leaving with blue packets of material. At midnight the night before, cadets had been given digital access to the files they needed for their classes, but having a physical packet always seemed to make it more real. He walked down to the bottom level and stepped into line. On the broad display wall, a single line of text read, "United Against Terror: A History of International Domestic Terrorism." The class, according to the description available in the catalogue, aimed to "Analyze the roots of the biggest threats to Stability following the Decline."

When Zak reached the desk, he pressed his thumb onto a pad to sign in. He exchanged a nod with the man sitting behind the desk and took one of the offered packets. He turned and made his way up a few rows into an open seat close to one wall. From here he was able to see well but wouldn't be singled out easily from the crowd. Zak knew many of the people in the classroom and exchanged a polite wave with a woman he'd had in a Gov-NET Systems course previously. There wasn't anyone he knew well enough to sit with though. Instead of talking and joking with his peers, he flipped absentmindedly through the materials. Words, phrases, and diagrams drifted by as he turned the pages.

A preface said something about the origins of "The Great Shift" and several images stuck out to him as he skimmed the packet. One image showed a group of protesters on the original Wall Street in New York, burning something that looked suspiciously like a human body hung from the neck. The humanoid figure was wrapped in something and suspended from a street-light. On another page, a graph showed the sudden spike in anti-government groups that had congregated and organized on un-secured digital networks before the Decline. Another image depicted police in riot gear. A very early mechanized crowd control unit could be seen in the background.

Zak looked at this image for a while. The police were pushing through what looked like a massive temporary encampment. The light mech resembled the much larger units in use today, but only in form. He knew that the armor used by this crowd control force would have been flimsy by comparison. The controls would have been clunky at best, resembling construction equipment of the day. The offensive capabilities would have been even worse, but the units had a place in history. Indeed, without them, the Mechanized Warfare Academy wouldn't exist. And, if the school's understanding of history was to be believed, the Decline would have resulted in a complete societal collapse.

This image was as far as Zak got before the large display on the main wall changed to a graphic of a timeline. The teacher, a man with glasses dangling from a gold chain on his chest, stood to address the class.

"Good afternoon, and welcome to History of IDT. I am Professor Kamal. I don't plan to waste your time, so do not waste mine." He paused to scan the room, seeming to search out anyone that might be a problem student. "Please either key your optics to your desk or open to page six in your packets."

The sound of rustling paper and cadets shifting in their seats rose and then faded gradually. Professor Kamal took his glasses and cleaned them with a small cloth removed from a shirt pocket until the class had quieted completely. He let his glasses dangle once more at his chest.

"This first class will bring you up to speed on some history you should already know," Kamal leaned back on his desk and spread his arms wide. "However, experience has taught me that a surprising number of you do not even have a grasp on the basics of how our current social and political structure came to be.

"On the screen behind me is a timeline ranging from the beginning of the last century, up to the Decline. Marked along this line are the formative points of inspiration for many groups which would eventually become the backbone of the so called 'revolutionary movements' still currently operating across the globe. In your packets, this information corresponds to the Preface and Section One."

Zak looked back down at the image of the crowd burning a body. These early groups were what eventually led to the rise of the Harbingers of the Fall, a particularly hard to eradicate group that incorporated a broad range of tactics and people. Zak had spent a lot of time researching the group during his time at the academy, and this course would offer him the closest look he'd had yet at the way they operated.

"We see the first two major conflicts over here at the beginning of the last century. Don't feel the need to take notes on any of this yet. I just want you to know what the political climate was like in the time just before the Decline."

Zak, unable to help himself, had already pulled out his pencil and was taking notes on the pad of paper he had brought with him. The notes were more to help him maintain attention. He often found himself drifting away on currents of thought if he didn't actively engage with whatever was being taught.

"The first events in the overarching conflict are often regarded by historians as stemming from a series of initial attacks perpetrated against the former United States. What began as a conflict in *response* to an attack slowly transformed into a conflict waged in *defense against* another attack. The distinction hardly matters to the boots on the ground, but it greatly affected the way in which the conflict was managed at home. A steady decline in the stability of governments worldwide led to the

formation of new and dangerous alliances, and similarly dangerous chasms of antagonism.

"The political temperament worldwide was a powder keg of
loose alliances, understandings, truces, and deep-rooted animosity. Fears of an international war were on the rise, and citizen
groups were growing more distrustful of their home governments the world over. This was not simply a passing phase for
these governments as you should, hopefully, already know."

Zak looked around the classroom and saw many of the cadets
nodding in agreement. One or two, however, seemed to be paying very close attention to the lesson. He wondered if his note
taking made him look like one of the uninformed, and self-con-
sciously put the pencil away and sat up in his chair.

"This is the climate in which many broad shifts in power occurred. A relatively short period of peaceful protest and then violent uprisings led to drastic shifts in the political organization
of governments in several key countries. These new and hastily
reformed governments were soon deemed incompetent by many
of the same people who had installed them."

As Professor Kamal spoke, he brought up images of protests
and conflicts in chronological order along the timeline. Zak recognized most of them from the social integration courses he'd
taken in his preselection schooling. A few of the images were
new to him, however, showing some of the more brutal aspects
of the Decline. Most of what they showed in preselection school
was sanitized and ubiquitously optimistic. These, however, were
much more grim. He got the sense that these images were only
available to them because they were in an advanced social studies
course.

"In short, that was the state of the world as dissident groups within the United States began to mobilize. This movement, peaceful at first, showed the first signs of a coal fire deep underground. An animosity for authority that crossed traditional political lines was burning and was nearly impossible to put out by the time the full measure of it was known. Once this fire eventually reached the surface in the form of the Harbingers of the Fall, it brought about the Decline. This period of chaos very nearly led to the full collapse of our mother nation and with it, the world as a whole. Concentrated organizational power from corporate entities, paired with the might of government-led military and infrastructure allowed for the strategic defeat of these radical forces. The tactics employed to maintain Stability, and the eventual formation of the United Entities, are what we will be studying in this course.

"In our next class, we'll be taking a closer look at how the original peaceful movements splintered and eventually initiated the Decline."

As Professor Kamal finished talking, an image familiar to many of the cadets appeared on the screen. In it, a green street sign was laying on the asphalt with one boot obscuring the first letter of "Wall Street." In the background were a riotous crowd, burning buildings, and blurred bodies. On a tattered black and white leaflet poking from underneath the downed street sign was a single line of text: *"BRING DOWN THE WALL"*

The image was often carted out during any discussion of the Decline. It had become emblematic, the way images often do, of the day that terrorists violently occupied and destroyed much of the New York Financial District. It had also come to represent the broad destruction that followed not only in the United States, but also around the world.

"That's all I have." Professor Kamal turned the screen off. "Short class today, please do not get used to it. I want you to read the preface and study the political climate that led up to the Decline before we meet again. I won't be covering today's history lesson in any further detail. The rest of the course will deal with the Decline itself and the intricacies of how it was reversed, how Stability was ultimately achieved. If you feel confident in your knowledge, feel free to skip this assignment. However, I am allotting each of you thirty minutes of CorNET time to access the archives should you choose to use it."

Zak picked up his packet, and with a deft gesture of his free hand, keyed his optics off the desk. He left with the rest of the cadets. Corporate Network time was valuable, and not often granted to cadets. Even if the class skipped the assigned reading, the professor could be sure that each of them would use their allotted thirty minutes for something.

Mark sat along the back wall of a small classroom. The room was nearly full but only held about fifteen cadets. The front wall had a display panel that wasn't being used. The cadets instead had their blue packets open and listened to their instructor as she spoke at the front of the class. Her name was displayed as Vice Admiral Katherine Scholl on the front of the packet. This was the only course she taught at the Academy, as she spent most of her time as the school's superintendent. She wore a crisp dark teal officer's uniform, in contrast to the faded and frayed one that Phillips had worn during their Live Piloting class. Stepping from behind her desk, she began walking back and forth as she answered a question asked by a cadet.

"To answer your question simply: no. This isn't a class about tactics as you'd normally think of it. The course title 'Application of Tactical Analogies' refers to the theory that analogies, when applied, have a high statistical likelihood of being accurate further than initially intended. While this concept does have practical applications on a battlefield, it's not the only place it can be used. Put simply, analogies can serve as tools for working out problems. It sounds simple, and that's because it is in many ways. But, if you're trained specifically to think this way, studies have found that reasoning skills in high stress situations are greatly improved.

"For instance." She stopped pacing and leaned back against her desk. "This is a fairly common example used to explain the principle. Let's say you compare an incoming force of enemy troops to a wave. The theory this class works with says that the properties of a wave can be even further analogous to the incoming force of enemy units if the analogy is explored fully.

"The math, and the studies that support this assertion, aren't exactly riveting, but the results can be. In the wave example, we can posit that the incoming force will behave in a fluid way, and therefore what happens in a fluid might also happen with the incoming force as well. If we block the center of a wave, the two sides will spill to either side of the obstacle."

Scholl mimed these fluid examples with her hands as she spoke. She clearly cared about the subject, and it was apparent that there was a reason this was the only class she taught.

"After that, the wave may spread out again once around the obstacle. However, if you were to block two outside edges of the incoming wave simultaneously, it may cause the wave to gravitate inward and bottleneck. Applying this idea to the incoming force, you can create a strategy that is easy to convey to your subordinates: Concentrate fire on the sides and draw the enemy in toward the middle. Then, once they've bottlenecked, concentrate fire in the middle."

Scholl pushed away from her desk and returned to her chair. Mark imagined the scenario she described. In it, he was on the command deck of a massive Neith class command unit with more controls than he knew what to do with at his fingertips. The enemy forces she talked about were numerous, and he had to convey to the other mechs under his command what to do. He shook his head to clear the image. He wasn't quite ready to accept his mech designation yet.

"This course will prepare you to think critically in high-stress situations," she said. "Your traditional tactics courses will focus on more standard tried-and-true themes and will teach you many of the same methods we'll discuss here. This course, however, will allow you to link those common methods in ways that are new and innovative. It also aims to help you work through those new problems which have no proven solutions."

Scholl finished speaking and looked over the class, examining the look of stern confusion on many of their faces in apparent amusement. She used the display panel on the wall behind her for the first time. A new block of text filled the screen.

"Aside from the example given, how else might the properties of a fluid make an analogous comparison for an advancing force of enemy troops?"

"I expect a thorough response on any of the ways you might expand this example. It will constitute a significant portion of your overall assessment, so be sure of it before you turn it in. The deadline for this is the end of the course but you may submit it earlier if you wish.

"There are entire dissertations on applying fluid dynamics and wave theory to group behavior, so I expect that I'll have some well-thought-out responses to look forward to." She made a few movements on her desk and transmitted the assignment. "You're dismissed."

CHAPTER 4

After class, Mark walked the floor of the massive main garage space. Around him, the fleet of armored giants slept. Most of the units in the main garage were new, or at least recently retrofitted with the newest technology. Every unit was slightly different, modified to suit the pilots and technical teams who operated them. One day he would be in one of these machines, deployed somewhere to help defend Stability. He looked up at them and marveled at the myriad pistons and joints that gave them life. The dormant power of a fleet this big was intoxicating. He imagined being part of a large core of mechs, pushing through enemy forces and securing some valuable outpost.

Ahead, he saw the familiar shape of Brooke working high up on her mech, a sleek Avian class unit. She was slated to deploy officially with it after she graduated later that year.

She wore her welding helmet, and a periodic shower of sparks rained down on the concrete floor where they bounced and eventually disappeared in the darkness. He liked to watch her while she worked, though he technically wasn't supposed to be down here. There was something about her concentration that was special. It was as if she slipped into a separate reality, simultaneously more and less complex than the one he inhabited. He spent a few moments looking up as she finished a weld. She stopped and flipped up her welding hood. She scrutinized the result, looking for some flaw that might need mending, biting her lip and leaning in to get a good look at her work. Her welding torch cast soft warm light onto her face, and Mark admired the look of stern concentration that bloomed into a smile when she evidently decided she was satisfied with her work. She reached up to pull her hood back down.

"Hey, you're late!" he called up to her before she could start another weld. "We were supposed to meet in Rec. Five an hour ago."

"What?" Brooke let go of her hood and looked down. "Oh shit, I'm sorry. I just need to get this done. I completely lost track of the time."

"This thing looks immaculate. What the hell else could even need to be done?" he asked as he looked over the mech. It truly was one of the most stunning pieces of machinery in the garage.

"Well, for starters, command updated a couple of the parameters on what we're likely to encounter once I head out. So, I've got to get the hull reinforced for burst plasma and not a direct beam. And you know they've always got some update for the Isolation Protocol.

"On top of that, some cadet assholes tried to boot one of the older units the other day, so they've got us putting *padlocks* on all the doors." This last remark she punctuated with a wink.

"Okay, okay. I get it, lots to do." Mark laughed. "I guess I'll take the heat for that last bit, too. Come down here so I can give you a present."

"Sure, why didn't you open with that?" Brooke swung off her platform and, using footholds on the mech itself she must have remembered by reflex, deftly climbed down. "What'd you get me?"

"Don't laugh, okay?" Mark said, putting his hand in his pocket. "You know how you've got that coin collection you don't like anyone to know about?"

"Sure. No idea where this is going, but yeah I still have it in my bunk," Brooke said.

"Well, I know you keep a coin for the important moments in your life." Mark removed something on a short length of chain and held it out.

"I was sort of hoping the day we met might make the cut for one of those moments. This one's got that year's date, and I figured you might not be able to take your whole collection with you when you go. Maybe this can help serve as a reminder for all of them too, but mostly of me, I guess. And, I'm going to miss you, see. A lot. And I think I'm rambling."

"You done?" Brooke asked.

"I think so, yes," Mark said.

"I love it." She reached out and took the necklace from him. She immediately put it on and then held it up to look at it more closely. "You even drilled a hole in it. You know that's illegal, right? Defacing currency."

"Well, you're dating a serious badass," Mark said. "Committing crimes in the name of love and all that."

"I love you too, Mark," Brooke said.

Zak headed straight to one of the specialized CorNET stations on the third level of the library building. It was a small brightly lit room with screens integrated into three of the four walls. These screens projected information around the user in an immersive environment that was directed with hand movements in much the same way that his optical display was. However, this room was set up specifically for access to the CorNET and wasn't physically linked with the GovNET network that his optics and the rest of the base operated on.

The unsecured networks in use before the Decline had been weaponized beyond usefulness, and existed now only in small pockets that were frequently used by terror organizations like the Harbingers of the Fall. The three major networks engineered after the Decline, GovNET, CorNET, and CivNET, had been designed to be incompatible with one another to establish a more secure platform for society to build an information system.

Zak logged into the CorNET station with a username and password, followed by a relatively antiquated handprint analysis. Once logged on, he was presented with projected icons for the programs he had been given access to. The icon he was expected to use for his assignment was a simple triangle, the logo for information conglomerate Delta Sieve. Information was valuable, and companies like Delta Sieve that survived the Decline often charged a high premium for verified data and analysis. Other icons gave access to various entertainment libraries and other programs. He'd gotten there before any of the other cadets from his class to make sure he got one of the available slots. Zak reached out, tapped the triangle icon, and the screens around him presented the user interface for Delta Sieve.

A simple search bar hovered in front of him, awaiting his first input. He was confident in his knowledge of Pre-Decline political tensions and didn't plan to study exactly what he'd been assigned. The information Zak was most interested in, current mech designs and theoretical research into advanced weaponry, were undoubtedly off limits to him. There were ways for him to find research that would be at least moderately interesting, but it would still need to fit within the scope of his search limitations.

He input a search, 'Mechanized Weapon Technology Pre-Collapse', and a projected web of research papers populated the air in front of him. Good, this subject fell within whatever limits his professor had set. Zak scanned through the web, looking for anything that sounded interesting. Related documents had lines that connected them, so it was easy to narrow the search as he navigated.

From the web, he selected one paper titled "Mechanized Weapons Technology Evolution: A Comparison Study of Modern and Initial Designs". When the document opened, he was presented with an abstract that went over the main points of what was contained in the document.

"While mechanized combat armor units today work well in a vast range of combat scenarios, designs were initially meant to cope with violent uprisings inside the United States. Their use in these fields was successful, but experienced limitations in their size and firepower.

"These first mechanized weapons were relatively lightweight from a modern standpoint, consisting mainly of ballistic plastics and lightweight metals. Early units were meant to be worn by a pilot and used to clear public areas of rioting civilians. They were intended to be an upgrade from the cumbersome riot gear typically used in crowd control situations to that date.

"The armored suits were eventually fitted more aggressively and used in tactical police operations as well as overseas combat zones.

"Those that used them soon found that the units were slow and had a travel radius much smaller than that of equivalent firepower trucks and tanks already in use. These initial MCA units also lacked the maneuverability required for dynamic and changing scenarios. For these reasons, the units were used infrequently until innovations in robotics technology made them viable assets.

"The beginning of the Decline also marked a dramatic shift in energy alternatives. These new power systems were small enough to power the larger mechanized weapons demanded by the military as the chaos of the Decline continued. The design and implementation of advanced new mechanized weaponry are largely credited with the success of campaigns against various terrorist groups during the Decline.

"This study gathers relevant information following the evolution of design and use of mechanized weaponry from inception into the modern era. The study also pulls relevant historical data on the real-world tactical applications of the machines to provide a broad understanding of the history and composition of mechanized weaponry."

The abstract was interesting enough. Zak wished it focused more on the current state of the technology, but a lot could be learned from studying the past. With a hand movement, he moved the projected article into a file to request it for transfer. GovNET was a closed network, but files could be transferred manually from one to the other following a rigorous process that involved manual human transcription. The only thing he had to do was place it in his transfer file. If it was approved, it would show up in his personal files later.

Taking a chance, he spent some time trying to push the limits of his search parameters. Several searches regarding more direct queries for information about current and experimental technology produced no results. Just as his allotted time had nearly elapsed, he caught the thread of something at the very fringes of his access. He found a paper titled, *"Theoretical Applications of Gravitational Lensing on Airborne Threat Vectors."* Zak opened the abstract and read what he could as a small timer ticked away the seconds. The paper seemed to describe highly theoretical gravitational wave generators and how they might interfere with or even destroy military targets. Zak wasn't sure why he'd been able to access it, but the concept was very interesting.

He dragged the paper over to the transfer request file and then went back to see what else he could find as a related topic. But, before he could try another search term, the screens went dark. His time was up.

"I think that all sounds fine." Mark sighed deeply and rubbed his eyes. He was sitting with Zimmer at a small table at the back of the room in his barracks. The lights were out, and the rest of the cadets had turned in for the night already. "I honestly don't know why we have to do this every week. Why don't we just have some sort of rotation set up? If anyone needs to change their duty assignments for the week, they can submit a request."

"That's a great idea," Zimmer said. "You should draw something up and submit it to me for approval."

"Oh dammit," Mark pointed at Zimmer and smiled. "I knew I should have kept my mouth shut. Fine, I'll have something for you by next week."

Mark had thought that being Zimmer's second in command would be a good way to boost his resumé with minimal effort. He'd been mostly correct in assuming the job wouldn't be very demanding. His only real complaint was the late-night meetings where he and Zimmer assigned duties to each of the other cadets for the week. Occasionally they would have to schedule or plan some larger event as well.

Mark looked down the long room at the two rows of bunk beds. His bed seemed to be calling him, and he looked at Zimmer with what he hoped were adequately pathetic and tired eyes.

"Fine." Zimmer was engrossed in something on his optics and waved his hand dismissively at Mark. "Go to bed. I can take care of the rest of this."

"Did the requisitions for our camping trip come through?" Mark asked with a wink.

Zimmer smiled and pulled up a document with his optics and it floated in the air where Mark could see it. At the bottom, he could see that it had been approved two days before.

"Why didn't you tell me?" he asked. "Everyone is going to be thrilled."

"More fun this way," Zimmer said with a shrug. "Consider it a reward for getting me a concrete duty assignment schedule."

"Sold," Mark said. "This will be the best schedule you've ever seen."

"Just make sure I get it before next week," Zimmer said. "And don't go giving yourself or Zak all the light duties either."

Mark looked down the rows of bunks and found Zak. He was still awake, studying with his optics. The blue light from the projected diagrams and papers flickered in the darkness. He wondered how Zak managed to function on so little sleep. Even on the nights when Mark had to meet with Zimmer, Zak was always still awake when he went to bed.

"You can clock out," Zimmer said. "You look like you're going to fall asleep in that chair."

"Thanks," Mark said and stood up.

Zimmer continued with whatever task he was engaged in, and Mark shook his head. He also wasn't sure how Zimmer managed to keep up with all the work of maintaining order in their little group, but he was good at it. Mark wasn't sure if he would be able to do it, if he ever got the chance.

When he got to his bunk, he took a quick look at what Zak was working on. He was sitting up in his bunk studying something about the history of mech design. A dozen or more projected schematics were open in various positions around him.

"Gonna build one yourself or something?" Mark smirked and put his hand on the ladder up to his bunk.

"I just like to know how things work," Zak said distantly.

Mark knew he wasn't being short with him on purpose. Zak simply disappeared into his studies in a way that could look like he didn't care. By tomorrow he would be rattling off the most interesting statistics and facts from the projections in front of him. Mark looked forward to those conversations, so he left him alone. He always learned a lot just by listening to Zak recount all of it.

"Can't wait to hear about it, man," Mark said and climbed into his bunk.

Smoke billowed from a point on the horizon. Turner was driving an open-air armored truck rapidly down an uneven dirt road, cresting a hill in a plume of dust. Shielding his eyes from the sun, he looked out at the horizon as the rest of the cadets in the vehicle amused themselves.

"It's just up ahead!" Mark yelled from his position, standing in the back of the vehicle. He pointed grandly in the direction they were headed and took a long, exaggerated, drink from a bottle.

"No shit!" Turner yelled from the driver's seat. He gave the wheel a good tug to put Mark off balance. Zak reached up from the backseat to punch Turner in the arm, and then turned to make sure Mark hadn't been left in the dust behind them.

As the truck cleared the next rise, the source of the smoke became apparent: a bonfire with a dozen or so trucks and cars parked around it. They were about thirty miles from Taycher approaching a group of locals holding a party in the desert. While not technically allowed to partake in the kinds of activities bound to occur at such an event, the cadets were authorized to check out vehicles and camping equipment for use during longer stretches of recreation time. They also hadn't technically been invited to this event, but previous excursions of this nature had yielded positive results.

The truck arrived with its load of cadets and skidded to a halt, bringing up a cloud of dust. Mark was the first to hop out and survey the scene. Many women, some too young to be considered, glanced approvingly at the new arrivals. The local men cast glances at one another and straightened up at the prospect of new competition.

The sounds of the party died down only momentarily before festivities began at a higher pitch than before. Many of the locals knew these cadets and welcomed them with a beer or a handshake. Mark approached a rough, bearded man in his late twenties, sitting on the tailgate of a truck, and shook his hand.

"Jim, how has everything been?" Mark asked.

"You promised you'd bring ladies the next time we saw you," Jim said. "Looks like a truckload of assholes to me."

"On their way, Jim." Mark took a homemade beer offered from a cooler. "You know, makeup and all that crap. One of them is with me. So, don't go picking before I've pointed her out."

As if on cue, a second truck came over the closest rise carrying a group of female cadets. Driving even more dangerously than the men's vehicle, they gained a significant amount of altitude as they crested the hill. The change in the crowd of locals was the inverse of the first arrivals.

"Gotta lay claim before your boys get any ideas, Jim!" Mark pushed away from the tailgate and walked over to the new truck.

He approached Brooke as she stepped out from the driver's seat. Mark gave her a brief and calculated kiss as she shut her door.

"Fuck you." She scanned the crowd and sighed. "I was hoping to get a bit of fun in before you marked your territory."

"Am I that obvious?" Mark asked, giving her his practiced crooked grin.

She rolled her eyes and turned away from him. "I'm getting a drink. From the taste of your mouth, I've got some catching up to do."

~

The party was filled with music and laughter. Groups formed, broke, and then formed again, like the ebb and flow of a social tide. A group of cadets and local men took turns jumping over the roaring fire. It went well until one cadet found that his legs weren't as long as he'd hoped and fell backward. The resulting burn wasn't serious and was remedied with a cool beer in the offended hand.

As the night stretched on, an occasional duo was missed from the party. Rumors flew like sparks and were remembered a dozen different ways by the next day. In some memories, Zimmer slipped off into the night with Kalen. In others, they slipped off twice.

~

"Wait. So, you're serious?" Jim asked loudly, taking a step away from Zak. It was late and the party was dying down, so his tone immediately drew the attention of those around him. "Never? You have *never* been in a *real* fight?" He took another dramatic step back, drained the remainder of his beer, and tossed the bottle into the fire. "That's okay, you're trained. You'll do fine."

Jim lunged at Zak. Having had a bit less to drink than Jim, Zak dodged smoothly and took a few quick steps out into the open desert. He laughed and motioned for Jim to come at him.

"Bring it, farm boy." Zak winked at him.

"Fuck you, Officer Bitchass." Jim pursued him with a smile on his face as the crowd took notice and gathered around the two. Some appeared more concerned than others. The most concerned was Mark, having just returned from relieving himself behind a truck.

"What the hell is going on?" he yelled to anyone who would listen.

"Fight!" blurted a man with only a cursory understanding of the situation. "Jim's gonna' kick the shit outta' your cadet boy."

Before anyone could correct the misunderstanding, Mark sprinted at full speed toward Jim. He landed a kick square in the small of Jim's back that sent him sprawling in the dust.

"Ah, god!" Jim rolled over and climbed back onto his feet. "Who the hell?"

In an instant, a rift was torn between the cadets and locals. One local, who worked with Jim in a repair shop, broke from the crowd and headed for Mark. Zak was paralyzed by confusion, and looked from face to face, sizing up his options.

"Herm, it was a joke!" Jim yelled at his friend, but it was too late to stop what had already begun. Several smaller skirmishes had already broken out among the crowd, most of them verbal. These were short-lived, as the fight between Herm and Mark quickly became the main attraction.

Herm laid a solid punch into Mark's chest. Instead of pulling back from the blow, Mark leaned into his assailant, pushing him to the ground. The flurry of kicks, punches, and dust was cut short when Zak, finally breaking from his paralysis, managed to reach in and pull his friend out of the fray. Unfortunately, Mark thought he was being pulled back by an enemy and retaliated by sending an elbow into Zak's ribs.

"Joking, it was a joke." Jim approached with his hands up, palms out, in a sign of peace. "Everyone calm the hell down."

This seemed to have an immediate effect. Mark turned to Zak for confirmation and saw him nodding in agreement while holding his ribs. Unaware of the peace treaty being forged, Herm scrambled up from the ground and again headed for Mark. Zak saw the danger, stepped in between the two of them, and made Herm an unwilling participant of a collision between forearm and face. Dazed, Herm took a wild swing and missed everyone completely. His second attempt was less clouded and connected with Zak's jaw. The two fell to the ground yet another scuffle of violence.

"Ah, fuck's *sake*," Jim said, holding back laughter. "It was a joke!" He threw his hands up in defeat and stepped away from Zak and Herm, pulling Mark along with him. "He'll get his first fight after all, I guess."

Herm was fully committed to the moment and was unmoved by the increasing shouts to stop. Zak, laying on the ground with his forearms up in a defensive position, blocked one blow from Herm and then another. Then he charged up, got an arm around Herm's midsection, and shoved him back into the dirt. He rolled into a kneeling position and pressed his arm into Herm's neck, catching an incoming punch with his other hand.

Now Herm began to take stock of the situation. He turned his head and saw Jim and Mark standing off to one side. Evidently, he saw that no one else was fighting. Indeed, they were all smiling and drinking together again.

Zak released the pressure on Herm's neck and stood up. He offered Herm a hand to help him up, which he accepted. The two spent a few moments catching their breath, checking for blood, and dusting themselves off.

"Skinny little privvie's got some fight in him, eh?" Jim laughed, looking approvingly at Zak. He walked over to Herm and handed him a fresh drink. "We've got to work on your form man."

It was quiet, and what was once a sizeable blaze was now a pile of ash and embers. Zak, complete with fresh bruises, was using a long stick to turn the few remaining pieces of wood in the fire. Jim stood close by, warming his hands. Mark was laying with his head in Brooke's lap. She stroked his hair absently as they all listened to the radio in Jim's truck as it played a soft, classic song from before the Decline about coming home.

Most of the civilian trucks and other vehicles had made their way back up the road toward Tonopah, leaving only three vehicles behind. Only one of the cadet's trucks remained. A mixed group of cadets had headed back across the desert to the base just before midnight.

"So, when do you guys finish up?" Jim asked, gesturing around at the remaining cadets.

"I finish up in about four months," Brooke said. "I'll be in the field long before our pilot boys here."

Mark, coming out of a semiconscious state, mumbled something about mountains, then grew silent again.

"Yeah, about a year for us," Zak said, looking up from the fire over at Mark. "I'll make sure that asshole doesn't kill himself."

Silence washed back over the group, and the soft crackle of the dwindling fire occupied the night. Jim looked uncomfortable. He began to say something and paused, gathering the words from a half-drunk haze.

"Be careful, when you do get out there." He gestured vaguely to somewhere distant with one hand. "I don't really like much of who filters through here. I don't like a lot of things these days. But you guys, just be careful."

Zak nodded, and after a few more moments of silence, the soberest members of the remaining group began gathering their friends to ferry them back through the darkness, and get them home.

CHAPTER 5

A news program played along one wall of the bar in Rec. Six. The cadets sitting and talking during their free time paid little attention to it, as what was normally background noise droned on. Mark, Brooke, and Zak were crowded around a small table drinking coffee and discussing their various lessons and progress in their fields.

"So how does this sound?" Mark asked and closed his eyes, trying to remember something. "Supposing that a group of enemy forces can be assumed to have an analogous relationship to a liquid, we can also posit that applying force at the front of a column will cause compression. This compression can be exploited by targeting the areas where there are more forces."

"Isn't that the same thing your professor said, but with different words?" Brooke asked, with a smirk.

"Hey, it was either that or talk about how maybe freezing a liquid might translate into a battlefield analogy, but I couldn't get that to work," Mark said.

"That's actually not bad if you think about it," Zak said holding up one finger while he collected his thoughts. "If you think of immobilized and densely packed units as your 'ice' in that analogy, you could apply 'heat', bullets and what have you, to cause it to 'melt'. It's not perfect but it's better than just restating what was already said in your class."

"Oh, I like that," Brooke said excitedly. "Maybe think about how when something freezes, the particles will lose kinetic energy. They don't move as much. It could be like mechs that haven't been activated or soldiers who are asleep. Low kinetic energy."

"That's great," Zak said leaning in. "So, when forces 'melt' maybe the 'heat' would be more closely linked to awareness, not bullets and all that. So, what happens if you apply heat in only certain areas? Hey, Mark, this could work."

"What would I ever do without you two?" Mark had leaned back and watched them work on the idea as soon as he'd given the prompt.

"You knew we'd work it out, you jerk." Brooke smiled and pushed him lightly with her shoulder.

"Leadership is ninety percent delegation of duties," Mark said and laughed. "Anyway, thanks. You're right, that's a lot more interesting than my other idea. What are your courses looking like Zak?"

"They're fine. A bit dry so far, but I did get some CorNET time a while back to do some research. They denied one of my document transfer requests though," Zak said. "Actually, they didn't even acknowledge that I'd put in for it, which was weird."

"What was it?" Mark raised an eyebrow. "Ten Most Boring Things to Do With CorNET Time? I swear, you're given time on the CorNET and you use it for research?"

"Leave him alone Mark," Brooke gave him another gentle nudge. "He's got actual interests. What would you have done with CorNET time?"

"I certainly wouldn't have spent it looking up research papers for one thing. You know they've got all the…" Mark stopped talking as Brooke held one hand up to quiet him.

She pointed at the display wall as a red band scrolled along the bottom. A startling image was displayed above it, and a gradual silence crept around the room. The image looked like the ones they had all seen from the time of the Decline, but this one was new. A large building was completely engulfed in flames and the headline, *"Breaking News: Explosions Rock New Wall Street in Washington"* scrolled across the bottom of the screen.

Someone must have noticed and turned the volume up a bit, and all conversation died completely. The practiced rhythm and even tone of a reporter's voice could finally be heard coming from the display.

"…today. At this point, it is not known whether or not the attack was carried out by domestic or foreign agents. All that we know at present is that multiple explosions have occurred on New Wall Street, causing major damage to at least two buildings. No casualties have yet been reported as the plaza was closed for the weekend some hours earlier."

"The buildings affected include the Office for Civil Complaint, and the trading floor of the Securities Exchange. Authorities close to the situation, who asked not to be named because they are not authorized to comment, confirm that preliminary investigations point to the prolific domestic terrorist group known as the Harbingers of the Fall. For a live update, we turn to Jamie Colbourne who is at the scene of the attack. Jamie."

"Thank you, Don," a reporter said as the feed switched to a live view in front of a police barricade. Behind the reporter, a thick plume of black smoke rose from a building as numerous fire truck ladders poured water down onto it.

"The scene here is frantic," the woman continued. "Rescue crews are attempting to get close to the buildings behind me to begin their effort to put out the flames. They have yet to ascertain if there were people in any of the buildings when the explosions occurred.

"A local CorNET server building was also one of the targets. Because of the local disruption this has caused, we are only able to broadcast through an unsecured channel. At any moment we may disconnect."

She turned away from the camera momentarily and nodded as someone talked with her from off screen.

"Now we are being told to move back by Civil Defense Enforcement. There is fear that another explosive device may be hidden somewhere nearby."

Almost as if in response, another explosion bloomed in the background. The reporter fell to the ground, and the camera operator followed her down. The camera impacted the ground but continued broadcasting. The screen showed only her lower half as she lay on the ground. Her audio feed was still connected, and her frantic updates came through clearly.

"Another explosion! Maybe two blocks away, I'm not sure." She paused for breath. "Crews are moving us back Don! I have to leave."

The sound of her microphone hitting the ground was followed by the news feed suddenly cutting back to the newsroom. The shocked anchor shuffled his papers and coughed.

"More on this harrowing story as it develops, and we try to get back in touch with our sources in the field." He turned to face off screen and began asking what to do.

A commercial break interrupted; a dancing sponge fired a beam of light that burned away dirt from a tabletop. Mark, Brooke, and Zak all began talking at once. The rest of the room erupted with conversation as well.

"What the hell is happening?" Mark asked. "I thought the Harbingers had been contained."

"I don't know," Brooke said, still looking at the screen. The advertisement continued to allege that it cleaned better than any other. "There hasn't been an attack like this since I was a kid. The seed bank attack. I think there are still some species of plant we haven't been able to bring back from that."

Zak looked furious; his eyes focused down on the table in front of him. He gripped his drink between his hands so tightly it could have cracked the glass. "Maybe we can graduate in time to take these assholes out."

"I'm sure we will Zak." Brooke broke her gaze away from the screen and looked at the others. "Don't worry, we'll all be out there soon enough."

"You're getting a head start though," Mark said. He looked at Brooke with concern and made an effort to push past it. "Just make sure you leave some for us to handle when we get out there. I can't have you hogging all the glory. It's not our fault we were born a year late."

"I wouldn't be surprised if there was nothing left of the Harbingers before I'm even able to graduate." Brooke's eyes were fixed on the screen as she waited for coverage to return. "An attack like this is way more than I thought they were capable of. I thought we'd almost wiped them out."

"It's what they do when they're cornered," Zak said, barely audible through the din of other cadet's conversations. "They kick out like wounded animals."

Before Mark could ask him if he was okay, the red banner on the screen returned, cutting off an advertisement for a personal massager. The newscaster looked more composed and had set his face with what Mark assumed was supposed to be a reassuring smile. The man's eyes were concerned however, he could see fear in them.

~

"Try it now!" Hartley, a strong cadet with her sleeves rolled up, called down from her position on top of their mech. She gripped a large wrench in one hand and held on to the mech for support with the other. The mech's right arm made a jerking, but mostly controlled set of movements. A significant amount of chalky red rust fell out in the process.

"We have arm calibration!" Kalen called from inside the cockpit.

The class let out a communal cheer, gathered around their project. What was once a barely serviceable assemblage of parts had become an almost fully operational unit. The left arm, which was in the worst shape to begin with, was nearing completion now. With some tweaks to the calibration parameters, it should be working smoothly in just a few hours. The mech, which was now neatly stenciled with the name "Cronus," looked unlike any other in the fleet. While it still retained the general shape of an early model Jotun class, namely its vaguely humanoid bipedal frame, they had modified it with a patchwork of armor and weaponry from other models and classes of mech.

The more critical areas, the ones surrounding the core, were taken from a massive Neith class command mech. The cadets made up for the added weight by using lightweight Avian class armor in other less critical areas. When the cadets finished restoring the Cronus and presented it in two weeks, it would join the ranks of the dozen or so training mechs they used frequently during their real world-combat simulations. Also two weeks away was the annual graduation ceremony for older cadets. None of the cadets in Mark and Zak's class would be graduating, of course, but the ceremony would mark their ascension to the final stages of their education at the United Entities Mechanized Warfare Academy. It also meant that many of them would have to say goodbye to good friends, and in some cases lovers, who were graduating and moving on.

The mech continued making movements as it calibrated to commands from Kalen in the cockpit. The tweaked design specifications on the Cronus weren't unprecedented. Customizing a class mech had been the way to prove skill and ingenuity throughout the years, and many of the mechs in the training fleet were unique. One class had installed lift packs on the eight-legged Neith class mech and named it the "Maratus" after a particular species of jumping spider. Unfortunately, that alteration only allowed it to jump a few times before the propellant was exhausted due to the sheer mass of the unit. Still, it was always a thrill to engage jets on something that big.

Many classes also made more subtle design changes, such as a hidden compartment in a cockpit chair that fit a cigar and lighter perfectly, or a cup holder where there really should have been one anyway.

At the base of their mech, while everyone else was admiring the efforts to calibrate the arm, Mark was in an animated discussion with Zimmer. He was trying to convince Zimmer on the merits of installing a coin-operated condom dispenser, lifted from an old, abandoned bar, inside the cockpit of the Cronus.

"It takes up too much room, and it's pointless," Zimmer said. "And the condoms in it are expired anyway."

"It's about making this thing ours, with its own sense of personality and identity." Zak chimed in, turning away from the calibration to help Mark's case.

"And it's funny!" Mark insisted. "Get it? It's a cockpit. And condoms are for…"

"Yes, we get it," Zimmer relented. He rolled his eyes and threw up his hands. "Cocks. Condoms. Hilarious, just put the thing in and shut the hell up."

"Hooray!" Mark replied and was subsequently unable to be persuaded out of it.

The sun rose over the ridge that surrounded the base in the distance, bringing the practice field into stark contrast. Mark was sitting in the pilot seat on the command deck of the Maratus, the eight-legged command mech. He examined a recent scan of the area ahead of his mech and found what he was looking for to the north. Two heat signatures stood out against a relatively cool image, faint but definitely there. The signatures were positioned behind a large outcrop of rock. It was not easy to hide in an open battlefield like the one they were in, but the outcrop was one of the better positions available.

Mark's mech was impossible to hide, but the point of the exercise for his team wasn't to hide. In their final assignment from Phillips, Mark and his crew were supposed to defend a single truck idling down below them from the rest of the class piloting four of the smaller mechs.

He positioned two of the mech's massive legs close together, shielding the truck from any rounds that might come from the new heat signatures' location. He had a small crew with him on the command deck. Zak was at the weapons station near the back of the command deck, and Hartley was closer to the front at the sensor and communications panels.

"You see them, right?" Mark called back to Zak and pointed to the outcrop on the sensor image. "Get the main gun targeted there and get ready to fire at anything that tries to come around it."

The main gun on top of the mech was like something taken directly from the deck of a battleship. It could move independently of the mech's heading, and they felt the rumble of it as it swung into position overhead.

"Mark we've got incoming," Hartley said from the comms and sensor station. "How the hell did we miss them? It's like they came out of the ground."

Mark looked at the fresh scans and saw two mechs coming at them from the east. Zimmer and his team had been preparing for this exercise for a week prior to the exam, and Mark was seeing the result of that preparation as it unfolded. As he turned the mech to face the new targets, yet another pair of units came up on scans from the west.

"I thought we only had four enemy units in this drill," Mark said, trying to sort out the situation quickly. "Just fire on the outcrop and get the gun turned behind us to the west. Hit them as fast as you can and get turned to the east. If we can time this right, we can have them all down in less than a minute."

The gun on top of their mech blasted a shot toward the outcrop. Mark didn't see the impact because he'd already started turning toward the two units to the east. While Zak positioned the main gun behind them, Mark began acquiring a target lock on one of his new targets. The moment he had a lock on one, he let loose a barrage from the forward-mounted guns. An explosion of green paint indicated he'd hit one of them, and it fell to the ground, disabled. The other enemy unit let loose a barrage of paint-filled rounds and then slipped behind a rise in the earth, disappearing from his direct line of sight. One of the massive legs he'd positioned to protect the truck took a direct hit from the barrage, sending red paint cascading into the air around his mech. It buckled instantly, having been disabled by the training program.

The mech's systems made an automatic adjustment and stopped the unit from pitching forward into the ground.

"There's that automatic background correction I've been telling you about." Zak laughed as he continued to get the main gun oriented. "I told you it would come in handy!"

"Worry about gloating later and take care of those units behind us," Mark grumbled. He glared at the ABC light that had come on and saved the mech. The gun on top of the Maratus fired again and he refocused on his displays.

"Direct hit on the targets to the west," Zak called out. "Both units are down. I'll get the main gun ready for whenever our last target shows up again."

Mark felt the main gun move to intercept the final mech that had disappeared behind the hill ahead of him. There was nowhere for the unit to go, except out into the wide sagebrush field, so he held his ground and waited.

Out the front windshield, a thin white smoke began to rise from the desert sage. The smoke thickened and blossomed, slowly overtaking the entire field of view.

"Still no movement from those rocks to the north," Hartley said, shaking her head. "It must've been a diversion."

"Zimmer is never going to let me live this down," Mark said. "Do you have any new scans, where's the last unit?"

"I lost it, but it's got to be out there somewhere." Hartley examined a fresh scan and zoomed in on an area with some confusing heat. "I don't know what I'm looking at here, Mark. There's heat everywhere out there."

"Just look out the front glass." Mark's eyes darted around the landscape, looking for movement as the smoke continued to thicken. "They started a brushfire. A goddamn smokescreen. Where are you, asshole?"

For what seemed an eternity, nothing but the slowly rising smoke moved. Then, a fast-moving Lupine class on all fours bounded from the wall of smoke directly for them. Mark fired the forward-facing guns at the same time as Zak let a round out of the gun up top. The Lupine mech made a sudden change in direction and avoided any direct damage. It managed to close the distance to only a few hundred yards before releasing a burst of rounds toward the truck below them.

A second shot from the gun up top caught the enemy mech mid-stride and the explosion of green paint indicated another direct hit. The Lupine class mech went down, pulling up a cloud of dust. Mark turned around to the others with his arms in the air to celebrate their victory. He was greeted not with elation but despair on their faces.

"What?" he asked, slowly lowering his arms. "We got them, right?"

"That last barrage got the asset." Hartley tapped one of the indicators on her sensor panel and pulled up a status report on the truck below. A red light flashed, indicating that it had been hit. "We lost."

"Shit!" Mark shook his head. "We were that close. How did they get around us like that?"

"I don't know," Zak said. "But I sure as hell want to find out."

"Thank you, cadets." Phillips' voice came over the radio. If he was impressed or disappointed, his tone didn't betray it. "I'll have your final evaluations available by the end of the day today.

Please put out that fire before it becomes a problem, Zimmer. All of you return your units to the training hangar and make sure to get them cleaned off."

"Losers clean," Zimmer said over the radio with a mocking tone. His mech righted itself and bounded over to the source of the flames. With some short work, he trampled them out. "I'll see you guys tonight in Rec. Five. And, before you get all bent out of shape, we set off some flares behind the rocks out there and dug some trenches last week. Just because tactics are old doesn't mean they're not still useful."

"Oh, goddamnit," Mark said to his crew. "That can't be legal."

"You're just mad you didn't think of it," Zak said as he powered down the main gun. "Let's get back to the hangar before the paint dries on these things. I don't want to be cleaning them all day."

With courses ended and many cadets preparing for graduation in the morning, Rec. Five was teeming with vibrant and excessive personality. That night, the secret spaces on base, those dark corners without surveillance, were booked until dawn. It was even rumored that Phillips was known to take the night before graduation off from his usual rounds. Cadets would fail to check in at their barracks. The night held one last chance before friendships were torn apart. Before relationships, private and public, became nothing but memories and a string of decreasing correspondence from afar.

74

Brooke leaned against a tall table in the back of the bar, illuminated only by a small candle. She sipped a drink and watched in amusement as Mark and Zak, roaring drunk and riding a wave of confidence, tore through the bar, half-blind and half-blurred in an attempt to get Zak laid.

"He's fine, look at him," Mark said to a woman, a petty redhead, possibly too sober for much of the happenings in the bar that night. "He told me, yeah. He told me like three weeks ago that you're at least the fourth hottest person on base." A confused expression came over Mark's face. "You know, it sounded like a compliment when he told me. Zak, tell her like you told me."

The woman, Rooney her uniform said, raised an eyebrow and turned to Zak. He looked as if he were brand new to the conversation.

"Well?" She asked him and leaned back on the bar. "How *did* you say it to him?"

"Well yes." Zak stood up straighter and looked her in the eyes. "What I said was that you're super hot, and that, uh. You know I don't actually remember what I said." Then, suddenly regaining perspective, "No, no. Yeah. What I said was that you're hot like the sun. Like there's all these moons and planets and asteroids and stuff, but you're like a *sun*. All fire." Zak paused, losing his words again, and instead mimed flames by flailing his arms.

"Exactly!" Mark said. "That's, well, that's basically what he said. I'm just going to leave him here with you if that's all right."

With that, Mark motioned the bartender toward Zak and Rooney. He mimed a drink and pointed to the two of them before grandly stepping away. Once he was separated from the two of them, he looked across the room at Brooke who was quietly applauding his heroic victory. In jaunty strides, he walked over to her and leaned against the table. He waved his hands over the candle flame, letting the flames touch his fingertips, and then looked up at Brooke.

"That should keep him busy for at least four minutes," Mark said.

"Four? I don't know that he'll even be awake four minutes from now." Brooke gestured at Zak with her glass.

"Well, then we'd better get out of here before he comes back." Mark slid his arm around her waist.

"Mark, we should probably talk." She moved in close to him. "I'm done tomorrow. You know that. And then I'll be shipped off. My bags are literally packed already." The smile had left Brooke's face, and she stared down at her glass.

"I guess we should." He pulled one of her hands away from her glass and held it firmly in his. "It's hard. I know, but we could at least try, yeah?" he said in a whisper.

"And what are you going to do? Live vicariously through Zak?" she said, the hint of a smile returning.

"Hey, he's got more potential than you give him credit for. Secret swaggery charm. Just have to coax it out of the bastard." Mark smiled back. "But I think we should at least try."

"Sure, we'll see." Brooke allowed her shoulders to drop and leaned into him. "Just don't get all pissed off when I'm right."

"I'm always pissed off when you're right," he said, and kissed her.

Their lips parted, and after a moment of quiet contemplation, Mark spun toward the bar. He made a show of trying to pick someone out of the crowd.

"What'd I tell you? The man's got secret swaggery charm!"

"What are you talking about?" Brooke followed his gaze.

Mark straightened his shoulders and gestured toward the room as if revealing his newest invention.

"Zak and fire-girl are gone. My work here is done; we would do well to imitate."

"I suppose we should," Brooke smirked and extended her hand.

"There's a very good chance my barracks is completely empty right now," Mark said, leading her quickly out of the bar.

CHAPTER 6

The sun was so bright. It seemed like white had never been this white before. Even the shadows were teeming with reflections and unforgiving stabs of the stuff. Zak couldn't remember how he got there, or even where here was. The ground felt unsteady, like an earthquake, but less rhythmic and altogether more violent. All of this was bad, but it was the noise that truly smashed his brain into mush. Everything sounded like a recording pushed beyond a speaker's limits. It was hard to focus on anything, but with great effort, some individual sounds began to register and come through.

"Fall…" a disembodied voice said from somewhere.

Then, a series of rapid and concussive explosions, followed by shrill screams, washed over him.

It sounded like the simulations and exercises he had worked through in his final round of exams. A thought drifted through his mind; *thank god I'll never have to do that again.* Zak sat up, taking a brief inventory of his surroundings. He was outside, on the ground near the vehicle garage at the north end of the base. Another cadet was lying beside him. He reached over and shook the cadet to get them up. It must have been almost time for morning call.

He mounted his unsteady legs and looked around, trying to figure out what was happening. His vision was unnaturally obscured by something. Fog? No, he had that back in Seattle. But this was the desert, there was scarcely enough water there for the ribbon-thin stream that ran by the base.

What, then? Smoke? Before he could conclusively decide that yes, it was smoke, he was blown back by a hot stinging wind. All at once the world around him came into focus. The cadet he had tried to shake awake still hadn't gotten up. The position they were lying in was wrong, and several other cadets were lying motionless around him. At the far wall, or what was left of the far wall, a massive fire was working toward him. Muscle memory forced Zak to reach down to the cadet lying at his feet and remove the sidearm from the holster he found there. Only now did the voice he'd heard upon waking make sense. It had been the call to fall back. They must have assumed he was one of the dead.

Zak did not have much of any gear. Last night's clothes, soiled with sweat and spilled beer, and the newly acquired sidearm were all he had. Another explosion, this time muffled by distance, woke him further. He realized that the base had already been under attack for quite some time. No doubt the enemy was behind him, already deeper inside the base. Quickly, Zak concealed himself as best as possible inside one of the impossibly bright shadows of a storage shed and vomited.

Beads of black crept in from the edges of his vision. The smell of his own vomit and the oily smoke coming from the hole in the courtyard wall caused him to retch again. He took four rapid breaths to gather himself before standing again. The faint patter of distant gunfire unnerved him, but also reassured him that others were, for the moment at least, still alive.

He checked the digital readout of the pistol he had commandeered. Eighty five percent power and nineteen rounds. It would have to do. He began to quietly move into the base.

Mark woke with his arm around Brooke. Her even breathing and soft skin tempted him to close his eyes and drift back to sleep. Also, his head was pounding. Maybe just a little more rest would help that too.

"Mark!" Zimmer yelled from beside his bunk. "Brooke. You guys, get the hell up! Someone's here!"

"What?" Mark asked. "Where are my pants?"

"I don't know," Zimmer called. "Just get dressed. You too Brooke."

Mark looked over at Brooke, who seemed less confused and altogether more concerned.

"It's fine, babe," Mark said. "These guys are cool. We'll cover for you, get you back into your barracks without anyone noticing."

"No, Mark," Brooke said, ignoring propriety and stepping out of bed while still pulling on her shirt. "This is bad. They're not talking about an inspection."

This broke through the haze in Mark's head, and the next few minutes were spent gearing up. He gave Brooke his pistol and a spare set of combat armor from his locker. The armor didn't fit her well, but it was better than what little she brought from the bar.

He pulled his rifle from his locker and busied himself strapping on his second set of armor. Gunshots pounded out a concentrated burst at the steel door of the room. Someone was trying to get in. Luckily, some of the more sober cadets had already locked and barricaded the room with some of the bunks.

Whoever was on the other side of the door recognized the preparedness of this particular room, and the gunfire outside ceased. An uncanny silence rang harshly in Mark's ears. In a corner of the room, a cadet was crying. Muffled commands came from the other side of the door.

Mark took a moment to look around and saw that Brooke was not the only cadet to have strayed from their barracks last night. There were two more cadets in patchwork dress at the front of the room.

"What the hell is happening?" Mark asked in a hoarse whisper.

Zimmer brought a finger to his lips at the front of the room. Outside there were more commands and shuffling noises. Mark was relieved to see that Zimmer was there. A sense of leadership was welcome in the unfamiliar chaos. As comforting as seeing Zimmer had been, a chill ran through his insides as he realized that Zak's bed was still made. He hadn't made it back into the barracks.

"Zak's not here," he said quietly.

"I know," Brooke put a hand on his shoulder and shook him briefly. "Focus up. Worrying about him now won't do anyone any good."

81

Mark was forced to take her advice as the sounds of someone trying to force their way into the room came in rhythmic beats. He checked that his rifle was loaded and shouldered it, prepared to fire if the barricade should fail. Three attempts were made on the door, and then silence fell again. Zimmer quietly approached it and pressed an ear to the cold steel. He held up one hand and strained to hear what was happening outside.

After a moment, he pulled his head away and motioned for everyone to pay attention. He pressed one finger to his temple and pulled up his optical display. He used a simple program to project words in front of him.

"Enemy pushing on," he typed out. "Heard: Move to the target zone for withdrawal."

The group took a collective sigh, and the first mutters of conversation began. Zimmer spread his hands to quiet them, then returned to typing words onto his optical display.

"Use optics. Do not talk," he typed. "IRD should be safe."

The cadets obeyed, turning on their optical displays and setting them to project onto their retina only. Unlike the kind of display many cadets used for studying, games, and other needs, this mode was a customized heads-up-display rather than a projection out onto the environment. The internal retinal display could send and receive messages among several other tactical uses in a trusted user group. Geotagging enemy forces, for instance, would make it so that everyone on your frequency could see where the enemy was located.

Once everyone had their optics online, they began sending messages to one another. The general lack of information, and the frantic anxiety meant that the sheer abundance of communication rendered most conversation little more than iterations of "What the *hell*?" "What do we *do*?" and, "I have no idea."

As the frustrated messages flew across their displays, Mark stood up and put both hands out toward the group around him. He paused, reached into a small pocket on his ballistic vest, and produced a piece of chalk. He then knelt on the grey concrete floor and drew a small rectangle. Inside, he wrote the word, "us."

He spent the next few minutes sketching a map of the school and the base. Near the rectangle he'd marked as their barracks, he also drew seven more shapes, representing the other barracks around them. He drew in the central tower, and the main assembly hall where they would have had the graduation ceremony. Around these shapes, he laid down lines representing the walls that surrounded the base.

Mark looked around at the cadets, then motioned for Zimmer to join him on the floor. He handed him the piece of chalk. Zimmer drew what looked like a cloud near the north wall of the base and wrote the words, "Explosion here, breach point?"

One by one, the group took the chalk and, together, they created an expanding picture of what little they knew.

~

Zak tried to move fluidly and without sound from shadow to shadow. He remembered then that he'd left the bar with Rooney. After some extracurricular activity, they had parted and headed for their respective bunks with promises that they would continue later. He remembered sitting down on the ground for a minute to clear his head and had apparently spent the rest of the night there.

Training had prepared him for the uncertainty of what he was now facing, but putting that training into practice was new. The sun was out, but smoke from the countless fires provided cover for much of his movement as he made his way into the base. From what he could see, the enemy forces had come in through the hole blown through the vehicle port of the base. The crumbling wall he'd woken up in front of was enough evidence of that. The forces must have then pushed through to get to the west side of the base, where the largest concentration of mechs in the region was housed in the massive hangar. By forcing their entry on the cadet side, the invading forces had secured a significant measure of surprise.

The sound of gunfire had been steadily ahead of him as he continued working his way in. The invading forces seemed to be moving at least as fast as he was. He stopped in a shadow of a building to catch his breath and took stock of his surroundings. The building across from him, a cadet barracks, was on fire. His hand smeared through something cold and wet on the cement behind him. Bringing his hand around, he feared for a moment that the sticky substance was blood. Zak took a step out into the light and saw that it wasn't. Someone has scrawled a message in red paint on the cool concrete, *"The Fall Begins."*

CHAPTER 7

Mark, Brooke, and the other cadets stood around the chalk diagram on the floor that had slowly become a plan. They had decided that two groups would leave at different times, taking separate routes to where the training mechs were stored out on the practice fields. The hope was that the invading forces would have overlooked those units. The other hope was that if one team didn't make it, the other might.

The first group, a larger party, would be led by Zimmer. They would take a direct path through the main courtyard, then out toward the training mechs. The second team, led by Mark, would take a more roundabout path, hoping to gather cadets who were willing to join along the way. Zimmer's group was gearing up at the front end of the room and talking about tactics in hushed tones. Mark's team was doing the same near the back of the room.

"I want to hit any buildings we can," Mark said. "I haven't heard a lot of activity over the past twenty minutes. After we heard those mechs power up, it sounded like those assholes withdrew. We'll be careful, of course. Who knows what they've left behind for us. We'll circle the inside of the east end of the base and check buildings as we move, then end back here and exit the same way we would for class."

"I'm not sure we're going to find anyone out there," Brooke said. "You said it yourself, it's been really quiet. Anyone left has probably barricaded themselves just like we have."

"I'd almost rather we heard something," Hartley said, adjusting a strap on her ballistic vest, cinching it tighter. "It's unnerving."

"We'll be okay," Mark said. "Just remember our training and we will get out of this fine. Zimmer and his team are about to leave. Give them a hand unblocking the door."

Everyone quietly helped to pull the bunks and other items away from the door. When it was finished, the first team slipped into the hall. No shots were fired, a good sign. Mark risked a glance outside the door and watched as Zimmer led his team quickly to the end of the hallway and the exterior door. They stopped for a moment and checked for tripwires. When they didn't find any, they opened the door. Blinding light spilled into the corridor.

Turner, bringing up the tail end of the first team, looked back at the room and locked eyes with Mark. Turner put on a fake looking smile and made a cocky shooing motion with his hand. Mark lingered for a moment out of spite, then returned to the room.

"They made it out fine," Mark said. "The door didn't blow up on them on the way out, so I suppose there's some good news."

Mark's team consisted of himself, Brooke, and five other cadets from his class. Hartley and Baker had always been competent in urban combat simulations, but he knew less about the others. One of them was a second year cadet that had made it into the room before their barricade went up.

The team suited up with what little gear they had and prepared to leave when he heard a sudden, muffled series of gunshots. The shots were brief and evenly timed. It sounded like Zimmer and his team had found something out there.

Zak heard a burst of gunfire and quickly ducked into the open doorway of an intact barracks building. He held his breath as a group passed by outside, their footsteps barely audible. Clenching his teeth and taking a deep breath, Zak chanced a glance out from the shadows. Nothing. They had already moved on. As he waited in silence, his eyes slowly adjusted to the darkness inside the building. He wondered for a moment where he was even going, but quickly realized that he was trying to find Mark. He had been heading toward their barracks from the moment he woke up. He checked the wall in this hallway and saw that he had already made it to barracks five. His room was inside barracks seven and would be just a few yards away, across a wide path that ran between two rows of buildings.

He looked away from the stenciled number and up the hallway, toward the various rooms further in. Instantly, he wished he hadn't. The entire hallway was littered with the bodies of fallen cadets. Some were half dressed for battle. Others were still in bedclothes. His mind clouded over, and he felt like he was going to pass out. Instead, he stepped quickly back into the light.

It was careless, but he couldn't stand the sight of the hallway. Thankfully, the group that he heard passing by wasn't lying in wait. He stood alone along the path that ran between the cadet barracks. Three of them were already fully engulfed in flames.

~

Mark motioned for Shakey, a quiet and capable cadet, to open the door. His squad fanned out of the room carefully, covering every angle with their weapons. The hallway ran north to south along the full length of the barracks, with doorways to other rooms opening along the way. At the north end was the door that Zimmer and his team had left through. On the other was the one that Mark and his team would take. Mark signaled for his team to move toward the first doorway ahead of them, a bunk room that should've housed a number of younger cadets.

His team moved smoothly behind him as they approached the room. On the wall opposite the door, they noticed a cluster of bullet holes in the cement. Someone had fired from inside. Mark and Shakey, at the head of the group, tightened their grips and prepared to enter the room. Counting down from three, they swung into the room, sweeping the area with the mounted lights on their rifles. The others stayed in the hall, waiting for orders.

Before Mark could register what he was seeing in the room, he heard a scream from somewhere near the back. A shock of bullets cut past Mark, and out into the hallway behind him. Shakey dropped to the floor and pushed himself behind a metal wardrobe, and Mark did the same with an overturned bunk. The scream did not stop, but simply faded in and out with labored breathing and what might have been words.

"Goddamn!" Shakey yelled as he tried to flatten himself against the ground behind the wardrobe.

The scream stopped suddenly as whoever was making it began to cough violently from deep inside the shadows at the far end of the room. The cough faded and was replaced by the sound of sobbing.

"We're friendlies! Please, stop shooting!" Mark called from behind cover.

No verbal response came from the figure huddled at the end of the room, but the faint clatter of metal on concrete signaled that the weapon had been dropped to the ground. Another sound began, rhythmic and soft, at the end of the room. Mark looked across to Shakey and nodded. They both stood and pointed their rifles toward the shadows. Their mounted flashlights illuminated a cadet curled against the far wall. He was rocking back and forth, his head lightly tapping the cement each time.

Mark and Shakey approached the cadet and moved the discarded weapon away from him. He looked completely absent, almost catatonic.

"If everyone we find is like this, I don't know how much help they're going to be," Shakey said.

Mark slung his rifle onto his back. "Shut up and help me get him up."

They each pried one of the cadet's arms from around his knees and lifted him to a swaying, standing position. When they turned around to lead him out of the room, the light on Shakey's rifle revealed a bloody scene. Bodies were strewn around the room in various stages of undress. Sheets from beds had been pulled off and were spattered with blood. Several cadets were crumpled in a heap, and others were laying singly on the ground. One was still in a bed, almost as if asleep.

"Oh my god, Mark," Shakey said. "Look at this, some of these guys were killed..." Shakey began, but then motioned toward the swaying cadet.

Mark shook his head and looked Shakey in the eyes. "Gather what you can from the lockers and move it into the hall," he said quietly. Then, to the group, "All right, it's pretty messed up in here guys. We're going to bring the gear we find out to you."

Mark nodded to Shakey. They led the trembling cadet through the room and out into the hall. Mark handed him over to Brooke who sat him down against the wall. The bullet holes in the cement hung like a twisted constellation above him.

"Can you check him out, make sure he's not bleeding or anything?" Mark read the name on the cadet's uniform. "I think his last name is Payne, if this is his uniform."

"Sure." Brooke reached out and took Mark's hand briefly. "Hey, are you okay?"

"I'm fine. It's..." Mark took a deep breath, his eyes darting back to the dark doorway. "It's not good in there."

He headed back into the room to help Shakey retrieve what gear was inside lockers and scattered around the room. Once it was all out in the hallway, they divided it up between them. There was enough gear to give each of them a full set of combat armor, a rifle, and a sidearm. Fully outfitted and feeling much more secure, the team moved to the south end of the hallway.

Baker and Shakey prepared to lead the team out. Mark stuck to the back of the formation with Brooke and Payne, who still hadn't said a word. Mark cast a look back at the holes punched into the wall of the hallway.

"Fuck me," he whispered. If he had been standing a few inches to the right, he'd be dead.

"Not right now jackass," Brooke said with a troubled smile. "We're kind of fucking busy."

Zak made his way down the central walkway and needed to go past the smoldering rubble of a troop transport vehicle to get into his barracks. There, he hoped to find Mark and anyone else left alive. He crouched behind a short wall and examined the area. Nothing moved but thick curls of smoke drifting across the empty spaces and into the sky. He stepped from behind the wall and moved toward his barracks when another series of shots stopped him cold. These shots were different than the controlled burst that he'd heard before. The long stream of pops from inside building seven was mingled with a chilling scream. He nervously checked his pistol again to verify that it did indeed have ammunition left. The scream stopped suddenly. Could that have been Mark? It was possible.

He pushed on toward the building. A dozen yards were between him and the south door. He covered the distance quickly, stepping over more of his fellow cadets than he cared to count along the way. Once at the door, he pressed himself flat against the wall to one side. The door was open. He realized it was possible he was following directly in line with one of the enemy groups working through the base. He closed his eyes for a moment, trying to remember the layout of their barracks. There were two doors leading into the building. One to the north and another to the south. Inside there were two main bunk rooms and a communal bathroom. Was there another way in? He clutched at the thread of an idea and seized on a memory. Another time he'd been trying to sneak into the barracks, but under much lighter circumstances.

Zak and Mark had stood in the shadows outside their barracks after curfew during their second year at the Academy, their clandestine shenanigans of whatever sort now complete. They'd become almost a single unit as they had progressed in their schooling. Mark pulled Zak into various schemes and debauchery and Zak always found a way to pull them back out again. The building was locked up tight, and no one had come looking for them yet.

"Someone must have covered for us," Zak said. "Said we were already in our bunks."

"Good man, whoever that was," Mark said.

They were both very cold and very drunk, so breaking in seemed like the logical course of action. Shivering, they walked around the building until they discovered a roof access ladder. It was latched so that it didn't come all the way down to the ground, presumably to stop wayward cadets from climbing up.

"Here, get me up there," Zak said and pushed Mark toward the ladder.

Mark knelt and laced his fingers together to create a platform for Zak to stand on. He lifted, and Zak was just able to reach the latch and release it. The ladder began to clatter down with a deafening racket. Mark had let go of Zak to catch it, and he tumbled into the dirt.

"Shit, sorry," Mark said, now holding the ladder still. "Give me a hand with this?"

Zak stood up, brushed himself off, and together they lowered it the rest of the way to the ground with minimal noise.

Once they were on the roof there wasn't a lot to see. Air conditioning units, bird excrement, a sun scorched football, and in the corner, there was a door. They crept toward it, careful to keep their footfalls as light as possible on the thin roof. When they arrived, they found it was already unlocked. They walked down a set of stairs and ended up cramped inside the janitorial closet in their communal bathroom. The door of this room was also unlocked.

"What luck," Mark said, holding back laughter. "Someone should really tighten security around here."

He shifted and knocked a broom from the wall, which in turn swiped a pile of cleaning products from a shelf. Mark let out a peel of startled laughter that he quickly rectified by placing his hand over his mouth.

"Quiet down," Zak said, shaking his head. He opened the janitor's closet carefully and peered out into the communal bathroom. It was empty. "We owe someone big for this."

The barracks were completely silent, and with a few additional tiptoe dashes, they were safely in their bunks.

They both woke up the next day with vicious hangovers. Even Zak had some trouble getting dressed on time, but they both made it. As they exited the building, heading for company inspection, Zak chanced a glance back at the ladder on the side of their building. Zimmer was putting it back in place with the help of Kalen. Kalen caught his glance and wagged a finger at him in mock admonishment. Later, Zimmer quietly assigned both Zak and Mark an extended stint of janitorial duties. Neither Zak nor Mark had asked him why.

Zak quickly pulled away from the south door and headed to the side of the building. He found the ladder right where he'd remembered it. It was hanging on the building at a strange angle, and it didn't look particularly sturdy. At least whatever blast caused the damage had also broken the latch to release the full length of the ladder. Zak tested it gingerly, then decided to chance it. The ladder held. Once he was on the roof, he saw the familiar access door. It was open and spattered with blood. Just outside the door was the figure of someone he knew. Ariana, a cadet from the room next to his. She must have heard about this door and thought it would make a good escape route. Zak closed his eyes as he stepped over her body.

Before he descended the darkened stairwell, he turned to look out over what he could see of the base. Thick black smoke rose on the wind, and bright orange sparks drifted by like shooting stars. He stood for a moment, watching the smoke pass by, when a sudden roar shook the building. Engines, churning at full tilt, beat at the air, pulling up curls of the smoke. A squadron of jets streaked by in a blink and suddenly climbed in altitude.

"Finally," Zak said under his breath. Someone was here and this nightmare could end.

He stood inside the doorway, watching as the jets broke formation and spun down. Their contrails looked like the tentacles of some giant octopus in the sky as they began firing. These jets would be manned. Research had proven, luckily for Zak and his fellow cadets, that even the most complex artificial intelligence still lacked the decision-making power of the human mind. The inherent instability of long-distance information transfer meant they were also not being controlled by a joystick from hundreds of miles away.

As the fighters approached the ground, something happened. None of the rounds fired from the jets made it to the ground. He watched as one plane exploded in midair, while another seemed to bounce off something, then lose control and slam into the desert floor. Others, seeing the danger ahead of them, attempted to pull out of their attack trajectories, but it was too late.

In seconds, more jets had either exploded against the invisible barrier or lost control and plummeted. The world shook as the concussive blasts of the planes hitting the ground rolled through the air, low like thunder. One plane pulled up a fraction of a second earlier than the others but was still unable to control itself. It hurtled through the air back toward the base.

The plane dropped and impacted the barracks building across from his. The shock wave and intense heat knocked him down the first flight of stairs. The smoke that followed was thick. It enveloped him, and he lost consciousness.

CHAPTER 8

Mark, Brooke, and the rest of their team exited the building just as the jets roared by overhead. They stood in the courtyard, completely visible from several angles, but for this moment they felt protected. Finally, someone had come to put an end to this chaos and bring back the structure they'd been conditioned for since childhood.

Their comfort was short-lived as one plane after another exploded, slamming into something in the sky. One jet managed to make a last-second change in direction and was headed directly for them. They scattered as the plane impacted a building near the barracks they had just exited. The explosion sent all of them sprawling as flaming debris rained down.

Payne began to wail in agonized fear again, his eyes focused on some point only he could see. The scream was unsettling, but more unsettling was the urge to join him.

"Is everyone all right?" Mark yelled. His own voice sounded muffled. A pervasive ringing seemed to drown much of the detail from his voice. He looked around, checking to make sure everyone was okay. Everyone seemed unharmed until his eyes landed on Shakey. He'd been further behind, busy repacking a bag that had come undone closer to the barracks. He sprinted the distance to Shakey, who was lying on the ground now, blood already seeping through his clenched teeth.

"Man, this really hurts guys," Shakey said, clutching at a hole torn through one of his pant legs. Blood soaked through the fabric, and his eyes began to lose focus.

"Who has medical training?" Mark asked frantically.

Hartley and Larson pushed past him and began to tear away Shakey's pant leg to reveal the injury. The wound they found was severe, and they continued to find more wounds as they cut away the rest of his clothing. He began to gasp for air.

"Shakey, stay with us man. Please," Mark said while crouching over his head. "It's going to be okay, just hold on."

He watched, powerless, as Shakey's eyes seemed to catch a faraway object and focus there. The cadets tending his wounds stopped, as the blood flowing out of him stopped coming in force. His breathing came to a halt and his body became limp. There was silence, unbroken for a long time. It had only been a few moments, but that's all it had taken for one of their own to die. Hartley checked to make sure his pulse was gone.

"He's dead," she said simply. Hartley crossed Shakey's arms on his chest and pulled his dog tags out where they could be seen. She read them aloud.

"Shawn H. Shakley, ID number 276198-DHZ." She coughed as smoke continued to fill the area. "Blood type, A positive. Faith, Christian"

Shakey hadn't said anything during the last few moments of his life. No words of encouragement to his fellow comrades, just frantic breathing, and fear. Mark felt like something should be said but didn't have the words for the moment. He had never been faced with death this closely before. He had spent most of his life believing that when he was faced with it, he would remain cold and rational. But something needed to be said, and he was without words for what felt like the first time.

"Yea, though I walk through the valley of the shadow of death," Payne spoke in a low whisper, his eyes closed, and his head bowed. Everyone turned to him, shocked. Mark lowered his head as Payne continued. "I will fear no evil, for you are with me. Your rod and staff comfort me. You prepare a table before me in the presence of my enemies. You anoint my head with oil, and my cup runs over. Surely goodness and mercy shall follow me all the days of my life. And I will dwell in the house of the Lord, forever."

Payne opened his eyes and looked around, his eyes growing distant again. "That's how it goes, I think. I think that's right."

"Thank you." Mark looked up and found their barracks. He pointed toward the building that had been their home for months. It was on fire, a result of the fallen jet. "It's the best we can do right now. Give me a hand and let's get him back inside."

They lifted Shakey's body and carried it toward the burning barracks. As they got close, the smell of burning wood, plaster, and bodies caused Mark to retch. They approached the open door and carried his body a few yards into the hallway. Mark took one last look and retreated from the hall, coughing, and rubbing his eyes. From the shade of an overturned transport truck, Mark and the others watched as the barracks was completely engulfed in flames. The heat started to become too much to bear, and Mark stood up.

"Let's get going," Mark said, shouldering his rifle. "We still have a rendezvous to make."

Zak woke with a start at the bottom of the stairs from the roof. A layer of rubble and thick smoke were all around him. As he tried to push himself up, pain shot from his wrist through his right arm. He couldn't tell if it was broken, and there was no time to check. He pushed with his other arm, hoping this one would support him. It did.

Getting up revealed some other minor injuries, but the most severe seemed to be his right wrist. Once he was standing, he focused on his surroundings. The first thing he noticed was that dense smoke was now seeping up the stairwell from the main floor. The explosion must have ignited the barracks.

He looked back up toward the roof. The door was still open, a rectangle of light intermittently obscured by smoke. With nowhere else to go, he ran back out onto the roof. The trees around the building were also on fire. The side of the building with the ladder was fully engulfed in flames, and Zak began to panic. He coughed violently from the smoke as he struggled to think of a way off the roof. It was only one story tall, and he'd heard of people surviving much worse.

He walked to the edge of the building least impacted by the falling jet and looked over the edge. Below, there were two damaged vehicles and a large dumpster. The plastic lid seemed like his best bet.

Something inside the building exploded below him. He took this as a sign and stepped off the edge. As he fell the short distance, he cradled his injured wrist. He landed on the dumpster, uncomfortably twisting as the lid collapsed, and he fell into what little trash was inside. He was on the ground floor now, covered in garbage. His wrist was possibly broken, and his lungs felt like they were on fire, but at least he was on the ground. Once out of the dumpster, he ran across the pavement, away from the flames that roared up through the roof of the building. He headed toward the grand assembly hall at the center of the cadet's side of the base.

He had all but forgotten about concealment and stealth. Now he just wanted to be somewhere safe where he could take stock of his situation. He reached the hall and pushed through a partially open door and stood inside the grand room. All the usual chairs and tables, which would on any other day have been filled with cadets eating breakfast, were neatly stacked against one wall. In their place were rows and rows of empty white chairs, all facing a temporary stage set up against the far wall.

Above the stage was a banner, "Congratulations Graduates!"

A thin haze of smoke had found its way inside the hall, and shafts of light poured in through the skylights. The room was still, the scene eerily untouched. The attack must have started too early for anyone to have made their way in here. Zak walked softly in the cavernous space, toward where he had been instructed to sit during a rehearsal for the ceremony the week before. Zak could imagine the room, filled with the cadets. Those graduating would have been sitting in the front rows, with subsequent classes filling in toward the back. He shuffled down his row and sat in the fourth seat from the center aisle.

He looked around, taking in the empty chairs, each one held space for some cadet outside. How many could have filled the seats then? From what he had seen, there couldn't be many left. A few isolated pockets were waiting for rescue, no doubt. Some might even be out wandering the compound just like him. He hoped Mark was alive but feared the worst. The building they had lived in for months was now a burned-out shell.

Zak didn't remember when he started crying. The smoke had made his eyes water so much that the difference was only now occurring to him. He held his head in his hands and closed his eyes, trying to think of what to do next.

Mark led his group through the battle-torn base. The cadets were silent as they moved tactically from building to building, weapons trained in all directions. Payne occasionally muttered something and followed well but had returned to a completely dethatched state.

After searching two buildings, they stopped any effort to search for survivors. In the first, they saw just how unprepared almost everyone was when the attack happened. The scene was reminiscent of where they'd found Payne. Some buildings they passed seemed to have been lit on fire intentionally, while others were virtually undamaged.

A pocket of survivors they did come across fired warning shots from a hole in one wall. Any subsequent attempt to communicate was cut short by another burst of gunfire. Their gathering of reinforcements, therefore, had stalled with Payne. As they continued to push through the base, Mark fell back and met up with Brooke, who was still keeping an eye on the rescued cadet.

"I don't feel right leaving without Zak," he said. "He could be in any one of those buildings we didn't check. Hell, he might even be in one of the ones we did check."

"I don't feel right, either." Brooke nodded. "But if he's alive, we're not going to find him. And if he's not..." She stopped to look at him, catching his arm and holding him in place. "If he's not, do you really want to know?"

Mark rubbed his eyes with one hand and shrugged.

"I don't know. I guess not, not right now." He looked back in the direction they'd come. "Go ahead. I'll catch up."

"All right Mark," Brooke took his hand for a moment. "Be fast. It's a one in a hundred shot we've even made it this far."

She held onto his hand for a moment longer and then released it, turning back to the group and ushering Payne along with her. Once she was gone, he knelt and put his rife down on the cement.

"Zak, I hope you can't hear this. Because if you can, it means they got you. It also means there's a God, and I have some shit to atone for." Mark shook his head. Now was not the time for jokes. "If you're gone, I swear I'll kill every last one of these assholes. Hell, I'll probably do that anyway. Just please don't be dead."

He reached down for his rifle and, as an afterthought, took out a piece of chalk and scrawled a message on the ground.

Mark turned away and hurried back to the group. They'd just come upon the hangar that opened onto the training fields. This was the same room where they'd begun their official pilot training with Phillips. It was completely intact, but the room felt different without Phillips parading back and forth, trying to hide his limp. The power had failed in the attack, and so the room was dark.

They worked together to pry a smaller door beside the massive bay door open. The very fact that they had to open it this way left hope that no one else had come through during the attack. Once they had beaten and bent a corner enough, Mark crawled outside carefully. Sweaty from exertion, he examined the long stretch of barren desert hardpan in front of him. He took a deep breath of fresh air. He hadn't realized just how much the air inside the base had been choking him until now. The stench of burning flesh and spent explosives was almost completely absent out here. Brooke slipped underneath the door next and looked relieved to be outside as well. Soon, they were all leaning against the outer wall, breathing in deep gulps.

A few hundred yards across the open desert was the hangar that should contain the dozen or so cadet-built mechs of the training fleet. With any luck, Zimmer and his team would already be inside, getting a small core of mechs ready to leave.

Unlike most of the landscape, the open desert in front of them was only sparsely populated with sagebrush. Years of mechs trampling the earth in this area had left the ground barren and chalky. Covering the distance across to the building would be risky, but they had to chance it. They left in two groups. Mark led the first group in a sprint ahead and then turned them around, ordering them to keep their rifles trained on the ledges and windows of the high base walls. Brooke and Payne headed out with the second group, moving toward the first, also sweeping the walls with their rifles. In this fashion they traded off, sprinting and covering each other until they reached the outside of the hangar. Fresh footprints indicated that they were not the first to arrive.

Pressed against the wall beside one of the outer doors, Mark knocked three times on the hard steel. For too long there was no reply. The cadets tightened their grips on their weapons. Then, one knock came back from inside. After a pause, two more came through. Mark sighed with relief, recognizing the agreed pattern. It was Zimmer and his team. The cadets outside dropped their stances slightly but held their positions.

The door creaked open, and a visibly shaken cadet stood in the doorway. Inside, Mark was relieved to see Zimmer's team. He counted even more cadets than they'd left with. They must have had more luck in finding willing survivors than he had. Mark scanned the room, looking for Zimmer, and found him. He was laid flat on a table with his vest removed and his shirt ripped open. Blood-soaked bandages had been applied to his chest, but it was too late. Kalen was sitting with him. He stroked Zimmer's forehead and was whispering something, over and over, under his breath. Mark could only guess what he was saying, but he knew it was a goodbye of some kind.

Everyone in the room turned to look at Mark. For a few moments, he looked around to see why, until he remembered that he was the next in line for command. He'd been elected to the position at the same time they elected Zimmer but never thought he'd be asked to lead. His duties had mostly consisted of late-night meetings and standing beside Zimmer during company inspections.

Brooke gave him a gentle push, and Mark stepped out ahead of his team. The heaps of the training mechs loomed all around them. The hangar was large. Nowhere near as massive as the main garage on the active side of the base, but he still felt small in the stillness.

"What..." he started to ask, and then took a deeper, more authoritative tone. "What happened? Was there someone still out there?" He reflexively turned toward the door, expecting it to burst open and for all of this to end before it had begun.

"We caught some stragglers still in the base," said Turner, stepping into the center of the group. "They were looting the medical supplies. We took them out, but..." He looked over toward Kalen who was still sitting with Zimmer's body.

"I'm so sorry," Mark said. It was his plan that caused this. If they'd stayed barricaded in their room, it was possible both Zimmer and Shakey would still be alive. "I know it's hard. You probably noticed that Shakey. Uh. He didn't make it either."

Mark watched as cadets around the room looked to find Shakey, as if to prove him wrong.

"We have to move on," Mark said, trying to sound sure of his decision. In truth, he had decided to press on with the plan because he wasn't sure what to do. "Anyone who's trained on a specific mech, get it prepped to go. Someone help me move Zimmer upstairs. We'll leave him on the table inside the classroom."

No one moved immediately. Mark could see that they needed something from him, so he took two more steps into the center of the group, and Turner moved back into the crowd reluctantly. Mark felt the absence of words returning to him, but pushed past it, searching for anything to get them moving.

"This is hard," Mark began. He looked over at Zimmer's body for a moment and continued. "Jakob Zimmer and Shawn Shackley were good men, but we need to move if we're going to get the people that did this. What we've seen is true evil. We've trained to be the forces against that evil, and we need to do our jobs. Our creed, we memorized it, and I hope every one of you still has it in your heart. I will fight the enemy of Stability, even if it should cost me my life."

Mark took a moment for the group to reach back through their memories to when they'd each recited the creed in front of the class.

"As far as we know, we're the only United Entities soldiers in the entire region with any access to mechanized combat armor. I'm not sure if you saw what happened to those jets, but whatever the Harbingers have is too dangerous." He saw members of Zimmer's team nodding. Good, so they had seen it too. "If we're going to do anything at all, if we're going to get the people that did this, we have to do it now. Let's get started."

The group dispersed and preparations began on several of the mechs. They wouldn't be able to take them all, but they would fully outfit as many as they could and strip the remaining mechs for valuable parts and supplies.

Mark and two other cadets helped Kalen move Zimmer's body upstairs into a classroom. After they placed him on the desk at the front of the room, Kalen removed a United Entities flag from the wall and draped it over Zimmer's body. On that flag, the dual figures of a phoenix and a bald eagle fiercely protected a single star in the center of a field of deep crimson. On a banner below these figures were the words that also ended the Armored Soldier's Creed: "Stability before self."

CHAPTER 9

As the sun reached its highest point in the sky, they'd nearly finished outfitting seven mechs and a handful of armored trucks with everything they could find. A typical core of mechs would usually contain a dozen mechs and up to ten support vehicles at the least, but what they had would have to do. The hardest unit to equip was the Neith class command mech, the Maratus. The main challenge was its size. It took up a large portion of the hangar even in compressed form. They had to hook onto it with two trucks in order to pull it outside, and then spent time opening each of the eight legs. Once it was fully revealed, however, it was clear why they had taken the time. It was by far the largest and most armored unit they had access to, and the sensor array would be invaluable.

An ugly four-legged Lupine class mech called the Kapu was outfitted. Turner had lobbied for it because its smaller frame and wide stance made it the best suited for stealth infiltration. An Ursidae class named the Nanook didn't require much to get it fully equipped and ready to go. Also moving on four legs when traveling, this mech was designed to rear up during battle, becoming a sort of massive turret. It was a bit more worn down than the others, but the firepower it offered was worth the risk.

They hauled out two huge, blocky Jotun class mechs designed for deliberate, steady progress on a battlefield. One was their very own Cronus. The other was named Craig, and no one knew quite why. The last two mechs they added to their core were two lightweight Aves class mechs, Iris and Icarus, that were completed in the same year.

The trucks they selected each had an enclosed cargo bed and a large caliber gun mounted to the top. These were loaded with any supplies that could be found in the hangar. The training mech hangar also served as auxiliary storage for the base, so some basic medical supplies and other items were easy to find. One thing they were in short supply of was ammunition for the mechs. They had performed live-fire drills as a part of their training, but they weren't fully outfitted and would need to use it sparingly if they ever came to need it.

Once complete, their core of mechs looked formidable out in front of the hangar. The work of preparing them seemed to have focused the cadets. They were all actively strapping in and securing cargo wherever possible. Occasionally someone would look off in the direction of the enemy, and then refocus on their work.

As the sun fell beneath the horizon, the world became a series of layered silhouettes. Mark gave the order to move out, and everyone boarded the mech or truck they would be traveling in. They powered up with all exterior lights off to attract the least amount of attention. Their activity would have been noticed by then if anyone had been watching, so Mark wasn't too concerned.

Mark strapped himself into the pilot chair on the command deck. He used the mech's eight powerful legs to raise the central command module of the Maratus off the desert sand and into the air. He was familiar with this mech, having trained with this specific beast for months both in his designation course and in various exercises drawn up by Phillips. As he finished the power-up sequences, he wondered briefly how the enemy forces had been able to get through these security measures but was quickly distracted by the rest of the activity going on around him. Brooke and Kalen were on the command deck with him and occupied the weapons and sensor stations.

The command deck was large compared to the cramped quarters of the other mech units. There was room to move around if the need arose. The forward end was dominated by a reinforced transparent windscreen capable of displaying information. The pilot seat was positioned at the center of this and had an additional smooth panel in front of it for controls. In the center of the room, a small rectangular table displayed a map of the terrain around them in three dimensions on top of it. There were two decks below them. One held crew quarters and a mess hall, and below that was a cargo area that could be used as additional accommodations if needed.

Mark input their first heading, and it was transmitted via low frequency coded radio signals to the other mechs in the core. Inside each unit, the command would need to be manually applied by the pilots.

The plan Mark had drawn out as they were doing final preparations had them moving as discreetly as possible in the direction of the stolen mechs and the rebels who stole them. Once they got far enough away from the base, they would make camp and figure out the next step. Mark hoped that someone with authority would have reached them by that point but was beginning to worry it might not happen.

His mech lurched into motion. This sensation was always a bit disorienting, as each leg calibrated and adjusted for the movement of the huge machine. But, as they got up to speed, the movements became barely perceptible. Their entire group moved as one into the desert as the brilliant yellows and reds of the sunset began to fade into oranges and deep purples. The trucks, much less armored and far more vulnerable, rode directly beneath Mark's command mech. The other mechs traveled in a loose and constantly shifting pattern around him.

Slowly, the group made their way away from Taycher Mechanized Armor Base, leaving Zimmer's body draped in a flag in the upper classroom of the training mech hangar. Once they were moving smoothly, Kalen stepped away from his console and walked toward the back of the room. He sat against the wall and took a private moment. The constant activity had kept them all busy, and Kalen hadn't had enough time to process Zimmer's loss. Perhaps he would never fully recover. Mark did nothing to interrupt him. Instead, he busied himself by verifying the locations of everyone now under his command. He checked with Brooke to make sure the sensor sweeps were coming up clean and to see if any friendly communications had come through. There was nothing on any of the encrypted communications channels.

Mark had been careful not to broadcast or sweep too broadly, fearing they might alert the enemy mechs up ahead. There was a good chance they were monitoring communications and signals in much the same way that Brooke was. If there were any government forces out there, they were being just as careful.

As with all technology following the Decline, mechanized combat armor had very little in the way of direct connections with other information systems. While advances in security had been positive since the creation of the three-net system, the military had been steadfast in the use of isolated units connected only by low frequency radio communications. As a result, commanders relied heavily on the pilots in each mech to relay information verbally and carry out orders manually. Not much other than their positions were available from the command displays. Mark remembered that, because of this lack of communication, their group would be indistinguishable from the enemy right now to anyone else.

"Brooke, watch this for a minute," he said, gesturing at the control screen. He swung out of his chair and headed for the back of the room. "Gotta send a message to anyone passing over."

Brooke nodded and assumed control of the mech, sitting at the panel positioned in the center of the windscreen. Most of the systems were in autonomous mode, so she didn't have to do much other than watch the ground ahead for major obstacles. While she examined the various numbers on the display, Mark passed by Kalen and climbed a ladder at the far end of the room. He opened a hatch in the roof and pulled himself out into the cool evening air. The center module was remarkably steady, considering how much weight was being shifted around with each step.

Mark stood for a moment, admiring the deepening purple of the sky. The observation deck took up about half of the top of the central module. The other half was occupied by the sensor array and the large main gun. The deck was large enough for a helipad, used for resupply when on longer missions, with some room to spare. A steady breeze from their forward movement rustled his uniform as he walked to the supply box mounted near the front railing. Flares, rain gear, medical kits, and other loose supplies were haphazardly strewn inside. At the top, he found six cans of fluorescent marking paint. He'd stored them there at the last minute after realizing the problem of being mistaken for the enemy. He used them to paint a large rectangle with an oval inside it onto the top of the mech. It was a symbol he had hastily looked up in a book he'd found in one of the classrooms. If he was right, it meant 'friendly armor'. Hopefully, if anyone was watching them from above, they would see the symbol and think twice before bombing them.

When he was done, he tossed the cans back into the box and closed the lid. Before heading back to the hatch, he stopped and sat down against the supply box, facing back toward the base. Without realizing it at first, he began to cry. He wiped at the tears rolling from his eyes and tightened his jaw. Through the blur, he could see faint lights out toward the base. Fires were still burning in the place where he'd learned more than just battle tactics and military protocol. It was also the place where he'd met both Zak and Brooke, two people who believed in him in a way no one else in his life had to that point. It had become a place where he was good at something.

Mark's mother had pulled strings to even get him admitted, and that had bothered him for a while. With Zak's help, he'd eventually determined that he wanted to be there. But, more recently, Mark had begun to actually believe he might make a competent leader someday. He just hadn't realized his chance would come this soon.

~

Zak opened his eyes and forced himself to stand. The light that filtered in through the windows and skylights was already tinged with orange. He swore under his breath and walked to an outer door, accidentally pushing it open with his injured hand. He winced at the sharp pain but realized it might not actually be broken. He looked out toward what remained of his barracks. Smoke still billowed from the various holes and windows, but the fire seemed to have run its course. It looked like it might even be cool enough to see if there was anything left inside.

Zak walked slowly across the lawn. This time he didn't ignore the bodies that lay strewn on the ground. As he threaded his way through them, he saw that some weren't wearing cadet uniforms. They must have been some of the invading forces, he realized. The clothes these bodies wore were dark grey and black with no insignias or indication of rank. They were a utilitarian design that looked easy to produce in large numbers. He moved his uninjured left hand down to where he had the pistol tucked into an oversized pocket of his jacket and took it out. He had been careless since the plane crashed, but his mind was clearing.

Zak crouched and moved toward what remained of his barracks. When he reached the burned and reeking building, he had to focus hard to stop himself from dry heaving. There was a smell like cooked meat on the air. A burned corpse was laid inside the doorway with the arms folded neatly on its chest. There wasn't much left, but it looked like the body was laid there with the purpose of letting it burn. A glint of metal reflected in the dying light of day, and he leaned down to see what it was. There he found dog tags that identified the corpse as Shawn Shakley, a cadet he'd known for years. Zak closed his eyes for a moment, repressing the urge to scream in anger, then moved further into what remained of the building.

The room he'd stayed in with Mark and the others was ahead. A smell of burnt flesh was stronger from a room further up the hall. He remembered those cadets, nice but a bit antisocial, and faced the doorway of his own room. He pushed open the door slowly, his heart pounding hard in his chest.

One golden beam of light cut through the room from a hole that had been opened in the far wall. The first thing he noticed was that there were no bodies. Zak let out a sigh and dropped his shoulders. Some of the bunks and cabinets were piled on either side just inside the doorway. Carefully, he made his way to the remains of his bunk and ran his hand along the scorched rails where the mattress used to be. He looked up, toward where Mark had slept, and found a piece of chalk that must have fallen beneath the now absent mattress. He picked it up. It looked good, considering the damage done to the rest of the room.

Zak turned to leave and looked down at where his footfalls had swept away a layer of soot on the floor. He noticed faint markings in these cleared tracks, froze, and backed away. Removing his jacket, he fanned the cement floor, revealing an expanse of words and marks beneath. Zak examined them, trying to piece together the fragments of a plan from curved lines, partial phrases, and an occasional diagram. He followed one line, clearly laid in with purpose, and found that it ended in an arrow, pointing at a shape out beyond the map of the main base.

It pointed to what must be the training mech hangar. It had to be if he was reading it correctly. They must have decided to load up in the training mechs. That was the plan. Zak resisted the urge to yell out in triumph. Mark must have still been alive, at least when the map was made. No other jackass he knew carried chalk around. Zak stood and put his jacket back on. He placed the single piece of chalk in his front breast pocket and headed for the door.

He worked his way through the base with a destination now securely in mind. As he slipped across the base, he heard what he feared was enemy activity in the crumbling debris. Some sounds might have been survivors, as the rebels couldn't possibly have killed everyone on base during their relatively short attack. Either way, fear kept him from investigating, and he worked his way out toward the training fields without confrontation. When Zak finally approached the garage leading out to the fields, it was already after sunset.

As he got closer, he came across a chalk message scrawled on the pavement. Again, he knew that this was Mark's work. Who else would carry a surprisingly effective and useful thing like chalk? Zak smiled as he read the message.

"Fuck You," it read.

No exclamation point, no underline, just the phrase scrawled hastily on the ground. Zak tried to parse the meaning from the simple phrase. It could have been aimed at the rebel forces, but if Mark were going to leave a message for them, it would have been much more profane. Perhaps it was for any government forces that came to the rescue, too late to do any good. Zak, however, felt that the message was for him.

"Fuck you for dying," the message was saying, or possibly, "Fuck you for staying out all night and not being here with us."

Either way, it was good natured, in a grim way. Zak smiled again before exiting through a door that had been pried up just far enough for one person to slip underneath.

He leaned against the outside wall, enjoying the crisp and clean air for a moment. He let it fill his lungs, then exhaled, almost feeling the ash and smoke leave his body. With nothing for protection, he made a dash for the training hangar, intending to spend as little time in the open as possible. He slowed down when he got close and listened as the wind rattled the corrugated metal roof of the building. It was the only sound out here, and his hopes dropped.

Zak crept up to a side door that hung open and peered into the gloom. The remaining faint light of day filtered in through large dusty windows high in the hangar. There was just enough light to see that several of the mechs were missing. The ones that remained had been stripped of anything useful. He moved quietly through the strangely empty space and walked into the vehicle garage. Here too he found missing equipment and vehicles. Some smaller vehicles remained, and he tried each one in turn only to find that they'd also been relieved of most useful supplies. He couldn't find a single one with enough power left to drive any extended distance.

"Well crap," Zak said, his voice echoing. He started the truck with the most energy left in its emergency cells and managed to get it outside before it shut down completely. Its solar panels would need to charge the main power cells in the morning before he would be able to leave.

Not wanting to sleep in the truck, Zak headed back inside the hangar. While most of the supplies had been taken, he was able to pull together a bag of items that might prove useful. He felt safe enough now to use a flashlight he managed to find and headed upstairs to the classrooms. He regretted the decision when he saw a body, draped in the flag of the United Entities, lying on the main table.

"Oh man. No," he whispered as he approached. "Please."

He folded back the fabric, revealing Zimmer's face. Zak turned away instinctively and shut his eyes. He looked back for a moment, mentally saying goodbye to another friend, and then folded the flag back over Zimmer's face. The room was clearly not where he would be sleeping that night, if he could sleep at all.

Zak moved to leave the room and glanced back at Zimmer's form beneath the flag. If Mark was still alive, like his message indicated, he would now be leading whatever group got the units up and running. Zak quietly closed the door to the classroom, as if not to wake Zimmer. He walked down the hall to one of the smaller classrooms and pulled the large desk at the front of the room over to one corner. Climbing into the triangle of space this made, he leaned into the corner of the wall and tried to calm his nerves.

At earlier points in his life, he'd similarly sought out places where he could be concealed. He had made a game out of it, though it hadn't been one any of his caretakers had liked very much.

Once, in a particularly overcrowded home, he'd been but one of over a dozen children taken in from the state system. The guardians, Zak rarely took the time to remember their names, were often absent from the house. Even when they were there, they hadn't been particularly caring or attentive. This suited most of the children, because without adult supervision they were allowed to do whatever they wanted.

The house was old but much larger than anything given to most families. It had been given to the guardian couple because of their considerable contribution to Stability by taking in so many wards of the state. Of course, they'd been also compensated generously for their contribution. Zak had explored every inch of the house, discovering every entrance and exit. He could access each of the three floors, the basement, and the attic without anyone ever seeing him. Some of the children had taken to calling him the Ghost Kid.

Zak liked the name. A ghost could disappear. A ghost didn't have to worry about pain or suffering. What he hadn't liked was the other children themselves. Occasionally, when Zak had bothered to be present around anyone else, they would all suddenly turn on him. Often, they'd lift him up and carry him somewhere in the house and lock him inside a closet, cupboard, or other small place. Sometimes he found a way out, and they'd call him Ghost Kid again. Other times he'd just had to wait until someone remembered and came to get him. There had been instances where he'd slept in a cramped space for almost an entire day before being released.

Once someone from the state had come to make sure that everything was in order. The guardians arrived the day before and ordered all of them to clean the house. Zak had instead disappeared into his secret places and avoided everyone. The guardians asked the other children where he was, but they all said they never knew where Ghost Kid was.

As the hour of the official walkthrough approached, the guardians became more and more frantic in their search for Zak. As they'd grown angrier, Zak had burrowed deeper into his dark, quiet places. He ended up as far down as he could go, inside a crawlspace under the stairs in the basement. The inspector had questioned them about Zak's whereabouts. When neither the guardians nor the other children could produce the Ghost Kid, the routine investigation became a criminal one. The other children quickly told a team of investigators that had shown up how the house was run.

Eventually, when the team of investigators swept the house with blinding flashlights, they'd found Zak sleeping under the stairs. He and the other children were swept back into the system and filtered out to other foster homes. Zak never hid from people in quite the same way, but he'd remained distant from almost everyone until he got to the Academy. Mark had somehow brought him out of his secret places, and he'd begun to feel almost normal.

But there he was again, curled into another dark corner, alone. He tried to focus on the prospect of catching back up to Mark and the others but felt the urge to stay in the corner. He wanted to wait until someone came to rescue him from the new nightmare he was living. Opposing impulses sparred in his mind and, with some false starts, he eventually drifted into sleep.

The next morning, Zak was awakened by a harsh light streaming in through the windows along one wall. The building was silent and still. The light of day solidified his resolve, and he decided he would try to catch up to the other cadets. Rather than climb back over the desk, he pushed it out with his boots slowly. He had to get moving if he wanted any hope of catching up to Mark and the rest of the survivors. Any possibility of being swept up in a wave of friendly reinforcements now seemed like a fantasy. Since the squadron of planes that had screamed across the sky and then crashed, there had been no sounds of air traffic.

He walked across the room to the window and looked out at the base. The scene was largely the same, though the fires had mostly burned themselves out inside the compound. The truck he parked outside was still there, soaking up power from the morning sun. Zak walked carefully past the room where Zimmer's body was laid on a table and made his way downstairs. The space was a bit less threatening in the daylight. It didn't seem to contain unseen terrors, but now felt as if it contained nothing at all. In the daylight, the hangar was reminiscent of the days he and the others had spent here in training. On those days, many of the mechs would have been out in the training fields, performing whatever maneuvers or operations Phillips had them practicing. The mechs wouldn't be coming back inside that day at sunset though. They'd probably never be back again.

Zak strode outside into the warm light and put his meager pack of supplies onto the passenger seat of the vehicle. He checked the battery charge and saw that it would be able to cover some ground while the sun continued to charge the cells. Taking one look back at the base, he started the truck and began driving. He was following along the beaten tracks in the desert earth that both the enemy and Mark's group had made.

His hands moved automatically down to the radio and turned it on. Nothing but static came through on the open channels. It wasn't surprising, really. Everyone would be keeping quiet on any high frequency channels. He was surprised there wasn't even an emergency broadcast on the civilian bands, however. If he knew what specific isolation protocols anyone was using to hide their communications in the white noise, he might have been able to pick up short bursts of communication. Those protocols were only decided in person between those who wanted to communicate, though.

He let the radio play out its static hum, taking comfort in the thought that somewhere in there were voices. The sound allowed him to drift and disconnect from reality as he pushed through the desert toward his friends.

CHAPTER 10

The sun rose as Mark's small group began to pack their camp back into the mechs and trucks. They had stopped to make a quick camp near midnight, after putting in what felt like enough distance between themselves and the base. No one had the energy to set up a full campsite, however, and most of them slept inside their vehicles.

Mark ate a meager breakfast on the command deck as he examined the map for obstacles along the current path of the enemy. He could see on his map that they were headed north toward Tonopah, a moderate urban center that had grown quickly after the end of the Decline. The United Entities had set up major CorNET and GovNET facilities there to facilitate communication across the vast empty stretches of desert in the western region. Most of the people they had seen back at the bonfire party lived in or near the city.

Mark used the comms station to call for a meeting beneath the bulk of his command mech, making sure to leave the crew of the Cronus to keep their eyes on the horizon. After waiting a sufficient time for the cadets to assemble below, Mark descended to the ground using a long cable and metal-rung ladder instead of dropping the entire center module down to the ground.

"Alright, guys," Mark said once everyone was clustered around him. "We're headed out toward Tonopah. We should be getting a lot closer to the enemy today, so we'll have to be more careful. We still don't know who we're dealing with, but they've already proven to be exceptionally prepared. Assume the city itself is occupied until we know one way or the other. I don't expect them to have stopped there, but who knows."

"Still running a wedge formation, or what?" Turner asked with a hint of resentment in his voice.

Mark looked up at Turner, and the rest of the cadets followed his gaze. Turner raised one eyebrow, as if to challenge Mark's authority.

"Let me get this out in the open." Mark spread his arms and then dropped them. "I'm about as experienced as everyone else here. The only reason I have command is because Zimmer is dead. I won't assume I know any more than any of you, because I don't. Until yesterday, we were all cadets back there." He gestured toward the thin column of smoke rising to the south. "But I do have command. Someone has to. I have trained extensively in the Maratus." He pointed above them. "I believe I will be able to keep us moving and keep our core as safe as possible out here. But I'm more than open to suggestions. So, on the table is wedge formation. Anyone else?"

"Sure, I don't like it," a cadet named Snell said. "It puts the single mech out in front at too much risk. And with our forces as thin as they are, we can't risk it. I say we put two mechs at the front of the formation instead. It would give us more coverage if we come up on anything unexpected."

"I agree," Turner said, with the first genuine smile Mark had seen in quite some time. "We can't risk mechs, not while we've got so few. That change to the formation ensures that we protect a wider area up front. It's not like we've got any replacements bringing up the rear."

"Sure, that makes sense to me," Mark said, attempting to reclaim some of his lost authority. Surrendering any of it to Turner may have been a mistake. "Turner, take the Kapu and one of the Aves class mechs up front. Either one, I don't care which. Hell, it might as well be the Iris. Probably shouldn't tempt fate with a name like Icarus up front. The rest of you fill out the formation with the trucks underneath me in the center. It's as good as we're going to get without a full core."

Many of the cadets looked to Turner, who read the situation and nodded his approval.

"Pack up," Mark said shortly. "We're moving within the hour."

Soon, their group was contained back in their various vehicles. Turner reported from the Kapu that he and the Iris were in position, and Mark ordered them to move out. To the broader group, he gave the general orders to stay in formation and to keep concealed from any direct lines of sight from the city.

"If you can't see them, they can't see you," he said over the radio. "But you already know that. Keep to your training and we'll all be fine."

He slumped back in his chair, sighed, and looked over at Brooke. She was smiling in a way that betrayed her amusement at his discomfort.

"They *want* someone to give them orders Mark. It's fine," she said. "Plus, it's hot when you get that commandery look. All determination and valor, like some kind of recruitment ad."

"You shut it," he said. "That's not appropriate to say to your commanding officer."

"She's right," Kalen said with a smile. It was the first time he had spoken without necessity since they'd left Zimmer behind. "There's a look you guys get. Zim always does. Well, did, I guess."

Kalen turned back to his console. Mark and Brooke pretended not to notice as he pressed his fingers into his eyes. Mark ordered the second group of mechs to head out, offering some more advice they probably already knew. This time he didn't second-guess himself and let the orders, hopefully, carry more weight.

Command had always seemed to come naturally to Zimmer, and Mark still wasn't sure if it did for him. It felt a bit like playing a role in a play. He was delivering the lines as well as he could. The difference was that if his audience didn't believe him, people might die.

Soon every mech was moving at an even pace toward the city. If there were enemy forces holding up in the city, they would be expecting some kind of ground force soon. The hills he'd plotted them toward provided relatively complete cover from anyone who might be looking out into the desert. As they got closer, their movements between dunes became more calculated. These maneuvers sometimes warped them out of their ideal formation, causing Mark some unease when they had blind spots in their scans.

Occasionally, based on this unease, he piloted his mech a bit higher on the dunes to get a clear view of the desert around them. It took only a moment for one of the visual sensors up top to rise above the hills. He timed these risky maneuvers with gusts of wind, hoping the chaos of sand coupled with the brevity of the moment would conceal the movement. Each time he did one of these sweeps, he was reassured when Brooke reported no anomalous readings in the desert ahead.

The sun began to throw color across the cloud-streaked sky as they neared the city. Mark brought the group to a halt behind the cover of the last range of hills, and they made camp. They set up in much the same way they did the night before, circling around Mark's command mech. They left the Icarus this time fully powered and manned. Throughout the night, the small crew of the Aves class mech would cycle through, keeping their eyes on the scans that came in.

Mark called another group meeting beneath his mech. They all clustered around a rough map on the ground, this one etched in the sand with sticks. Their group was represented by a cluster of rectangles. A dotted line, running between their group and the shapes of the buildings ahead, showed the proposed twelve-mile path across the last rolling low desert hills. The map wasn't strictly necessary, but the group didn't argue as he worked. Visuals had always helped him to work through problems, so their indulgence was appreciated.

"I've only been into Tonopah a handful of times," Mark said, pulling a line through the rough shape he'd drawn for the city. "But if I remember right, there's a main road through town with most of the larger buildings near the center. The center of the city is an Enclaved Zone. A few government offices, and the housing for key officials in the region. The CorNET and Gov-NET buildings are in the complex as well. Outside the Enclaved Zone will be less heavily populated. Some buildings were completely abandoned the last time I went through."

"That's how I remember it, too," Turner said. "Depopulated like most urban centers, but that leaves plenty of space to hide a mech." He paused for effect. "Or twenty."

"We don't even know if they're still in there," Brooke said. "I wouldn't be. If I were them, I'd put in as much distance from Taycher base as I could."

"Better assume they *are* though," Turner said with an angry look. "As much firepower as they took with them, even one or two units could be a huge problem. Have you seen the rust buckets we're dragging across the desert?"

Turner gestured toward the worst of them, the Nanook. The clunky mech they'd been keeping at the back of the formations even looked tired, on all fours and powered down for the night.

"Sure, yeah it's best to assume we've got enemies in the city," Mark said. "Anyone have any suggestions on how we approach?"

"One mech," Kalen said from a few steps outside the circle. The group turned in surprise as he moved in. "That's all we can spare for recon. There aren't enough of us to risk sending everyone, but we need someone to head in and scope it out." Then, without waiting for a vote, he said, "I'll do it."

Mark was surprised to have both a suggestion and an immediate volunteer. He'd been worried about a full-scale argument erupting over their next move. The silence around the circle was hard to read, but no one immediately offered another plan.

129

Mark waited a few moments for the silence to solidify and stood up from the sand map.

"Sounds reasonable," Mark said, brushing dust from his hands. "Take command of the Craig, and I'll fit the crew in somewhere. Get a full night's sleep Kalen, I need you alert for this. Hang back and we'll talk strategy, everyone else is dismissed."

Mark was surprised when the group responded to his commands immediately. The only grumble he heard came from the current crew of the mech he had given over to Kalen. Even these grumblings were minimal, and they each shook Kalen's hand before they left.

"Thank you, Sir," Kalen said after everyone else was out of earshot. "I just need to do something."

"Don't call me Sir, and you're doing just as much as everyone else," Mark said. "More, if I'm being honest."

"That's not what I mean, and you know it," Kalen said. "I need to do something real. Zimmer is dead. I'm not sure you really get that, but I have to do something besides sit inside a metal box and wait."

Mark started to compile a response, to warn him against picking a fight by himself in the city. Instead, he took a moment to consider the man in front of him. Kalen had been near the top of their class in every ranking board back at the Academy. The only reason he hadn't thrown his own name in for the position of Zimmer's second in command was because of their relationship. No, he would stick to protocol. For a man like Kalen, wasting resources on a fight he couldn't win would amount to a betrayal of Zimmer's legacy.

"Just be careful out there," Mark said instead.

~

Zak had driven all day, cresting hill after hill of dry desert earth. Each time, he had hoped to see some sign of his fellow cadets in the distance. Every time, he was disappointed by an empty horizon.

As the sun lowered on his first day of travel, he found himself drifting into sleep at the wheel, and then jolting awake. As he crested another of the seeming thousands of hills, he suddenly noted the absence of any of the tracks that had been his guide so far. He panicked before he was able to reassure himself that he was probably still going the right way. It was simply too dark to see them any longer. He could have gotten out of the truck and checked more carefully, but progress would have been too slow to make it worthwhile. At the bottom of a hill, he brought the truck to a halt. He turned off the engine and could see the gentle rise of dunes all around him.

After a full day of driving, the sounds of tires rolling over dirt, the steady whine of the electric engine, and the static hum of his radio had merged into one continuous sound. Now that they were gone, the silence around him was nearly tangible. What little wind there was at the base of the hill was hot and slow. Zak exited his vehicle and walked a few yards away. He urinated for what seemed like too long and returned to the confines of his vehicle to prepare a small meal from what he had found before he left. There was more than enough water in two large jugs he'd brought to help him out here in the desert. What he really wished he had found was some whiskey, or even just a beer or two. It was hard to believe it had only been two days since he and Mark toasted to Brooke's 'bright and wonderful future.' Zak didn't even know if either of them were alive.

He patted the pocket where he still had the piece of chalk tucked away. It was reassuring, but not enough. Zak wasn't even absolutely sure he was still following his friends. They could have veered off without him noticing, leaving him to follow the tracks of the enemy forces. He could be alone in the desert, racing toward an invincible core of rebel mechs.

For the first time since the attack, he allowed a flash of rage pass through him. Until now, he'd been coasting on instinct and training, taking the most logical next step. His hands began to shake, and he gripped the steering wheel tightly to center himself in the space. There was a definite possibility that these bastards, these rebels who believed their cause justified anything, had taken everything from him again. They'd killed his family when he was only a child, and now they'd killed scores of students in their sleep. It was even possible they'd taken the only people he had been able to get close to since that day in his first home.

White hot flashes burst in his mind, and he found it hard to filter the conflicting emotions raging up inside him. Memories that he'd rather not unbox right then became untethered. The wind outside gathered momentum and cast a soft mist of sand around the truck. For a moment, the sound took him off track. Then he was back, and his anger thickened into a choking fear.

"No, not now." Zak closed his eyes and began practicing the breathing exercises he'd been taught as a child. He couldn't remember how long it had been since he'd needed to try them.

Holes were ripped into the kitchen wall just as his mother began pouring milk into his cereal bowl. White glass, it had been one of the prettiest things his family owned. Zak always felt special when he'd been allowed to use it. It shattered in front of him, and he looked up to see his mother falling to the ground.

The screaming came instantly, but not from her. She never had the chance before she died. It was his voice, but he felt like he had no control over it.

"No!" Zak yelled into the dark quiet of his vehicle. His voice was enough to bring him partway out of the memory. "You're okay Zak. You're going to be fine."

His heart continued to beat erratically in his chest. He forced his eyes closed and brought his hands up to cover his face. Zak rocked gently in his chair as his muscles seemed to spasm with the effort of mentally lashing his memories and errant thoughts back into place.

Another clear flash came through. He saw himself as if from above, a child at the breakfast table. It was a well-worn collapsible card table adorned with salt and pepper shakers that were purely decorative. The child was frozen with a smile still on his face, not yet comprehending what has just happened. Slowly it seemed to dawn on him that something was wrong, and his face lost color. Then he was screaming again, the sound seeming to pierce through time.

"You're *fine*, Zak!" He opened his eyes and was back in his vehicle once again. The wind outside was being cut by one of the antennas outside, producing a strong, steady whine. The memory wasn't even a real memory, strictly speaking. He couldn't have seen those details. But these things rarely ever made sense.

'They don't have to make sense,' was what a faceless doctor had told him after it all happened. 'Everyone processes things differently,' Zak had been informed, and his experiences were completely normal. Something about depersonalization and trauma.

"Completely normal," Zak said aloud. "Right, because every kid watches his mother die."

Zak was calming down now. He knew how these things tended to work for him. The shakes would last a little while longer and he might have a few more minor muscle spasms. This one had been mild, compared to some that he'd suffered as a child. He was exhausted, partly from the panic attack, of course, but also from the day spent driving.

The thought to try and conceal his vehicle occurred to him, but in his depleted state, it seemed like too much work for little reward. The odds that anyone else was out this far were low. The wind continued to gather energy outside as night slipped across the sky, and the truck rocked gently with the bigger gusts. The path he was following was taking him toward Tonopah and he was probably only a few hours out. Tomorrow he would have to be more careful, but for tonight he could rest. Zak reclined his seat and closed his eyes, allowing the driving desert winds to rock him to sleep.

In the morning, Zak took the time to go through his gear. He might not have another chance to prepare before he got into a situation where he would need to make quick decisions. He packed as much equipment as he could into a single pack. Not so much that it would slow him down on foot, but enough to keep him sustained for a couple of days in a worst-case scenario. He still had only the partially charged pistol in the way of defense. He supposed a fold-up field shovel he'd strapped to one side of the pack might do for a backup weapon. Satisfied with these preparations, he filled a canteen with water for the drive and opened a dry granola bar for breakfast. He wasn't very hungry, so it eventually ended up in the passenger's seat, half eaten. Zak picked his way through the hills more carefully now, avoiding the taller ones, and sticking to routes between them wherever possible.

When his truck's shadow was directly beneath him, he began to pass by the first small signs of civilization. Zak had been able to avoid all major roads and most marked trails to this point, but he began to pass over some of the smaller trails then. They were little more than double ruts carved into the hardened ground but were unmistakably man made. Occasionally, trash caught in the sagebrush glinted in the midday sun.

If Mark and his group were alive, were even headed the same way, they should have been reaching the town about now. Traveling with a command mech, they would be moving quite a bit slower than his truck was able to do alone. Now would be a good time for a reunion, Zak thought.

CHAPTER 11

Mark spoke to his group again in the morning. This had become something of a ritual, gathering beneath the Maratus to plan the way forward. This morning, however, they'd opted to stay out of the wind and conduct their meeting through their encrypted comms. Yesterday, smooth sands had given way to the more rocky and stable earth ahead. Just beyond the next expanse of foothills was a dusty stretch of unused government farmland. Most open farmland had been abandoned when blight had destroyed entire crops year after year. Massively genetically modified crops had become the only way forward and most agriculture now took place inside heavily protected warehouses that stretched for miles.

The land ahead was mostly open space, populated only by the occasional abandoned barn or grain silo. Kalen had been right the night before. The whole core couldn't go across it at once, but it still seemed wrong to send anyone in without backup.

"Kalen, you ready?" Mark asked. After a moment of silence, Mark leaned forward to look for Kalen's mech through the windshield. He could see the Craig, a few hundred yards ahead of the main group, facing the foothills ahead. Mark put his finger back on the comm button ready to repeat his question.

"Ready, sir," Kalen said, his voice calm and confident, before Mark could ask him again. "I was just sending a few words upstairs. Wouldn't mind if you did the same for me."

"That's not normally my thing, but I'll see what I can do," Mark said. Kalen's mech, standing apart from the group, looked so fragile that Mark made a quick decision. "I'm sending someone with you over the hills. They'll come back when they see that you've cleared the first stretch of farmland."

Before anyone had the chance to object, he ordered the Icarus to accompany Kalen to the other side of the hills, and no further. No one came through the radio to object.

The two mechs set out slowly, and when they dropped over the nearest hill, Mark let out a sigh. He was not usually one to get caught up in prayers and religion, but he figured that it couldn't hurt and spent the next minute speaking internally to some vague power. Near the end, he threw in some prayer for his family. It surprised him that he'd mostly avoided thinking about them for this long. He had spent most of his life in various academies and preparatory programs, so perhaps the lapse was forgivable.

He tried to picture them in his mind and had more trouble than he liked. His mother had been away most of the time on whatever important business she'd been tasked with at the time. He'd been closer to his father as a result. They'd even managed to carve out time for the yearly boating excursions his father had hauled him out to the coast for.

The trips were some of the only times he and his father had ever had real conversations, and Mark looked forward to them as the weather warmed each year. Mark remembered the last trip they'd taken together, just after Mark had been accepted into the Academy. The boat had been in their family for generations, according to his father. They had sailed it into the wind away from the coast. The smell of wet dust overwhelmed him, as the spray of the ocean washed away the months of dust accumulated in quiet storage. Soon they were far enough from the shore that it was effectively gone. In all directions, the expanse of the ocean seemed limitless.

They turned the sail so that there was no longer any wind in it, and the boat had slowed on the choppy water. His father smiled in a conspiratorial way and opened the storage compartment beneath his seat. His father had insisted on pulling their lifejackets out of it himself before they set out, but Mark hadn't thought much of it at the time.

He withdrew a half empty bottle of amber colored liquid, some sort of spirit. There was no label, but the ornateness of the glass suggested that it was valuable.

"This bottle has been on the boat longer than I can remember," his father said. "My dad told me it was here even before he got the boat from his father."

His father put the bottle on the deck of the boat carefully and then retrieved two glasses wrapped in a clean white cloth. He handed one of the glasses to Mark and poured some of the amber spirits into each. After returning the bottle to the storage compartment, his father sat and looked at his glass.

"This whiskey was distilled before the Decline." He swirled it around in his glass and held it up to the sky to examine its color. "It's bad."

"Wait, seriously?" Mark laughed and looked down at his glass. "What happened to it?"

"It might not have even been very good to begin with." His father took a sip and grimaced. "But whiskey doesn't last forever, and neither will this boat. All we can do is try to preserve the things that matter most to us. That's what you're doing, going into military service."

Mark lifted his glass and took a drink. It was bad, just like his father had said, but he didn't have much of a comparison for it.

"I didn't earn it," he said quietly. "I should be headed to one of the production communities."

"You passed the entrance exam like everyone else." His father adjusted the sail as a rouge gust of wind tugged at the boat. "Your mom pulled in a favor to get you in a priority lane, sure. But I'm not convinced you wouldn't have gotten in even if she hadn't. You're a fine leader."

"I threw a ball and called some plays," Mark shook his head. "It's not the same thing."

"No, it's probably not," his father drained his glass and looked out over the water. "I never served so I don't really know. But you performed under pressure. You reacted to changing situations and gave orders. It sounds a lot like leadership to me."

Mark had wanted to thank him, but the wind shifted again. The boom whipped across the boat narrowly missing them both.

The boat began to tug and lean. Mark's father stood up and put his glass away.

"The boat is yours, Mark." His father began to set the sail to bear away from the wind and return them to shore. "Take good care of it and it will take you anywhere you want to go. Looks like a storm cell is coming."

Mark drank the rest of his glass of whiskey and returned his glass to the storage compartment with the other one. He had turned his attention to securing the rigging under his father's direction, and together they had worked their way ahead of the storm that had begun to form over their heads.

~

After an agonizing stretch of time, the Icarus returned unscathed from its trip over the hills.

"Kalen is across, sir," Carson said over the radio. "Didn't see anything suspicious. Unless you count a complete lack of activity, which I kind of do."

Mark ordered his team into a defensive shield and hoped for a report to come in from Kalen. After an hour of silence, the radio on the command deck crackled to life. Mark leaned in close to the speaker not wanting to miss a word of Kalen's report.

"I don't see anyone here," Kalen said, his voice faint. "This area is torn apart. Shit, this is terrible."

"We hear you out here," Mark said, keeping his voice steady. "Start your low frequency scan. Let's see what we've got to worry about in there."

"Who could do this to a civilian target?" Kalen asked, his voice distant. "I thought all of this ended with the Decline."

"Kalen, we read you. Keep off comms unless it's necessary. We need clear readings before we can do anything. We're blind back here. The longer you sit there, the more you build a heat signature. Reroute your power and scan, just like in training."

A few moments went by with the channel clear of conversation. A fine ash began to fall, slowly dusting the windshields of their small core of mechs as smoke from the city continued to rise like a pillar into the sky.

"All clear, guys," Kalen radioed back to the group. "I'm reading small signatures here and there but no mech-sized holes in my scans so far. Whoever's left here is more afraid of us than we are of them. Maybe a few scattered camps of civilian holdouts if I had to guess."

"Thank you, Kalen," Mark said. "Transmit your coordinates and cycle down. We'll come to you." Mark switched over to the local frequency. "Alright, let's get moving. Kalen hasn't seen anything yet, but we can't be sure. Keep your eyes open."

Spreading into a wide formation, their small force advanced on Tonopah. Mark maintained his position in the center, watching the rooftops and windows of the buildings as they approached. Anyone looking out from the city would have been able to see the crisp outlines of their mechs as they crested the hills and dropped into the farmland below. Mark hoped Kalen's scans were right and that no one surprised them.

After another anxious length of time, the formation crossed the open land and reached Kalen's mech. As they waited for him to power back up, Mark looked out at the city. Many of the structures ahead of them were little more than charcoal sketches of their former selves. There was a central path of destruction cutting linearly to the north through the entire city. Fires raged in buildings along the way, and some had completely collapsed.

While they waited, Mark had Brooke run scans with the more advanced technology of the command mech. The largest heat signatures were in the center of the city, the enclaved portion that housed several government and corporate offices. Massive fires there obscured the scans a bit, and Mark decided to keep their sweeps trained on the area. Based on what they could see when she finished, the population in the city had largely evacuated itself. They may have had some warning or noticed the smoke coming from Taycher Mechanized Armor Base. There wouldn't have been a large population there to begin with. As Turner had mentioned earlier, most urban centers were depopulated and moved into government-run communities once Stability had been restored. Mark just hoped that whatever population had stayed in the city had been able to get out of the way in time.

"Head for the open area to the northeast," Mark said to his team. "It looks like some kind of park or fairground. It looks empty. I don't want to walk through the city unless we have to."

Their mechs followed a curve around the edge of the city. This way they caused the least damage and also retained the highest range of movement. As they traveled, Mark continued to watch the scans as they came in from Brooke's terminal. Where there should have been a regional GovNET building, there was a hole in the skyline. That explained some of the communication blackout they were experiencing.

He remembered the attack on New Wall Street they had seen while talking in Rec. Five back at the Academy. That must have been a trial run for what they did at Taycher, he realized. The enemy had attacked during a time of decreased activity and moved quickly to destroy specific targets and move on.

As he looked over a new scan of the city, Brooke leaned over his chair and reached out onto his screen to pan back a few pages. She spent a moment toggling back and forth between two scans.

"Do you see that?" She asked, pointing at a seemingly innocuous blob of heat on the screen. "Check it out, one after another. What changes?"

Mark panned through the scans and saw it almost immediately. He'd been focusing so closely on each image as it came across his screen that he hadn't been watching for changes between frames.

"Something's moving in there," he said. "Staying just out of our line of sight. Brooke, someone's in there."

The blood rushed from his head as he said this. He couldn't tell anyone then; doing so might spoil any element of surprise they'd created with their ignorance. He reached for the radio and pressed the button.

"Assume our standard camp formation," he said, keeping his voice level. "Once we're settled, I'll need one person from each unit down at the trucks underneath my mech for a meeting."

"You can't be serious, Mark." Brooke flashed him a look of alarm. "It's not safe out there. Anyone outside is toast if whatever's in the city decides to start taking shots at us."

"Just keep a close eye on the city." He paused and looked out the windshield toward the buildings in the distance. "We'll keep the gun up top aimed toward the city. Alert me if there's movement out there, and we should have enough time to get back inside if anything happens."

Mark exited the mech, leaving Brooke inside at the controls. Below, he found one pilot from each mech already waiting for him. Turner walked toward him, catching him by the arm before he could reach the others.

"Look." He held firmly to Mark's arm. "There's something out there. I saw it on some scans I made as we were moving in. I'm not sure if you saw it, but we can't stay out in the open like this."

"I know." Mark pulled his arm away from Turner. "I didn't want to scare anyone into making any sudden moves. We should be well outside their range, and if they planned on attacking us, they would have already."

Turner looked at Mark for a long moment, decided that he wasn't lying, and nodded. Together, they walked a few paces to the others. Mark called them in close to discuss the situation.

"I'm not sure who else knows this, but there is something moving around near the center of the enclaved portion of the city." Mark waited a moment for this to sink in. A couple of the gathered cadets looked toward the city; others simply nodded. They all focused on Mark, awaiting a plan he did not have. He took a deep breath and focused on coming up with something quickly.

"My plan, if you can call it that, is to wait." He paused to gauge the response. When no one objected, he continued. "Whoever is in there hasn't made a move yet, which leads me to believe they're either waiting to attack or hoping we won't notice them. Both are to our advantage."

The others had been taking cues from Turner during the informal gatherings. Leaving him out of the discussion might widen the rift that was already forming. Mark made a decision and looked to Turner.

"Turner, you saw it too," he said, making a play. "Do you agree with the assessment?"

"Sure, yeah," Turner said, seemingly startled by the inclusion of his opinion. When Mark didn't say anything, Turner continued. "Whatever it is keeps creeping around behind those buildings so that we never get a clear look at it. Through the buildings, it sorta looks like fires and warm bodies on thermal scans. There can't be more than one or two of them at most. Even fully equipped, they couldn't take out our core. Not to mention our big gun."

He pointed above them, at the Maratus. "We could level the entire area they're in with a few good shots from the gun on this thing. They might even already be damaged. It would explain why they were left behind."

"Perfect," Mark said. "So, we wait and see what they do. Until then, I want everyone acting normally. Keep a watch as we would, but don't go doing anything that might tip our hand."

Mark dismissed the group and returned up to the command deck, where Brooke informed him that there had been no movement in the center of the city. He used the comm system to catch the rest of his crew up on the plan to wait. As he did, Brooke shifted uncomfortably in her seat but said nothing.

Zak drove carefully, following the clear path trampled by the large number of mechs toward the city. The tracks had become visible again when the sun cleared the horizon in the morning. Seeing the tracks had brought him great relief. The smoke that drifted over the horizon was white and steady, so it was safe to assume no new action had occurred so far. With any luck, the city would be clear of enemy forces, but it was still much too early to hope. He continued through the low hills, working a bit harder to select the best path over the rocky terrain.

Once he crested the final rise, he moved quickly down the other side, trying to minimize his time out in the open. Zak still wasn't sure that the tracks he was following were friendly. His gut said not to worry, and to relax a bit. However, he recalled something Phillips had said one day as they were storing the mechs in the hangar at the end of the day. He'd said that once you were a true soldier, you would never fully relax until you were dead. He'd said it in an offhand way, but the layered meanings had always stuck with Zak. His favorite interpretation was that Phillips had meant to say that if you relax on the field of battle, you will die. Mark had interpreted it to mean that soldiers never truly become anything but what their training has made them. Both seemed apt, so Zak had tried to internalize both lessons as well as he could.

At the bottom, Zak made short work of an open field in front of him. He tried to keep his speed low enough that he didn't pull up a lot of dust in the barren expanse of farmland. As he examined the landscape for cover, he spotted the leaning remnants of an ancient hayloft. He worked his way toward it. The building's stability was certainly an open question, as it visibly leaned to one side, but he pulled inside and was effectively hidden from view. Zak turned off the engine and took a moment to exit his truck to get a sense of the area without a dusty windshield in front of him.

The barn was heavily damaged. The roof far above had been clipped by something, leaving a jagged skylight. The clouds beyond this tear were fluffy, slow, and completely indifferent to the scene below. There was a roughly constructed ladder leading up to the loft in one corner. The wood was worn smooth in the areas where boots and gloved hands had been placed over decades of use. Zak tested the ladder and found that it felt structurally sound.

When he reached the top, he walked quietly to a broad open window facing toward the city. From there he could see the extent of the destruction the enemy had inflicted on Tonopah. The smoke was less obtrusive now, as the fires in the city had begun to die down. With the cooling air, however, ash that had been suspended high in the atmosphere had begun to come down like snow. Zak could see the clear path trampled through the fields ahead. Beyond that, the beaten track ripped through neighborhoods, office buildings, and everything else in a direct line through the heart of the city. The enemy could have gone around. They could have even made better time if they had. Zak wondered if they were hiding among the taller buildings in the enclaved portion of the city but brushed the thought aside for now. They had taken too many units to effectively conceal them all, even in a city this size. Tonopah had grown when part of it was enclaved and the government had built a GovNET communication transfer station, but it was still nothing compared to other sprawling metropolises.

He'd spent most of his life in one of them, and still found the openness of the western landscape disquieting at times. In a city, walls, buildings, and fences created a maze of entrances and exits that could be exploited. Out in the open desert, however, there was too much open space to hide.

Scanning the fields closer to him, he could see one of the downed jets that had dropped from the sky when he was standing on the roof of the barracks. The jet, surprisingly intact, glinted in the sunlight at the end of a dark gash churned into the earth. From here, he could even see the pilot, motionless, still inside the cockpit. He wondered again what could have caused an entire fighter squadron to simply lose control in mid-air. Whatever the enemy was traveling with must significantly limit attacks from the air. It could also have explained why there weren't more fighters in the area, mopping up whoever had torn the base apart.

Even if manned aerial attacks were blocked, he wondered why airstrikes or ground forces weren't coming in to box the assholes in. It must have been much worse than just this one attack, he realized. It must have been happening all over the country, maybe even globally. It explained how brazen the attack was and why no one had shown up since the jets.

"Who *are* these people?" Zak asked himself.

He shook his head to clear it and turned away from the window. These questions were important but wasting time thinking about them here wouldn't bring him any closer to the answers.

Mark and whoever was with him would have more information. If they didn't, maybe they could figure it out together.

Zak left the window and went back downstairs. He got into the truck and made his way toward the downed jet, hoping some supplies had been left undamaged. The jet had a matte grey finish, marred, and burned in places. It was a wonder that whatever explosive payload it was carrying hadn't detonated. One of the wings was completely gone, but everything else was recognizable as a plane.

Zak climbed up the side of the jet to reach the cockpit. He peered through the curved glass at the pilot, still motionless in his seat. Zak released the latches on the glass dome and lifted it open. As he surveyed the cockpit, he noted that the contents of the medical kit and several other items were strewn around. He lifted one of his legs over and into the jet to get a better reach on the supplies. He lifted the metal case for the medical kit and began scooping up the scattered contents. When he came across a bloodied bandage, he froze.

An impact caught him off guard, and he tumbled backward out of the cockpit. He had little more than a moment to assess the situation before he hit the ground. He landed on the scorched earth and immediately scrambled on all fours back toward his truck. Once he was around to the far side of his truck, he remembered his pistol and took it out. It hummed to life and the small display reminded him that it was still at half capacity.

A shot fired from the cockpit impacted the truck on the other side. It cracked flatly in the open silence of the field. A moment passed, and another shot plowed through both the passenger's side window and the driver's, sending shattered glass raining down on him. Another moment passed, and then another, and silence returned to the field.

"Just go," someone yelled out from the cockpit. "Fuck off and let me die in peace you..."

The voice stopped, and a wet, hacking cough followed.

"You, fucks," the voice finished, somewhat less energetically.

"Friendly! I'm a friendly!" Zak yelled.

"How the hell would you know?" asked the pilot.

It was true. The group that had stormed the base took a lot of things with them. It wasn't hard to believe that, somewhere else, The Harbingers had gotten ahold of a few jets. If Zak told the pilot his affiliation, he tipped his hand. Or the pilot might just believe he was lying. They would be at square one again.

"Prove you're one of us," the pilot called. "What's the password we're using?"

A password was something the rebels might use to identify themselves out on the battlefield. It would make sense with everyone moving the same gear around. Zak tightened his grip on his pistol and decided.

"I don't have a password, asshole!" Zak yelled. It was either that or make one up, which the pilot would have obviously caught; also, this felt better.

"Good," was the response from the pilot, followed by another fit of coughing. "I killed the last guy that gave me a password. Take a look yourself. The other side of the plane."

"You know I can't do that," Zak said. "Put your hands in the air and I'll check."

There was a metal thud as the pilot put his weapon down. Zak looked over the truck and saw two hands come up out of the cockpit, one bloody and trembling. "Hurry. I can't hold them up long."

Zak moved out from behind the truck, keeping his pistol aimed at the cockpit. He made his way around the plane and was relieved to see that the pilot was telling the truth. The body was there, just as he had said, dressed in a dull grey and black military style uniform. Small details, like where the holster was positioned on the tactical vest, assured Zak that this wasn't someone carefully trained. The poor position of the holster may have been what gave the pilot enough time to get off a clear shot. Zak reached down and relieved the body of the weapon and the holster.

"Okay," Zak called up to the pilot. "I think I believe you, but I'm going to need a bit more information before I climb back up there and get you out."

"No," came a weak response from above. The pilot dropped his hands, and Zak experienced a moment of panic. "Like I said before. Go away and let me die."

The pilot hadn't gone for his weapon. Zak relaxed.

"What's your name?" Zak asked. Keeping his weapon trained on the cockpit, he circled back around the plane.

"Captain Joseph Barkley. Why?" he asked.

"My name is Zakary Lockwood." Zak approached the cockpit again. "A third-year cadet from United Entities Mechanized Warfare Academy back that way."

Zak climbed the ladder carefully, listening for any movement in the cockpit. "Hands up again. I'm coming up".

The pilot's hands rose again, both trembling from the effort. Zak pulled himself over the edge and swung both his legs into

151

the cockpit. Barkley dropped his hands into his lap and breathed heavily.

"I'm going to get you out of here," Zak said. "A group of my friends are ahead somewhere, and we'll help you."

The pilot made no effort to speak, only continued breathing through his pain. Slowly, Barkley slumped forward in his seat. He was unconscious. Even if he were awake, it would be nearly impossible to get the man out safely. Zak briefly considered taking Barkley at his word and leaving him there but brushed the thought away.

Zak climbed back down and pulled his truck close alongside the jet. He slowly moved the unconscious pilot down onto the roof of the cab, then down the windshield to the hood, and finally onto the ground. The process wasn't graceful, but it was better than leaving the man to die.

Barkley had remained unconscious through most of the transfer, waking only once during his initial removal from the cockpit. He'd tried to fight Zak but had lost consciousness again quickly. Leaving him on the ground in front of the truck, Zak retrieved what supplies he could from the jet. He gathered medical supplies, food rations, and the weapon Barkley had used to shoot at him earlier. Before leaving, Zak also gathered some personal items he found stashed in a compartment underneath the control panel: a photograph of a woman holding a baby, and a worn brass lighter.

After the ordeal of getting the pilot down from the cockpit, getting him into the enclosed bed of the truck was easy. Once he had Barkley positioned inside, Zak busied himself with the man's injuries.

Barkley had done much of the work already, and most of what Zak could do was limited to changing out bandages. Barkley had even pulled a deep gash on his thigh together with crude stitches before Zak's arrival. Unfortunately, the transfer had reopened the wound partially. Zak brought it closed again with a few of his own crude stitches. Now that he was lying flat, Barkley seemed to be in remarkably good shape, given his fall from the sky.

If there were any internal injuries, they were well beyond Zak's expertise. Barkley's heartbeat was strong and steady, so he left the pilot in the back of the enclosed storage bed and returned to the cab. The best he could do was find Mark and the others, or they were both in trouble.

~

Mark took advantage of the time they were spending on the outskirts of Tonopah and made sure that everyone was active. Throughout the day they did their best to behave as if there was no danger lurking in the city. But all tasks were completed with one eye on the distant silhouetted buildings, searching for any sign of movement. On more than one occasion, Mark discovered someone idly staring directly into the city, paused in whatever work they were attempting to finish. Mark had to make a point to discourage this kind of activity.

Not only did these distractions potentially give away the advantage he was trying to cultivate, but there were also several important tasks to complete before any amount of travel, or other actions, could be taken. The mechs all needed routine calibration and maintenance, and there was always something to do in the way of organizing and rationing their ammunition, food, and medical supplies. Some mechs had payloads that weren't ideal for the fighting style typical of the unit, and some of the cadets were busy manually transporting ammunition from one mech to another. Light rounds and energy cells to the Lupine and Aves-Class mechs. Heavy artillery and missiles to the stockier Jotun and Ursidae classes.

By the time these tasks were completed, the sun had left the sky completely, bringing forth another watercolor of fire in the skies above.

Maybe Brooke was right about this desert, Mark thought as he watched his team working in the pink light. He caught sight of her, off near the edge of the camp, sitting with Payne. They were next to a tree that looked like it could use a good rain. He had almost forgotten about Payne, and he was glad Brooke had continued to look after him. Mark and his team had all been scarred by the attack, some more than others.

As he approached, he saw that Brooke was talking with Payne. He was also doing what he'd been doing since they left the base, staring off into the middle distance and fidgeting with his clothing. When Mark reached them, Brooke turned around to greet him. Her eyes told him the situation before he could even ask her what they were talking about. The cadet must have finally been telling his story. Brooke had a wonderful, and often annoying, talent for pulling things out of people. Mark sat with them under the tree, facing out toward the city.

"Beautiful," Mark said. "I'm actually starting to like these mountains."

"They really are wonderful," Brooke said. "Payne and I were just talking about them."

Mark turned and watched as Payne reached one trembling hand toward the city.

"I used to live *right* there." Payne grasped limply at the air in front of him, as if trying to bring something toward him, then dropped his hand back onto his lap. "My family wasn't important. It was just me, my mom, and my sister out there in one of the farm worker communities."

Mark looked out toward the community Payne had indicated. The area was directly in line with the path of destruction cut through the city. He could see that most of the homes were mere shattered remnants. It was possible that the area was evacuated, but there was no way to know. Mark thought about telling Payne that he was sorry, but Brooke leaned out and shook her head lightly. They waited for Payne to continue.

"My mom took the shuttle with the rest of the workers every morning. Came back smelling like strawberries. She brought some home one day for my birthday one year.

"I told her I didn't want to eat them. They were so pretty and red, and I knew how much she worked to make them grow. She worked so hard.

"She cried and said she worked hard so that I could have them, so that one day everyone could have them. Every year from then on, she would bring some home for my birthday. I knew she could get in trouble if anyone ever found out, but she did it anyway.

"They pulled my name after preselection school. My test scores were good, and she was so proud. She sent me away with some strawberries packed into my bags. When I got to the Academy, I couldn't bring myself to eat them. They sat in my locker for weeks, getting darker and darker until they weren't strawberries anymore."

He looked toward the ruined community in the distance and tears rolled down his face. His round face was bathed in the golden light of the falling sun, and in that moment, he looked so much like a child. Mark wanted to grab him and hold him, but he held back. Brooke reached one arm around Payne's shoulder, and he leaned into her and sobbed.

"I should have eaten them. I should have eaten them while I could." Payne brought his knees up to his chest and rocked gently.

No one spoke as the last wisps of color left the sky. Mark examined Brooke's face in the dying light. She was as beautiful as he had ever seen her, but her entire posture seemed harder now. She was somehow reinforced in the face of the ruined city in front of them. Mark had never known this side of her, and perhaps it was one new to her, as well. Maybe this was what happened to all soldiers when they encountered evil. Soft metal being forged into stronger, more resilient stuff.

Mark turned and looked back at his group. A similar look was reflected in all of them. Most of them had only seen war and its immediate effects from various safe distances until now. The horrors of losing family, friends, lovers, and even a home were now painfully real for this group. Somewhere along the line, they'd all transitioned from cadets into soldiers. There was no ceremony, but perhaps one wasn't necessary in war.

Sometime soon, he and his group would have their first chance to tip the scales back. Exactly when seemed to depend largely on what he decided to do about the enemy mech in the city. Mark looked back at the city and imagined it as his own city. He visualized the Harbingers tearing through his parent's house, his school, and his streets. It occurred to him for the first time that what he was imagining was completely possible. He hadn't heard anything from anyone outside of their group since the attack. The world could be crumbling around them, and they wouldn't even know.

The anger he was stoking in himself was fierce. He had the sudden irrational urge to power up his mech and charge into an unplanned battle with whatever was lurking around like vermin behind the buildings in the distance. This must have been what Brooke was holding back earlier.

"Tomorrow," Mark said. "We'll go get them tomorrow. Flush them out of whatever hole they think they can hide in."

He stood before either of them could respond and returned to the group to begin working up a plan. He started drawing a rough map of the area on the hood of a truck with a piece of chalk. Brooke brought Payne over and Mark set him to the task of finishing a map of the city and the surrounding area. As he worked, Turner came over with some other cadets to see what was going on.

"We're moving in tomorrow," Mark said. "We've waited long enough. Maybe we can capture whoever is piloting the mech in there and get some answers."

Once the map was done, a growing group used it to plan an attack. Based on their scans, they decided that it was likely the enemy would continue to hide for as long as possible. They would use this to their advantage and try to push the enemy into a position in the city where they wouldn't be able to defend themselves effectively. Using Payne's knowledge of the area, they would send two groups around the outside of the city, leaving one group to hold their current campsite. At some point, one of the advance groups would get a clear view of whatever was hiding in there. Once they had a visual, they would force it out of the claustrophobic downtown and out into the gash already trampled through the city. Scans from earlier in the day showed that area was largely empty. Hopefully, any civilians holding out would be smart enough to get out of the way before the action began.

It was nearly midnight when they put the final touches on the plan. Most of the time was spent talking about contingencies, should anything go wrong. Scans continued to show the enemy hadn't moved, so Mark sent most of the team to bed.

Zak had driven into the city with only dim light still in the sky. He passed by the shattered remnants of government housing that had once been neat and orderly. He had to pick his route carefully, as the damage to the roads was extensive. He looked for any clear signs that his team had stopped anywhere to rest. Given the average speed of mechanized combat armor, especially a Neith class, he should have come across them by now. He soon found the search hopeless, however, as darkness overtook the city.

None of the streetlights came on, and he pulled into a dark alley to spend the night. When he exited the truck, the sound of his door closing echoed in the empty city. There must have been some people still living there, but if they were, they weren't giving away their positions.

Zak walked to the back of his truck and climbed into the cargo area. Barkley was still asleep, likely had slept soundly through most of their journey so far.

"Hey," Mark shook Barkley's shoulder lightly. "You've got to take some food and water."

Barkley's eyes fluttered open, barely conscious. Then he gripped Zak's injured wrist so tightly it hurt. Barkley's eyes were fierce and dark in the gloom of the alley. His face looked like something out of a brochure for the Air Force. A tight blond haircut, and muscle tone in his jaw that spoke of a strict physical fitness regimen.

"It's me," Zak said. "You're safe. Everything is alright."

Barkley relaxed and released Zak's wrist. He looked around the interior of the enclosed cargo bed. In the dim light of the overhead lamp, there wasn't a lot for him to see. Zak handed him a canteen.

"I told you to leave me back there," Barkley said weakly. He took a drink to clear his throat. "I meant it."

"You're welcome." Zak opened the bag he had filled with rations and selected two granola bars. He also took out a packet of painkillers and offered them to Barkley.

"I'll be fine," Barkley pushed the offered food and pills away. "Save that stuff for someone else."

"There is no one else," Zak said. "It's just you and me out here."

Barkley hesitated but took the offered pills and left the granola bars. After swallowing the painkillers, he made an effort to sit up. Zak thought about trying to stop him, but Barkley gave up on the attempt himself and remained laying down.

"Where are we?" Barkley asked.

"Tonopah," Zak said.

He opened his mouth to continue but Barkley had already closed his eyes. If he was still awake, he wouldn't be for long. Instead, Zak turned and sat on the open tailgate and looked up. The dark buildings on either side of him loomed high like deep canyon walls. Beyond them was a strip of brilliant stars against the shadows of the city buildings. They were brighter than he'd ever remembered seeing them before. He watched as the galaxy slid by, a tapestry of luminous dust. He tried to find constellations, but his narrow view made it impossible to see the entirety of any particular formation of stars.

All of human civilization had looked up at the same stars, and many had ascribed some cosmic significance to their arrangement. Looking at them in this way, however, Zak could see them for what they were, countless points of indifferent light from billions of miles away. Their light wasn't directed at him or any place in particular. Each star shone in all directions at once, none more important than another.

He wasn't sure why, but this calmed him for some reason. The weight of expectation was not on him, or anyone else for that matter. None of it mattered to the grand expanse of the universe, and in a way that meant that he was allowed to focus

on what mattered to him. Finding Mark and Brooke mattered
to him. They were the only people who had focused their own
light on him.

CHAPTER 12

Mark found sleep elusive. So, instead of staring up at the bottom of another bunk, he headed to the command deck and disassembled and cleaned his rifle on the darkened map table in the center of the room. Brooke was also awake, sitting at the sensor display. When he was done with his rifle, he checked in with her. She brought up a diagnostic check of the Maratus' main systems. All systems were operating normally.

The sun crept up over the mountains in the east, casting a pale pastel version of yesterday's sunset over their camp. Mark still hadn't slept, and neither had Brooke. He left her to keep an eye on the scans of the city and descended from his mech onto the cool grass of the field they'd set up camp in. A fine dew had settled on the tips of every blade, giving the illusion that millions of stars had somehow fallen to Earth in the night. As he walked, he left a trail of dark prints where he snuffed the tiny lights. He took a breath of the crisp morning air and joined Kalen at the edge of camp for the final shift of the watch. The Nanook had taken up the usual watch position.

Kalen's post, out at the edge of camp with a pair of binoculars, was largely irrelevant considering how advanced the command mech scans were, but everyone had agreed that a pair of human eyes also keeping watch would make them feel better.

"All clear, Kalen?" Mark asked.

"Yes, sir." Kalen sat up a little straighter. "No movement that I can see."

Mark still wasn't used to being called sir as often as it was happening. It was starting to feel more natural, though, as everything progressed. His training up until the attack had been almost completely based on taking and executing orders from others. It must have been reassuring, in some way, for the others to have someone to call Sir. As part of his Neith class mech training, Mark had received a slate of separate leadership courses. Mark's position as second in command behind Zimmer may have been a formality of procedure and popularity, but in the chaos they were facing, it would do.

"Thank you, Kalen," Mark said as he took a seat beside him. "How are you coping?"

"I'm fine sir," Kalen said shortly. "Ready to get in and get started."

Mark put a hand on Kalen's shoulder, then turned him so they were facing each other.

"I'm serious. How are you coping, Sam?" Mark asked, hoping for a real answer.

Kalen let out a breath and looked up toward the brightening sky. He closed his eyes and seemed lost in thought, or prayer.

"It's terrible," Kalen said, with his face still elevated toward the clouds. "It's like there's a missing part of me, Mark. I keep forgetting Zim is gone. I want to ask him what he thinks about all of this, what he'd have us do next. And then I remember he's back there."

Mark said nothing to fill the gap in the conversation, letting Kalen have a moment to say whatever he needed to say.

"There are so many things we hoped we'd do after our service," Kalen continued, returning his gaze to the city. "We were going to make it work, you know? Deal with whatever distance bullshit we had to. We even had this plan to retire out near the coast. Get jobs fishing or something. How ridiculous does that sound?"

Mark thought of Brooke, and of how easily this could have happened to him, how it still could.

"It doesn't sound ridiculous at all," Mark said. "Brooke and I talk about a cabin in the forest, high up in the mountains where it would just be us. Maybe it is ridiculous, but we have to hope for something, right?"

Kalen nodded, and together they watched the city for movement as the sky began to turn a broad pale blue above them.

As the others woke, or simply got out of bed unrested, they began final preparations for departure. Just before the sun cleared the horizon, everyone who was leaving was fully outfitted and ready. They agreed on the coding structure to use for their radio transmissions and entered their mechs and trucks. Soon, the enemy would know something was happening if they hadn't figured it out already.

In the morning Zak was tending to the pilot's wounds before the sun rose. Barkley had slept soundly through the night and was more alert when he woke. He took food and water without complaint. When he had finished, Zak began to lay out the situation for Barkley.

"Taycher Base was attacked. They, the Harbingers of the Fall or whoever, took a whole bunch of mechs and headed in this direction. Some of my friends got hold of the mechs we use for training and followed them. What they plan to do if they catch the Harbingers, I have no idea. I got out late and I'm still trying to catch up. I'm sure you gathered or guessed most of that."

"Just about," Barkley said. His voice was still weak but gone was the sense that he might lapse into unconsciousness at any moment. "Smart thinking on your pal's part, taking your training mechs. You should have stayed back at the base, though. Waited for reinforcements."

"Reinforcements like you and your squadron?" Zak's comment was barbed. He regretted it immediately.

"Point taken, but it would've been the smart move for you." Barkley paused and looked at the sliver of pale blue sky between the buildings above them. "I understand why you did it. My squadron didn't have any official orders to fly, either. We were able to track down and eliminate a couple of enemy groups with what little information we gathered before we took off. We got word that enemy forces were moving north away from both Groom and Taycher bases just before all communications dropped off. We couldn't raise anyone on the radio, so we acted on what we had. We hoped that more information would come to us once we were airborne, but you know the rest of that."

"Damn," Zak said. "I was hoping you'd have more to tell me. Do you at least know what brought your plane down?"

"I have no idea," Barkley said. "Hoped you'd have some idea. They came from your base. We didn't come up against anything like that from the first group we took out at Groom. It was like there was a wall in front of us. I've never seen anything like it."

Zak thought on this in silence for a few moments while he finished packing the rations. Something about Barkley's description had reminded him of something, but he wasn't able to pin it down.

"I'm going to head up the banking tower here and get a look out at the city," he said pointing to an ornate concrete building nearby. "They can't be all that hidden if they're close, but I can't see a damn thing from down here. If I can't find them, we'll have to push on and catch them further up. I'm going to have to leave you here while I get a better look."

Zak pulled Barkley's weapon out from where he'd stored it and held it toward the pilot. Barkley took the pistol and checked the charge.

"I can handle myself. Just get back quick. I'm starting to think I want to make it out of here again."

Zak entered the partially damaged building. Broken glass cracked beneath his boots as he made his way across an open atrium. Color from the sunrise glinted across the shards from a gaping domed skylight far above. It looked like a brilliant floor mosaic. The power was still out in the city, so he walked past the elevators and made his way up an emergency stairwell. Checking for activity as he went, he made slow progress. As he reached the top floor, he noted that the doorway to the roof had already been forced open. The image of Ariana's body on the roof of his old barracks flashed through his mind. Zak shook it away and focused on the new rooftop. The door was only open halfway, leaving much of the area still obscured. He flattened himself against the wall beside the doorway to get a look at the roof. It looked empty, except for a few pigeons and large air conditioning units. He nudged the door open fully, keeping his gun out in front of him, ready for anyone lurking ahead.

He stepped out cautiously onto the gravel rooftop, taking care to check behind each of the air conditioning units. Some of the birds flapped away as he walked, and others remained obstinately still. As he moved around the last unit on the roof, he found a man lying on the ground, zipped into a sleeping bag. A small child was beside him, tucked into another. They were almost completely still, but the steady rise and fall of the man's chest told Zak they were alive. Keeping his gun trained on the pair, Zak stole a glance out at the city from this vantage point. He looked east toward the sunrise and saw something large moving immediately.

Zak had always been amazed by the unnerving grace of mechanized combat armor. Their sheer size and the smooth movements they made gave the impression of lumbering giants from a storybook. He recognized the familiar shapes of the not-quite-standard training mechs, and a wave of relief washed over him. Then he recognized the formation they were shifting into, and his relief was replaced by dread. They were flanking something in the city.

"Oh, no," Zak said aloud. "Oh, damn."

He watched as the mechs split into two groups and fanned out around him. They were trying to surround and trap something or someone very near him. Zak had just enough time to wonder at what they were after when a heavily damaged Jotun class mech stepped out from behind a building three blocks from his position. It was dragging one of its legs as it moved south, directly toward one of the flanking training mech teams. Between them were only a few buildings, one of which happened to be the one Zak was standing on.

He broke his gaze from the scene and looked back down at the sleeping forms on the rooftop. The man was awake now, covering the girl. His eyes were afraid, and Zak remembered he was holding a gun.

"Please," the man started to plead. "Leave us alone. We just needed a safe place to sleep."

"Oh no." Zak lowered his weapon and gestured wildly for the pair to get up. "You have to get out of here. We're right in the middle of a firefight, go!"

The man looked up at Zak, trying to decide what to do. When he saw that Zak's gun was lowered, he scrambled out of his sleeping bag and then pulled the little girl out of hers. She must have still been asleep before then because she began to cry in confusion.

"Just go, now!" Zak yelled at them. The man stood motionless, holding the screaming child, watching in awe as the damaged mech approached. Zak grabbed the man's free arm and dragged him three steps toward the roof access door. "Just follow me!"

168

This snapped the man out of his daze, and he obeyed without a word. Together they flew down the stairs, not checking for enemy forces this time. He needed to get back to Barkley and clear of the area before anything serious happened outside.

It was too late. They had only made it down three floors when an explosion tore a hole in the stairwell wall, slamming Zak against the railing. Through the fresh gash in the building, he could see the damaged mech working its way toward them, firing sporadically at the encroaching forces. Zak was slow to get up and waved at the man to move past him.

"We have to keep going," Zak said. "Get out of here."

The man didn't hesitate then and continued down the stairs. Zak shook off the debris and winced as he used his already injured wrist to pull himself up. He made his way down into the atrium as more explosions rocked the building. The man and child were already gone. Zak rushed for the exit and another explosion impacted the building across the street, high above, sending rubble and shattered glass raining down into the street. The truck was still where he had left it, but the exhaust steaming from behind it indicated that someone had started it up.

Zak bounded across to it and saw that Barkley had somehow managed to pull himself into the cab. The man and his child were also there, in the passenger's seat. Barkley was waving frantically at the mech still approaching from behind them. Zak covered the last few yards to the truck and threw himself into the back just as Barkley stepped on the gas. From this position, he could see the battle that was unfolding.

Closer than he could have imagined, the damaged enemy mech was firing everything it had toward the approaching

169

training mechs. Most of the shots were errant and only impacted the surrounding buildings. Barkley swerved to avoid a larger piece of concrete that smashed into the street in front of them, and Zak braced himself as well as he could.

The damaged mech lurched across the road near the banking building as a well-placed round impacted it directly in its center mass. The mech groped with one massive arm, attempting to stabilize itself while continuing to fire constantly from shoulder and arm mounted guns. The entire area was set ablaze with high caliber explosive rounds. Another precision round hit the damaged mech in its only good leg, sending it reeling backward and to one side. It slammed into the bank building, bringing the entire damaged structure down around it in a thunderous roar. A thick cloud of smoke and powdered concrete cascaded down the road toward Zak's truck.

Then, as suddenly as everything began, the firing stopped. Barkley continued driving for a couple of blocks and then brought the truck to a stop in the middle of an intersection. The debris cloud caught up and enveloped them. The dust coated Zak in a thick layer, and he used his arm to keep from inhaling too much of it. The only sound came from the rubble pile behind them settling and birds flying frantically from their roosts in the buildings on the street.

Zak pushed himself out the back of the truck and landed on the pavement. He opened the driver's side door and found Barkley breathing heavily behind the wheel.

"You." Zak realized he didn't know the name of the man with the little girl but pushed on. "Help me move Barkley into the back of the truck."

The man reluctantly let go of the girl to get out and help.

"Daddy, no!" the girl yelled and gripped the man's shirt tightly.

"She can come." Zak looked around the cab and pulled a canteen from the center console. He held it out for the girl to take. "Can you carry this for us?"

She took the water bottle cautiously and followed closely behind her father as they carried Barkley to the back of the truck. As they all situated themselves, Zak made Barkley comfortable in the limited space. He asked the girl for the water bottle and forced Barkley to take a long gulp while he regained his composure. His quick action in getting the truck moving had cost him most of his energy.

"My name is Brian, and this is Eva," the man said as they waited for Barkley's breathing to normalize. "Thank you for getting us out of there."

Zak opened his mouth to respond but was cut short by the harsh sound of rubber sliding on asphalt outside. Someone else had arrived.

"Get out of the truck, assholes!" an authoritative voice called out. "You've got ten seconds, or we light you up!"

The little girl buried herself into Brian's side and everyone looked to Zak. Outside, a countdown was shouted. He scooted to the edge of the tailgate and began to lower himself out slowly when he was thrown onto the ground and his arms were pinned behind his back. Flashlights mounted to their weapons blinded Zak and reminded him of the ones the investigators had used to find him when he was a child, huddled in the basement. He felt the same sense of powerless dread overtake him.

Then, from his position on the cold asphalt, he couldn't be sure, but the voices around him were familiar. Their movements were calculated and trained, the kinds of movements he himself spent years perfecting at the Academy. He felt the sense of hopelessness break. These were his people, and so he began laughing. He was covered in dust from the collapsed building, so he couldn't blame them for not recognizing him.

"The *hell* are you laughing at asshole?" This voice was close, coming from the man holding him down. "Answer me, right now! What's so goddamn funny?"

"It's just that…" Zak coughed as the man on top of him increased his pressure. "It's just that you gave me a countdown. How dramatic is that? A countdown, guys?"

"What the hell?" The pressure on Zak's back subsided. "It's Lockwood, guys."

Zak was pulled to his feet by a man he now recognized as Jensen, a cadet typically more interested in action than thought. He leaned back onto the tailgate of the truck rubbing at the spot where Jensen had been pressing down. The others in the group looked over Zak for a moment, and then lowered the weapons they'd had trained on him and the others inside the truck.

For the first time since he woke up inside the walls of his burning Academy, Zak began to feel safe. He looked down the street, through the chalky dust still hanging in the air, toward the downed enemy mech. When the pile of twisted metal beneath the collapsed building remained still, he allowed himself to relax.

172

CHAPTER 13

Mark had watched from the Maratus as the short battle in the city ensued. Just as he had hoped, their flanking maneuver drew the enemy out almost immediately. The mech had made a break for what must have looked like the safest route, firing off wildly as it did so. It hadn't tried to head for the open area as they had hoped, but his team had adapted well. Turner had managed to get a clean lock and fired calmly and precisely. They managed to take it out before it was able to get even four blocks. After the enemy mech was down, reports of a truck moving away from the scene called for immediate action. Mark had sent the two trucks to cut it off and neutralize the potential threat.

Scans from the site of the enemy mech revealed that no one inside had survived. He had hoped to take a prisoner, to glean information about the enemy forces, if possible, but this was only a secondary objective. As far as their first real-world combat maneuver went, they'd succeeded admirably. The mechs under his command had now completely circled the part of town where the enemy mech had been hiding, and everyone was on the lookout for new movement. As he checked in with each pilot in turn, a communication came across the main team frequency that he didn't completely understand. Had they said Zak's name? None of the words made sense to him in the current circumstances.

"Say again, ground team," Mark turned the main receiver volume up, abandoning his other conversations. "I heard you say something about civilians?"

The crackle of radio silence returned momentarily, and then Jensen's voice came in clearly. "You've got an extra incoming truck. The occupants are friendly. Got ourselves a flyboy, two civilians, and Zak Lockwood in route with us." Then, after another short moment of silence on the radio, "Yeah, I'm as shocked as you are."

Mark let out a held breath and collapsed into his seat, lightheaded. He'd thought he heard Zak's name the first time but didn't want to commit to believing it until he confirmed. Zak was alive. He made it out. Mark patted the armrests of his chair, then slapped them loudly and stood up, grinning. He turned to look at Brooke, who seemed to still be processing the message, and waved his hands in a childlike expression of excitement. He headed to an exterior door, threw it open, and climbed out. Precariously, he descended one of the mech's eight legs. As he reached the ground, he could see the small convoy of vehicles approaching. Three trucks, and inside one of them Zak was breathing, thinking, living. Mark leapt to the ground from an inadvisable height and adopted a suitably dramatic pose as the trucks arrived.

Mark noted a distinct smirk on Zak's face through the windshield of the first truck to arrive. He must have noted the dramatic pose. The trucks came to a halt underneath the Maratus, bringing with them a cloud of dust. Zak opened his door and stepped out. Mark covered the distance between them, and they embraced like siblings separated by years, instead of the mere days they had been apart.

"You jerks left without me." Zak pushed back from the hug, smiling.

"Yeah, well, you were late." Mark pointed one finger at him. "You look like shit."

"I barely escaped the building that came down back there," Zak wiped some of the dust from his face, his eyes growing a little distant. "Everything looks so much cleaner from inside a mech. From the ground, it's all a lot more chaotic."

"I'm just glad you made it out," Mark gripped his shoulder. A bit more of the dust puffed off as he did. "It hasn't been the same without you."

"This is touching and all, but we've got company." Zak pointed to where Brian and Eva were exiting one of the other vehicles. "We need to figure out what the hell to do with them. Not to mention the very injured Air Force pilot in the back."

"Right," Mark said, mentally reassuming his leadership role. He addressed the small group that had formed behind him. "Continue to keep all mechs manned and scanning for movement in all directions and recall the units still inside the city. Turner, take the pilot over to Hartley and Larson at the med tent. They'll do whatever they can for him."

"Yes, sir," Turner said, with a touch of sarcasm in his voice.

"Oh, and excellent work out there," Mark said as Turner walked away. If he heard the remark, he didn't show any indication.

175

Turner signaled for two other cadets to help him move the pilot. Mark knew that the camp wasn't particularly well equipped for major injuries, but Hartley and Larson were still by far the most qualified. They'd managed to put together a pretty comprehensive field medic operation.

With the pilot taken care of for the moment, Mark turned his attention to the two civilians. A man with a little girl clinging to him stood in the grass beneath the Maratus, looking around with an expression that was hard to read. He read anger there, but also relief and exhaustion.

"Why are they here?" he asked Zak quietly, turning away from them.

"They were on the rooftop I was using to scout your location when everything started," Zak said. "I didn't think too much, I just got them off the roof as fast as I could. Barkley, the Air Force pilot, he got them into the truck. We barely got clear before that enemy mech came crashing through the city. Don't ask me what we should do with them. I honestly didn't think that far ahead."

"Well, they sure as hell can't stay with us," Mark said. "There's no way we can keep them safe going where we're going. Maybe there's somewhere they can go?"

Mark nodded for Zak to follow him as he turned to the two civilians. He set his face with what he hoped was a reassuring smile and made his way over.

"Hello, I'm sorry for all the action today. My name is Mark Alder," he said and put out his hand. The man looked at the extended hand for a moment, then shook it briefly.

"Brian Caldwell," the man indicated himself. "And this is my daughter Eva. I don't mean to be rude, but are we free to go? I appreciate what your soldiers did for us, but this really isn't the place for us, especially her."

Mark looked at Eva, her head turned into Brian's chest. She looked to be about four or five. She had both of her arms around his neck. It looked uncomfortable, but Brian didn't seem to mind.

"You're right, but we can't just send you off into the city. There's a real possibility that rebel forces are making their way here as we speak. I'd hate for you to leave, just to get caught back up in our crossfire. You're our responsibility at this point. Is there anywhere we can take you? Somewhere you'll be safe?"

Brian looked around the ruined park they were in, then looked back.

"Is anywhere safe?" he asked, casting a genuinely confused look at Mark.

"Honestly, we're not exactly sure, but an escort is the most I can offer you at the moment. We're headed out tomorrow morning, so I could spare a team for the rest of the day. I'm sorry." Mark glanced at Zak for input.

"I'll go with them in the truck I brought." Zak shifted his weight uncomfortably. "Just give me a couple of hours and some extra hands to help, and maybe I can take them where they want to go."

"Sure, that will work," Brian said, stroking his daughter's hair. "There's a place just outside of town on the east side. If there's anything left of it, I'm sure we can stay there."

"That works," Mark said. "Is it family, a friend, something like that?"

"Something like that," Brian said shortly. Then his face softened a bit. "My ex-wife lives out there. My weekend is up anyway."

~

Zak walked toward the medical tent and sat down on a metal supply crate. Hartley saw him and gave him a surprised look.

"They said you'd made it, but wow," she walked over and crouched down to get into his line of sight. "You look like shit."

"Yeah, I've heard that." He looked out toward the man and child, who were being brought some food and water by another cadet. "I'm fine."

"Well, I'm glad you came over here," Hartley said. "I should at least give you a quick checkup. Make sure all your parts made it here intact."

"I'm really fine," Zak said. Then he remembered his wrist and shook his head. "Oh, actually. I messed up my wrist back at Taycher before I left. I don't think it's broken."

"I'll take a look." Hartley took his forearm and began working the wrist joint. "Does this hurt?"

"I mean, yes." His wrist was still swollen, but Hartley's manipulation of the joint didn't hurt as much as he'd thought it would. "It was worse earlier."

"Looks like a sprain to me," Hartley said. "Treatment would be pretty much the same either way, with the limited supplies we've got. I can get you a brace to immobilize the wrist. You should continue to use the arm and especially the fingers though. Don't go crazy or anything, but don't baby it either. If it is broken, keeping everything moving will preserve mobility down the road."

"You're a lot better off than your pilot friend," Hartley said. "He's pretty banged up."

Zak looked over to where Barkley was lying down. He was in the back of the tent on a cot set low to the ground. His eyes were closed, and his breathing was even.

"Is it okay if I talk to him?" Zak asked.

"Be my guest, but visiting hours are ending soon," Hartley smiled. "I'll go try and find you a wrist brace."

When Hartley left, Zak reached into his jacket pocket and pulled out Barkley's personal effects he'd taken from the downed jet. He looked at the metal lighter. It was made of tarnished brass but was worn clean and shiny in two places that indicated frequent use. Zak flipped the lid open and pressed the flint wheel. Sparks shot up but didn't catch the wick. He looked at the small photograph. It was also well worn but hadn't been folded. In it, a woman was standing in a green field holding a young child who looked out of the frame at something. Her smile was genuine and warm, and Zak felt a familiar sensation of dull bitterness rising in him.

He pushed off the supply crate and walked to the back of the medical tent. As he approached, Barkley turned his head and opened his eyes slowly.

"Well, if it isn't my goddamn guardian angel." Barkley tried to sit up on his cot but quickly gave up and rested his head back against the pillow.

"We'd both be crushed beneath a building if it weren't for you. So, let's just call it even yeah?" Zak sat down on the dirt floor in front of Barkley. "I managed to grab a couple of things from your plane before we left. I thought you might like to have them."

He extended the lighter and photograph toward Barkley and saw an immediate reaction. Barkley took the offered items and held them close to his chest. He took a few deep breaths and squeezed his eyes shut. A tear spilled from one of his eyes and disappeared into the brown and silver hair at his temple.

"Thank you," Barkley managed. He opened his eyes and looked at the photograph, idly turning the lighter over with his other hand. Barkley's thumb brushed over the faces of the people in the photograph and Zak moved to get up.

"Hey, are you okay?" Barkley asked before he could stand up. "That was all pretty close."

"Yeah, I'm okay." He thought about it for a minute and decided to continue. "Yeah, that was close. Too close. Do you think anyone got hurt?"

Barkley paused for a few moments and thought about it. He flipped open the lighter and closed it with a snap. "Probably," he said. "But your guys were doing what they thought was best. An enemy mech lurking in the city you're trying to get through is a pretty big unknown factor. They probably thought they had to do something about it before they could move on. And with whatever anti-aircraft thing they have, I'd say it's pretty important someone gets to them."

Something finally clicked into place when Barkley mentioned the unknown tech that had stopped his fighters in midair near the base. He needed to see Mark, but he wasn't sure how to get out of the conversation. He nodded toward the lighter and asked, "You smoke?"

"Oh, no." Barkley held up the lighter and it glinted in the light from the open tent flap. "Doesn't even work. It's just been in my family for generations. Good luck charm. Hope to give it to this little guy someday." He tapped the face of the child in the photograph.

"They look happy," Zak said.

"Yeah, we were." Barkley smiled at the image. "God, I hope they're okay."

Zak didn't know what to say. So instead, he said nothing, hoping that Barkley would fill the silence for him.

"I've got your brace, Zak." Hartley tapped Zak on the shoulder. "I think I grabbed the right one. Let me see if it fits."

Zak locked eyes with Barkley for a moment and nodded. Then he stood to be fitted with the wrist brace.

"Look at that," Hartley said. "Perfect fit. Do you need any painkillers, or will you be okay?"

"I'll be fine," Zak said. "Thanks."

"Good, because we don't have a lot," Hartley laughed. "If you really need them though, just say the word."

Zak headed out of the tent flap and out into the bright desert midday sun. He looked for and found Mark over by the command mech and walked over.

"You ready for your escort mission?" Mark nodded his head at the civilians as Zak approached.

Brian and Eva were still standing next to the truck. Eva was playing with a stick she'd found somewhere, drawing circles in the dust. Brian saw him and waved, looking eager to leave.

"Sure," Zak shook his head, not wanting to lose what little information he'd been able to recall. "Before I go, there was something that I just remembered from my research time back at Taycher."

"Even out in the field you've got the impulse to bore people," Mark smiled, and then must have seen the seriousness of Zak's expression. "I'm kidding. What's up?"

"Before everything..." Zak took a deep breath and urged himself past a flood of memories about the attack on the base. "Before the attack, I'd put in a request for a really specific research paper I probably shouldn't have been able to access. The request wasn't approved or denied though. When I went to check on it, the request was just gone."

"Do you think it was a glitch in the system?" Mark asked. "What was it about?"

"It was a highly theoretical paper on a hypothetical method of using gravitational waves to disrupt and destroy incoming enemy targets. Sounds familiar doesn't it?"

"Yeah, but you said the paper was only theoretical." Mark looked out to the north.

"Yes, theoretical, but also a few years old." Zak closed his eyes and tried to remember anything else about the document. "Its codename was Ston. And it was written by a researcher based at Taycher. Commander Sarah Black. I don't think the Harbingers were there for the mechs. They wanted the Ston, and the mechs were just their way out."

Zak traveled away from their camp in the park. He felt strange leaving after working so hard to find Mark and the others. Mark had given him one of the more heavily armored trucks to head into the city with, instead of the light vehicle he'd arrived in. The added armor and gun mounted on top would offer more protection should they encounter anyone as they made their way to drop Brian and Eva at their destination.

Brian and Eva sat up in the cab with him. In the storage bed in the back of the truck, he'd also brought two cadets, Lund and Manner. Lund was a broad woman with a steady hand. She'd been one of the best shots at the academy during Zak's time there. Manner was a quiet man but always seemed to know what was going on. Zak was glad to have them with him as he headed back into the city.

They wound through empty streets, occasionally working around derelict cars or heavily damaged sections of road. But, as they distanced themselves from the main line of destruction created by the enemy forces, one could almost have imagined that nothing had happened to the city. The streetlights didn't come on when the sun got low in the sky, but the city was otherwise undamaged by anything more than the elements and general neglect. As they continued, the buildings became less frequent, giving way to a series of walled-in government housing complexes, containing small homes and scared families.

The truck rumbled out into open fields and passed by abandoned farmhouses beside ancient grain silos and barns. They continued until Brian told him to make a turn near a row of mailboxes strung out along the side of the highway. There were more than a dozen of them, but they were relics of a time long past. They traveled along a dirt road as the sky above deepened into a bloated purple. They passed by what appeared to be abandoned homes in the twilight. Zak noticed the telltale signs of illegal occupancy, however, in the details he could see. A pair of all-terrain vehicles that looked to be in working condition were parked beside one of the homes, and the children's toys in front of another were not worn enough to have been abandoned back when this area would have been evacuated and relocated. No, these homes were likely filled with families who paid off the local patrols to look the other way. It was possible, even likely, that some of these homes had illegal crops growing behind a carefully tended copse of willow trees.

As they approached one of the homes, Zak caught a glimpse of warm light flickering in one of the windows through drawn curtains. Brian signaled for them to turn at the next road, so Zak drove off the dirt road, bumping onto an uneven gravel driveway. It ran through a thickly wooded area where the trees above laced together, giving the impression that they were driving through a tunnel. After about a hundred yards Zak pulled up outside a modest white house in a clearing.

The lights were off, as they had been in the other homes they passed by. Brian exited the vehicle with Eva, letting a rush of cool evening air into the cab. They walked out in front of the headlights casting their shadows onto the white house.

"Sandy, Jack, it's us!" Brian called out. Behind him, Lund and Manner exited the back of the truck with their weapons drawn, shouldered, but lowered. "Sandy, I've got Eva. She's okay!"

At the mention of Eva's name, the front door of the house swung open, and a woman rushed out into the yard.

"Mommy!" Eva yelled and tugged herself free from her father's hand.

Together they ran toward the woman. Brian was noticeably younger than Eva's mother, but not by any large margin. When they met, the woman swept Eva up into her arms and fell to her knees in the tall grass. There, the woman sobbed deeply as Brian stood to one side. The scene was beautiful, and Zak was happy to have played a part in making it, but he couldn't help the sting of jealousy that shifted uncomfortably within him.

After a few moments, another figure appeared, silhouetted in the doorway with a shotgun in hand. Zak heard two metallic clicks come from the back of the truck as Lund and Manner switched the safeties of their weapons off. Zak exited the vehicle and turned to face them, holding both of his hands up.

"That's it, guys," Zak said quietly. "Let's turn around and get back to camp before we're either invited to dinner or shot in the face."

The man with the shotgun leaned the gun against the wall inside. He walked down the front steps of the home toward Brian, who was still standing beside the woman cradling her daughter in the front yard. The two men shook hands, and engaged in a brief conversation, then looked back toward the truck. Zak gave them a wave and they waved back. The two men had another brief conversation, and Brian approached the truck.

"Shit guys, they're going to invite us in for dinner," Zak said under his breath. He stepped forward to meet Brian halfway.

"They, uh…" Brian rubbed the back of his head. "We want to know if you'd like to come inside. I told him you're with the military and that you saved our lives. Says you can stay here tonight, too, if you need a place to stay."

"That sounds great," came a voice from behind them. They turned and looked at Manner. "I could use a break after today. When's the next time we'll have the chance to sleep under a real roof?"

"Me too," Lund chimed in, engaging the safety on his rifle and dropping it to his side. "It's fine, I'll radio it into base. It was going to be hell finding our way back out there tonight, anyway."

Zak clenched his teeth. Domestic environments weren't historically where he performed best. But Lund was right, they were going to have trouble getting back in the dark. And they'd be able to get back to camp before anything important happened in the morning if they left early. Zak shrugged and nodded in approval.

Lund radioed the information to someone back at camp and waited for the short approval message before exiting the truck again. The mother and Eva had already gone inside the home, on the pretense of getting things ready for their unexpected company. More likely it was to take their personal moment of reunion out of the front yard. Brian and the second man were waiting for them to head inside.

"Name's Jack," the second man said as they approached. He was a large, heavily tanned man with calloused hands built for hard work. He eyed their sidearms with distrust. "We weren't exactly expecting company tonight. But I'm sure we've got enough for me to grill some burgers."

Jack wiped his hands on his jeans and extended his hand to each of them in turn.

"Thank you," Zak said as he shook the man's hand. "Anything at all will do. We understand that rations are short right now. We appreciate you opening your home to us."

"Hell, you're thanking me when…" Jack shook his head and wiped at his eyes vigorously for a few moments, betraying a level of emotion Zak hadn't expected. "When you've brought our Eva back. Thank you."

The five of them walked up to the house and went inside. The living room just inside the door was modest, with two couches of different colors facing one wall, presumably a broadcast display wall. Zak and the others with him took off their jackets and had a seat on one couch. Lund and Manner both removed their sidearms and placed them on a beat-up wooden coffee table. In another setting, this would have seemed aggressive, but in this context, it projected the opposite feeling. Zak looked toward the front door. He saw the shotgun leaning against the wall and decided to keep his sidearm strapped on. The shotgun was ancient, but still illegal, and leaving it out in the open was either a sign of trust or a warning. Possession of a firearm by someone not employed by the military was a serious crime.

Jack excused himself to begin cooking dinner outside, leaving Brian with the group. Once the four of them settled in better and a sufficient silence had passed through the room, Brian spoke.

"I don't think I've thanked you guys yet. Especially you. Lockwood, right? Thank you for saving me and my little girl. Thank you for getting her back here."

"It's no problem, and call me Zak, please," he said. "I'm sure I can speak for the others when I say it's just part of our job."

"I'm sure you've noticed." Brian looked around the living room. "This isn't quite a standard family unit we have here. It's complicated." He paused and took a moment to find the words to explain his situation.

"Not everyone's got the same story," Zak said, breaking the silence before Brian could continue. "You all care about each other, and that's all we can hope for, isn't it?"

"Yeah, we do." Brian smiled. "Can I get any of you anything to drink? I'm sure Jack has some beer around here somewhere."

"Absolutely," Manner said, speaking for the group again.

Brian left, returning a few minutes later with a box of dusty brown bottles. He was visibly comforted at the prospect of having something to put everyone at ease. The beer was homemade, as most alcohol outside the Enclaves was, but it was good. They talked together about the events of the day, skipping past the more emotionally dense material, and focusing instead on the action. A recurrent theme was just how grateful they all were to have made it through. After a while, the conversation dipped into the personal matters of where everyone was from, and they shared short autobiographies of how they came to be there.

Zak lied. Or he didn't lie exactly, but he found the socially acceptable parts of his life and stitched them into what he hoped created a complete tapestry of what a life should look like. While others talked and told their stories, Zak wondered whether they were leaving entire swaths of fabric on the floor as he had. What stories lay hidden beneath the table? An obvious omission was Brian shortening his marriage to, and subsequent divorce from, Sandy into two or three sentences. The star of the story was their daughter Eva, who he said had kept them all relatively friendly with one another.

Were Lund and Manner hiding their own pasts from the group? No doubt they were, but Zak didn't know them well enough to notice any skips or jumps in their narratives. Conversation had begun to wind down, and the beer was nearly gone when Sandy leaned into the room from the hall.

"Hey, everyone," she said as if she were addressing old friends. "Dinner's ready. It's not much, of course. I have no idea how long it'll be until the grocery store opens up again."

The group laughed nervously, unsure if it was a joke or an attempt at returning to some form of normalcy. There wasn't a grocery store in this area, or anywhere, for that matter. Even before the rebel mechs had come through, the only food that would be available would come directly from ration stations on a rigid schedule. The laugh, however stunted, was useful though. The group had loosened up a bit, with a more than plausible nudge from the now empty bottles on the coffee table. An old wooden dinner table in the next room had been extended with a fold out card table on one end to make room for the whole group. Together there were seven of them.

Jack sat at one head of the table, and before Zak had any say in the matter, seating worked out so that he was sitting at the head of the other end. To Zak's right was Eva, who stared at him and his two fellow soldiers with eyes the color of honey and the unashamed interest of a child.

"Hello, Eva," Zak said. "I'm sorry we haven't officially introduced ourselves yet. My name is Zak Lockwood, and this is Rebecca Lund and Colin Manner."

"Hi," she said, then quickly hopped out of her chair and went to help her mother who was in the kitchen.

"Is she always that shy?" Zak asked Jack from across the table.

"Sure, yeah," Jack responded shortly. "I mean, yes. She's kind of like that, interested in everyone until they actually talk to her, then she's off and away."

He smiled then and looked over at Eva, who was insisting that she bring the plates to the table. She partly got her way and was permitted to bring the mashed potatoes while Sandy finished up with the plates.

Soon they were all eating and engaging in dinner small talk. Much of it consisted of further condensing their lives for the benefit of Sandy and Jack, who hadn't had the opportunity to hear it earlier. After small talk subsided, Zak felt compelled to ask more substantive questions, if only to try and put the conversation on some track they could all follow easily.

"So, Mark and Sandy, why didn't you leave when the attack first started?" he asked, knowing their answer was sitting beside him.

"We couldn't leave without Eva. Even though we knew, we hoped, she would be safe with Brian." Sandy said, casting a warm smile at him. "But we knew we had to stay here in case she ended up needing us."

"It's a good thing, too," Brian said after clearing his throat. "Not sure where else we'd have gone to get a meal this good tonight. I just hope Alison is as safe as we are."

"I'm sure she is," Jack said, visibly surprised. "She's away at school. What do you mean you hope she's okay, Brian?"

"I just mean, who knows how far all this has gone?" Brian said, and then must have noticed the questioning expressions on Zak's face. He paused for a moment, seeming to organize his thoughts. "Alison is Sandy's first daughter. The father was out of the picture before I came in. You never really know what Alison will get into from one day to the next is all."

Zak thought this through, taking a moment to shuffle the family in front of him until the cards made sense again. The complicated story probably resulted from some infidelity somewhere along the line. Jack, sitting silently across the table, must have loved Sandy very much to have entered a family burdened with a history that predated his own.

"Stop it, Brian," Jack said, aiming his fork like a weapon. "I'm sure she's fine and safe, wherever she is."

"I'm sure she is." Brian clenched his teeth and looked down at his plate. An unspoken tension filled the room, outside the experience of Zak and the others.

"I made a mountain!" Eva shouted suddenly, gesturing at a massive pile of mashed potatoes she'd made on her plate. Then, noticing the instant attention, she clammed back up and began to mash the mountain back down to more manageable foothills. "Never mind, all gone now."

After a beat of silence, the room erupted into laughter. The tension dropped immediately. Maybe it was because they were all part of this new memory, when Eva made the mountain of potatoes. It was the kind of funny thing they'd be hard pressed to explain to anyone who was not in the room then. To everyone's relief, dinner finished smoothly, with conversation ebbing and flowing naturally around more traditional topics like weather and the food.

Once everyone had finished, Sandy cleared the table and refused to let anyone but Eva help her with the dishes. So, the rest of the group stepped outside to enjoy the cool night air. Conversation was weakened without Eva, and everyone lapsed into a brooding silence. Jack lit a hand-rolled cigarette and offered one to anyone else who wanted one. Brian accepted and sat with Jack on a short brick wall. Zak wandered out into the yard, just within the light cast by the back porch light, feeling the darkness pressing in on the group. He felt like a dog, patrolling the perimeter in search of some unseen enemy. As he walked, the subjects they hadn't talked about in the house turned through his mind. Slowly, thoughts about his own family history, the short battle today, his reunion with Mark, and seeing Eva reunited with her family began to whip up into an uneasy fog within him. Something wasn't quite adding up right, but inside the echo chamber of his skull, his thoughts lost coherent form. He was tired.

"Hey, guys," he said as he turned back toward the house. "I'm really tired. Anyway, could I take you up on that bed you offered earlier?"

"Sure, sir," Jack said. "We've got the three of you set up in the guest room. Hope that's alright. King bed and two cots. You can flip for who gets the bed, I suppose."

"Better than some places I've slept recently. You can be sure of that," Zak said, thinking of the rubble-strewn stairwell back at the Academy.

Jack led Zak through the house and to the guest bedroom, then left him there without a word. An old handwritten sign on the door read *"Allie's Room Do Not Enter!"* He disobeyed the sign and pushed the door open. He laid down on a cot positioned beneath a partially opened window, and eventually fell asleep.

He woke with a start and found his gun already in his hand. He was still fully dressed. Lund and Manner were asleep. They must have come in quietly enough not to disturb him. Zak holstered his pistol and listened as the house creaked in the night. He heard a sound coming from outside. It was a more rhythmic creaking than the sporadic ones the house made as it stood against the breeze. He laid awake for a few minutes, listening to the rhythm, hoping it would lull him back into his dreamless sleep. It didn't. For some reason the longer he listened, the more unnerving the noise became. He sat up and looked out the window, but still couldn't pinpoint the source of the sound.

He stood and slowly made his way out of the room, opening and closing the door as quietly as he could. The old wooden floorboards betrayed every move he made, and he wasn't sure why that seemed to concern him. When he reached the back door, he found it unlocked. It was possible that Sandy and Jack kept it that way, but he doubted it. Zak opened the door and stepped out into the night. The porch light still cast its limited semicircle of light out into the yard. The sound seemed to be coming from just beyond it, somewhere in the muted shadows. He walked out toward the sound, and as his eyes adjusted, he saw it. A wooden swing swayed back and forth gently. It was anchored to a twisted cottonwood tree that must have been older than the house itself. Jack was sitting in it, facing out into the black moonless woods that surrounded the house.

Zak stepped lightly through the dry grass. No matter how hard he tried, Jack would hear him at some point. Beside Jack was an empty expanse of wooden seat, and under different circumstances, Zak might have sat down next to him and had a deeper conversation about the day. But the uneasiness he carried away from the conversation at dinner had left him cautious. Something about how they'd all looked at him when he asked about their actions after the attack had been off. For a second, he had felt some boiling anger in the room.

The leaves in the trees rustled in the cold midnight breeze. In this light, it was hard to be sure, but it looked like Jack had his shotgun laid across his lap. As Zak approached from behind, he took his gun from his holster. There was an audible click as Zak turned off the safety. He was closer now, and yes, there was definitely a shotgun in Jack's lap.

"Put the gun on the ground, Jack," Zak said. "Now, or I'll have to shoot."

Jack complied, slowly lifting the shotgun from his lap and tossing it lightly into the tall grass a few feet in front of him. Zak moved around him, keeping his pistol raised. When he was in front of the man, Zak could see moonlight reflecting in tears as they coursed down his sun-worn face.

"You're a rebel sympathizer," as Zak said it, he knew it was true. "That's fine Jack, we'll call this one a draw. We've returned Eva and you'll let us leave. My soldiers and I will get out of here, and we'll leave you and your family alone."

"It's too late," Jack said, looking not at Zak, but into the trees beyond.

"What do you mean, too late? What have you done?" Zak looked quickly from side to side and saw nothing but tall grass fading into darkness. The shadows pressed in from the trees, and he quickly leaned down to pick up the shotgun from the grass.

"I called them after I left you in the living room with Brian, when I went to cook dinner. I can't be sure, but I think they're coming. They could be here already."

"Jack, your family is here. What the hell do you think is going to happen when your friends show up?" Zak's voice began to rise, so he made an effort to bring it back down. "You're putting your goddamn *family* at risk, you son of a bitch."

"I just wanted to tell her that we found Eva! I swear I didn't know they'd come!" Jack said.

Zak didn't know what to say. He began to run toward the house. He pointed the shotgun toward the stars and fired off one blast. It was the easiest way he could think to wake Lund and Manner. Jack made no attempt to run, or even leave his seat on the swing. As Zak reached the door, the first bullets began to pepper the house.

When Zak got inside, he ran for the guest room. He found his companions completely awake as the sounds of gunfire rose

195

outside. They were hastily putting on their gear and looking to Zak for orders. All the drills they had undergone while at the Academy seemed to have helped, as they were outfitted in moments. The three of them crouched in a formation around the inside of the bedroom door without even a word being spoken. Lund and Manner flanked either side of the door, and Zak stood away and to one side, each of them with their weapons drawn.

The house was filled with the wails of Eva and calls from Sandy. Sandy's voice stopped, and then so did Eva's. They must have been together then. That's what had to have happened. The gunfire stopped, and a moment of ringing silence hung in the house. Zak heard the wooden floorboards creak as booted feet entered the home from the rear door. Crickets outside the window had slowly begun to chirp again when glass exploded into the guest room. A canister spewing gas rattled on the floor. Zak, holding his breath as best he could, heaved it back through the shattered window before the room could fill completely. Even so, they couldn't stay there. Shouts came from all sides, both inside and outside of the house. Cutting through them all were renewed screams from Eva somewhere else in the home.

They were familiar to him, and not just because he had heard her make similar noises earlier. No, he remembered making these sounds himself, after his own mother had died. This couldn't be happening.

Zak squeezed his eyes shut to try and bring his focus back into the present moment. All it did was bring forward vivid flashes of holes punching through the wall into his childhood home. Zak's eyes sprung open, and he looked toward Lund and

Manner. Zak realized he hadn't even told them what was going on.

"Jack called in the Harbingers," he said simply. "I have no idea how many of them there are."

"We have to move now," Lund said. "Out to the truck if we can. It's our best chance. It could be our only chance."

Without another word, Zak pushed the door open. Together he and his team flowed into the hallway, an oiled machine honed by years of training. One shot from Lund's steady hand took down a shadowy figure on the way to the living room. As the figure fell, they managed to squeeze off two shots that destroyed a shelf of white ceramic animals.

"Fuck!" Zak yelled as the image of his shattered cereal bowl flashed through his mind. Manner applied pressure on Zak's shoulder and shook him back to reality.

The team moved into the living room, taking down two more rebels in dark uniforms without slowing down. Then they were outside, moving toward the truck at a sprint. Bullets flew by them, barely missing their mark and impacting the armor of the truck. The rebels were trained. If Lund hadn't gotten them out of the house when they did, they would have been trapped. Zak turned and fired two shots from his pistol into the darkness where he saw a muzzle flash moments before. One must have connected because no shots immediately answered his own. When they reached their truck, Lund opened the driver's side door and got inside just as two rounds impacted the reinforced windshield. The shots turned the glass into a spiderweb of cracks, but nothing got through to the cab. Zak and Manner moved around to the other side of the truck as Lund started the engine. When they got around, however, someone was waiting.

Before he could think, Zak raised the shotgun and fired, point blank, at Brian's form. The world seemed to slow down as Brian fell to the ground. From somewhere, Zak could hear the familiar screams begin again. The word Eva screamed was clear. Eva was calling out for her daddy. The moments that came next were blurry and disjointed. Zak stood for too long over the body of the girl's father. Then he looked up to see her, alone in the doorway of the home, silhouetted by the golden light spilling from inside. Something brutally explosive went off on one corner of the building, blowing the glass out of the front windows, and the girl crumpled to the ground.

A line of bullets peppered the truck, and Manner screamed at Zak to get in. The glass in the yard glittered with oranges and yellows as a fire bloomed. It took him a moment, but Zak realized Manner had already taken up position at the gun mounted on the roof from inside the truck. As if moving through water, Zak hoisted himself inside the truck, shut the door, and looked up at Manner. Half of his body was out through the roof hatch in the cold. His finger was pulling the trigger, firing round after explosive round at the incoming forces. Some, too many, impacted the home. Lund drove the truck away and the scene receded into the darkness. Manner's shots came less and less frequently.

Eventually, Lund brought the truck down to a more reasonable speed. Manner, visibly pale and shivering, crawled back into the truck and closed the roof hatch. Manner picked up the handset of the radio and called the main group.

"Whoever's on watch, we're coming in," Manner said. "Possible enemy targets in pursuit. Get up, these guys are not messing around."

"Say again, is this you, Manner?" a voice came in.

"Yes, it's me. Get everyone up. We were attacked out here. No injuries. Oh hell, wait a second while I double check that." Manner turned to Zak and Lund. "Yeah, no injuries, but Zak looks like that zombie kid we picked up in the base."

"I'm fine," Zak said quietly, almost entirely to himself, then looked down at his hands. He was still gripping the shotgun so tightly that it hurt when he stopped. "Mostly fine."

"Good to hear, man, good to hear," Manner said to Zak. Then, into the radio, "Repeat, no injuries, but possible enemy pursuit. We'll flash our lights when we get close, then check in with a quick radio burst to confirm it's us."

"We copy, Manner. We'll be ready for you." The voice that came through was muffled by the sound of mechs cycling up on the other end. "Be careful guys. Get home safe."

CHAPTER 14

It took them close to four hours to work their way back to the campsite. When they got close, Lund flashed the lights of the truck while Manner sent the brief radio signal.

When they reached the park, Zak saw that everyone was awake and busy. The Iris, Icarus, and Maratus were already actively sweeping the area. They appeared only as shadows against the deep purple sky ahead of them, but seeing them made him feel safer. Muscles he hadn't realized he was holding tight began to relax on their own. Fatigue set in like a fog, and he wasn't sure if he would be able to get out of the truck.

The truck crested a small hill and stopped near the center of camp. Somehow Zak found his way out of the truck and collapsed onto the heavily trampled grass, facing the clear sky. A broad expanse of stars hung over him, sparkling indifferently. He wasn't sure where Lund and Manner went, but he heard vomiting coming from somewhere close. After a while, someone came into view above him, blocking out a portion of the stars. It was Brooke. The look on her face said she was worried, and not entirely about him.

"Where's Mark?" Zak asked without moving from his position on the ground.

"He left a few hours after you did." Brooke glanced out at the darkness of the city, and then back down at Zak. Her hand unconsciously grasped a necklace that dangled loosely out of her uniform. It was the one Mark had given her as a graduation gift before everything came crashing down around them. "The plan was to leave in the morning when you guys got back. So, he took Turner and some of the others and went back out to scout that mech we brought down today. To see if there's anything useful to salvage."

"Have they reported in?" Zak knew the answer before she spoke.

"We haven't heard anything since you reported your situation." Brooke crouched down beside him.

Zak found the energy to lift his head and chest off the grass and looked out into the dark city with Brooke. Behind them, preparations continued for whatever would happen next. In the city, small fires still burned, mere flickers of light at varying distances. Zak found Brooke's hand in the grass and laid his hand on top of it. Her fingers were cold. She'd probably been standing out here looking at the city for hours.

"He'll come back," Zak said, squeezing her hand. "He'll come back."

~

Mark and his small group of fellow soldiers were working to remove the energy core of the downed mech. The work was hard, but the basics were easy to grasp. Mechs were designed with field repair and salvage in mind. Taking things out was easy, but plugging everything back in required a bit more care.

"You guys finish getting this thing unhooked," Mark said to the others. "I'll see if there is any unspent ammo in the arm over there. It looks to be pretty much intact."

"Yes, sir," Turner said. He wiped the sweat from his forehead with the back of one gloved hand. "We'll just finish with this three-hundred-pound energy core, no big deal."

"Thank you, Cadet Turner," Mark said. Let him fume on that for a bit, Mark thought. He was the commanding officer, however irritating that might have been for Turner. "I'll be back in time to help you lift it out and get it into the truck."

It was a miracle the core hadn't ruptured in the short battle. The resulting explosion would have rendered salvage impossible. Mark could almost hear Brooke's voice in his mind then, chastising him for not appreciating the work that went into the construction of a mech. The armor on those machines was *intended* to protect from catastrophic failures, so perhaps it was one of those miracles an engineer would hate being called as such.

Mark clambered off the twisted metal heap and walked down the street toward the huge, detached arm. He kicked idly at the spent large-caliber casings that littered the street. The metallic ringing echoed back from the vacant buildings around him. The arm was further away than Mark had guessed, almost a hundred yards. Even though they hadn't seen any enemy activity while they'd been here this time, he still began to feel uneasy in the open street. The buildings seemed to loom over him precariously, their shattered windows staring out like so many dark eyes. He raised his rifle, walked more carefully, kicked fewer shells, and avoided the larger pieces of broken glass.

When he got to the arm, he approached it slowly, looking for where the ammunition boxes might still be attached. With heavier mechs like this one, ammunition canisters typically detached automatically when they were empty, making the installation of new ones easier. It also had the added benefit of making the mech itself slightly lighter and more nimble during a firefight, right when it counted. He saw two boxes still attached and slung his rifle onto his back. Mark unsnapped the holster of his sidearm in case he needed quick access to it.

The first box came off easily, making a hard satisfying thud as he let it drop onto the street. It sounded mostly full. The second box must have taken a hit during the battle, because it wasn't coming off without a fight. He began pulling at the box to detach it from the arm and got progressively more frustrated as it resisted.

Mark yelled obscenities at the box, forgetting his uneasiness. The feeling returned as he heard something coming from back at the main bulk of the mech down the street. It could have been someone yelling to see if he was okay.

"It's fine!" Mark yelled across the space. "I'm fine, this goddamn box won't come off is all."

This must have eased their curiosity because he didn't get a response. Mark turned back to work on the box, then felt a sudden pain bloom in his ribs. Before he could draw his weapon, he hit the pavement, unable to breathe. Standing over him was the shape of a woman holding a sturdy length of pipe from some part of the wreckage. Mark attempted to yell out a warning to the others, but found that he still couldn't breathe.

He reached down for his pistol, but another blow from the pipe beat him there. Finally catching a short breath, Mark let out a cry of pain. The figure above him dropped the pipe, sending ringing melodic tones echoing down the artificial canyon. Mark made a second attempt to reach for his weapon but stopped when the figure pulled out a pistol of her own and aimed it at his head.

"Okay, okay," Mark said, scrambling backward. He put his hands up. "Look, let's talk for a minute. What the hell do you want?"

As an answer, the woman pulled the hammer back on her pistol, an antique piece with a rotating cylinder. Mark tensed all his muscles as he prepared to move. Before she could pull the trigger, the sound of shots being fired came from the wrecked mech down the street. The woman turned momentarily to look, and Mark kicked hard at her legs. She squeezed off an errant shot, which ricocheted off the metal arm and into the night. In these moments, Mark lunged to the other side of the arm and drew his own weapon.

"Put the gun down!" Mark yelled. "This isn't going to end well for you, I can promise you that."

There was no response from the other side. Mark glanced up the street where muzzle flashes illuminated the wreckage sporadically. The woman stepped around and into view, with her gun drawn. They each pointed their weapons at the other. The clouds shifted overhead, and the street was suddenly drenched in crisp moonlight. Mark could see that she wasn't much older than he was and didn't seem to have much military training. She was holding the gun too close to her body and hadn't adopted a stable shooting position. Her hands were shaking; from fear, anger, or simple adrenaline was hard to tell until he considered her eyes. It was grief.

"Hey, it's okay," Mark said in the calmest voice he could manage. "You don't have to do this. I don't know if you're with the Harbingers or if you're just pissed off. Just put the gun down and we'll figure this out together."

"You don't understand!" she yelled, the last word coming at him through clenched teeth. Her eyes were red with tears, and her voice was hoarse. For a moment, her pistol dropped slightly. He thought about firing then but thought better of it when she brought her weapon back up. "You've had it all! The care, the money, all you could ever want was *yours*. But us? No. No, we haven't earned our place among the elite."

She adjusted her grip on the revolver, gaining composure. "You murdered my family, and I'm supposed to understand? Stability? Recovery? Well, we don't want recovery. We don't *want* your Stability. We want all of this to stop."

"I understand," Mark said quietly. He didn't, but he just needed a few extra seconds to figure a way out of this. "But if you shoot me, your life is over. The rest of my squad is on the way and that…" He gestured at her gun. "That'll draw them in firing."

"You think I care! You do, don't you? That's a *fucking* mistake." Her hands shook, and she extended her pistol in front of her in a more traditional form, evidently remembering what someone must have taught her at some point. Tears forming in her eyes seemed to interfere with her sight, and with one hand she reached up to wipe them away. As she did, Mark ducked down and then leapt forward just as she fired off another shot that could have killed him. He hit her with one arm around her waist and slammed her to the ground. Her head hit the pavement with a sick, sharp smack. Her revolver went off one more time and then fell loosely from her hand. She wasn't unconscious, but she was dazed enough.

Mark quickly pushed her gun away, took hold of her hands, and applied wrist restraints he retrieved from his vest. Behind him, sporadic shots continued to be fired. These were followed by the short, even bursts he and his fellow cadets had been trained to use back at the Academy. They continued for a few moments, the flashes throwing elongated shadows across the vacant faces of the surrounding buildings. A final burst of shots came and went, the sound echoing on down the street, and then there was silence.

Mark looked down at the woman. She was still dazed but was gaining perspective and started struggling with her restraints. Mark retrieved her pistol and his own from the street. Hers was indeed a very old model, but it was well cared for, and every bit as lethal as his. Mark heard footsteps coming from the direction of the mech up the street and quickly got into a defensive position with his back pressed against the metal arm. He heard a muffled voice and recognized it immediately. It was Turner giving orders. It sounded natural, startlingly so, as if Turner had been practicing for a moment like this where he could take charge.

"Turner, it's me!" Mark yelled. "I've got a woman here, she's secured. Get over here and help me carry her, and let's get the hell out of here before more of them show up."

They abandoned the arduous task of removing the energy core and settled for the ammunition they'd been able to scrounge. Turner easily detached the second canister Mark had been struggling with.

"I loosened it for you," Mark said, flashing a grin. "I'll stay with her. You guys get the truck and pick us up on the way back out."

The woman stopped struggling with the restraints, and now simply glared up at everyone in their party. She was still visibly dazed, but her calculating eyes must have alarmed Turner because he glared right back down at her. He pulled Mark away a few steps.

"Just leave her here, Mark," Turner said. "We don't have room for one of these people."

"Turner, if there's anyone else watching us, a hostage may be our best chance of getting out of here," Mark said, his voice betraying more fear than he'd like.

Turner didn't seem completely convinced, but turned back to the others, "Let's get as much of this ammunition back to the truck as we can." Then, turning back to Mark, "Make sure no one else surprises you out here."

"Thank you, Turner," Mark said. "I'll keep that in mind. She'll also have information we can use if we can get it out of her."

This last point convinced Turner, and he nodded in affirmation. "Now that actually makes some damn sense."

Once Turner and the others returned with the truck, they fought with the woman to get her into the enclosed cargo area. During the scuffle, the radio in the front seat began to crackle as a distant voice came through. Mark left the struggle for Turner to handle and got into the cab of the truck.

"Say again," Mark said. "Repeat, say again."

"Thank God you're alive." Brooke's voice came through the receiver. "Get back here, now. Zak and the others were attacked out at that family's house. Whoever got to them might still be out there. There could be hostile forces headed your way."

"Brooke, is everyone alright?" he asked. "Did everyone make it back?"

"Mark, they're fine." Her voice was a pleasant mix of concern and exasperation. "Everyone is home and accounted for except for you guys, just get back."

"We got some heat here, too. It sounds like the same guys. Everything's quiet now, but we're bringing a captive with us."

"Say again, Mark?" Brooke sounded alarmed. "They got to you, too?"

"Turner and the others fought off the main bunch before they got close enough to do any damage," Mark said. "But listen, we've got a prisoner with us. She got the drop on me, but I managed it. We're bringing her in."

There was a silence on the radio, and his words hung in the dead air for a few moments.

"Mark, tell me she's not pretty," Brooke said, her tone hard to read. "Because I swear to god if this bitch tried to kill you, she had better not also be prettier than me."

"I have no idea Brooke," Mark said. "I was more focused on the gun in her hand than whether or not I'd run away with her."

CHAPTER 15

Once Mark and the others arrived back at their camp, Hartley and Larson met them at the truck and began checking them for injuries.

"I'm fine," Mark said as Larson prodded his ribs to find any breaks. "Just get her over to the medical tent. She hit her head pretty hard. And keep her under guard."

He waved his hand toward Turner who was leading the rebel woman by the arm. She handled the exchange without a struggle and let herself be led away, but her eyes darted around the camp, as if taking notes. As soon as Mark turned away from the exchange, Brooke was on him. She held his face between both of her hands and was gripping his head, hard.

"Don't ever go get yourself in danger like that." Her eyes were fiercely locked with his. "Promise me, Mark."

"Brooke." Mark placed his own hands over hers alongside his face and felt tears brimming in his own eyes. "You know I can't promise you that."

"Fine," she said, sliding her hands away. "I'll just make sure I get into some peril the next chance I get. Show you how it feels."

"How is everyone else?" He reached out and gently squeezed her hand. "You said Zak and the others ran into some trouble too?"

"Zak and the others were pretty shaken up." She nodded to where Zak was helping to pack up a field shower. "Especially him. From what I got out of the others, the Harbingers really did a number on the house where they dropped off that man and his girl. It sounded messy. They were lucky to get out of there at all."

Mark turned to take in his surroundings. The campsite had already been mostly packed away. The ammunition they salvaged was already being loaded into mechs that could take it. A few yards away, Zak continued with the field shower. When he saw that Mark and Brooke had finished talking for a moment, he broke away from the task and headed toward them.

"You two need to be more careful," Brooke said as Zak approached. "I can't leave either of you alone for more than a minute without you getting into trouble."

"You have absolutely no idea how pissed she was when you said you were bringing that woman back here," Zak said. His tone was light, but his eyes betrayed a deeper seriousness.

"Hell yes I'm pissed," Brooke said, looking toward the medical tent. "She tried to kill you, and now we're going to ferry her around? I should go over there right now and take care of the situation."

Mark shook his head. "She might have information we can use. Plus, we were safer getting out of there with her in tow."

"Shut up, I figured that out on my own." Brooke broke her gaze from the medical tent and let go of Mark's hand. "I get it.

It just doesn't feel right. I'll go help them finish packing up that shower. You were doing it wrong anyway, it was embarrassing. You boys catch up."

"So, you got some heat out there too?" Mark asked when she'd left. "I thought you were partaking in some rustic hospitality or whatever. What the hell happened?"

"I don't really know," Zak said, a distant expression washing across his face. "Everything was fine, and we were sleeping in their spare bedroom when I heard some noises outside. I went out there and the girl's stepfather, Jack, he was sitting on this swing. The kind you anchor to a tree branch. He called the rebels in. I don't know, man. The place was already surrounded. We had to get out of there. I killed that girl's father, Brian. I don't know how he got there. I think maybe he was trying to go with us, ask us to surrender maybe?"

"Zak, I'm so sorry." Mark reached out and placed a hand on Zak's shoulder. "I'm sure you all did what you thought was best. You were ambushed, who knows what he was trying to do."

"I didn't know what was best, Mark." Zak ran both of his hands through his hair. "We just shot our way out of there. I'm not sure if there's a *right* way to do that. I think that whole family might be dead because of me. We should have come back. I should have said no when they asked. It never felt right."

"Hey." Mark squeezed Zak's shoulder. "You're back. You're here. That's what counts. You did what you had to do to get back home. Why don't you head up to the command mech and get some rest before we head out?"

"Yeah, sure." Zak shook his head and forced a smile. "It's really good to see you, I'll see you up top."

212

"Sure," Mark said. "Come see me on the command deck when you feel up to it."

Once the camp was fully packed away into the various vehicles and mechs, Mark called a general meeting. He left a skeleton crew in each mech to keep them scanning the horizon.

"Our plan stays the same," Mark said to the group in a tone he hoped conveyed competency. He was standing on the hood of one of the trucks. It must have looked kind of showy, but sometimes the best way to project confidence was to play the part. "We follow, we keep our distance, and with any luck, we'll get official orders from someone on one of the main encrypted frequencies. Let's get moving."

He jumped from the hood of the truck and headed toward the lowered central module of the Maratus. Hartley and Larson kept the rebel woman in their care in their designated medical truck. From what Mark had heard, she'd been compliant in everything except speech. She hadn't said more than a few words to anyone, and those few were just to let them know that she needed to use the bathroom.

The mechs began churning forward, and Mark made sure to have the units at the front of the formation scan from higher ground whenever possible. The path they were following was easy to maintain. The destruction in the city gave way to trampled sagebrush and deep indentations in the ground from the heavier mechs.

"Take over control, would you, Kalen?" Mark exited the main control seat. "I think I might know where they're going, and I don't like it."

At the center display table, he brought up a topographical map of the area. He pulled back and got a wider view of the entire western United Entities. There was nothing of particular note in the direction the enemy was heading. The path had taken them just a few degrees off of due north, and when it had deviated to get around a larger obstacle, it always returned to the same heading.

Ahead were huge swathes of empty government land, an occasional small town, and patches of protected woodland. He set a projected course ahead of them and saw where the destination might be.

"I really should have seen this earlier," Mark mumbled under his breath. "This isn't going to be good."

"What won't be good?" Brooke asked from beside him.

"Shit, you scared me." Mark put his hands down on the map table and paused to compose his words carefully. "Brooke, you're not going to like this. I think they're headed for Ember Springs. It's the only thing in the direction we've been headed."

"Shut up. Why the hell would they be going there?" she asked. "There's nothing there but farms and mountains and old mines. Oh, and my goddamn family, there's that."

"I know, I'm sorry." He gave her hand a squeeze and then turned back to the map. "There's nothing out there ahead of us. The closest military installation is still actually the school. That has to be the reason they're going this way. They're looking to regroup somewhere safe and secluded. We've seen what they can do to incoming air power with that Ston device, so what they need is somewhere they can defend easily from ground attacks."

"Whatever, Mark. Sure. But why in hell would they go to Ember Springs?" Brooke looked with uncertainty at the map. The red heading line extended from their position directly toward Ember Springs. "There have to be a dozen little towns just like it out there."

"None of them are like yours though. Listen, this is still a guess. I could be wrong." Mark found and kept her gaze. "But none of those other towns are up in the mountains like yours, and it's backed up against a million square miles of empty protected forest. Plus, they could use those old mines you told me about if they had to retreat to safety. It's supremely defensible. It's where I'd go. If they're smart, they already have a place prepared for when the guys we're chasing arrive."

Brooke stepped back from the map and away from Mark. Confusion and anger played across her face. She closed her eyes and when she opened them, Mark could see that she was scared.

"I need some air," she said. Before he could stop her, she headed for the roof hatch at the back of the room.

~

Zak arrived on the command deck just as Brooke exited through the hatch to the observation deck. Mark was standing at the map table looking like he'd just lost an argument.

"What was that about?" Zak asked.

"I think they're headed for her hometown," Mark said. He pointed at the map of their current trajectory and showed him where Ember Springs was on the projected heading. "I'm not completely sure, but it's the only place ahead of us that makes any sense."

"Yeah," Zak said as he traced the line in the air with one hand. "They go off course occasionally, but they always return to a heading that points them right there. Are you going to go try and talk to her?"

"I don't think she wants to talk to me right now," Mark said. "I don't know how to handle any of this."

"None of us do." He looked back at the roof hatch. Fresh air sounded good. "Do you want me to try and talk to her?"

"Sure," Mark said. "Maybe you can help her. Get her to realize we're doing everything we can."

Zak waited a few moments, and then headed up the ladder. Once he was outside, he saw her leaning against the front railing. Ahead of their core, somewhere in the distance, an unknown number of enemy mechs armed with whatever they scooped up from Taycher Base was marching toward the square grey government housing complex where Brooke had grown up. They were also carrying some sort of anti-aircraft device he could only speculate about. Zak walked over and leaned against the railing next to her. He'd volunteered to talk to her, but now realized he wasn't sure what to say. Instead, he looked out over the landscape and hoped his presence with her would be enough.

"He told you?" Brooke didn't look at him.

"Yeah," was all he could manage at first. "I can't even imagine what you must be feeling."

It was true. Zak didn't have any family to worry about, and the idea was foreign to him. Everyone he cared about was either

216

dead or in the convoy with them. Even though Brooke was hurting, he felt a moment of envy that she had an external source of support. It would be nice, he thought, to be able to carry the thought that someone was waiting for him.

"It feels like I'm watching a train heading straight toward them," Brooke said. "And all I can do is run as fast as I can to catch up."

"We're doing everything we can." Zak looked out at the other mechs traveling with them across the desert. As far as they knew, they were the only friendly core of mechs in the western region. "At least we have a chance of stopping them."

As if in response to this, Zak felt their mech begin to slow down. The other units around them also lost speed. The core was stopping for the evening.

"No," Brooke looked around furiously. She pushed back from the railing and walked a few paces into the open space of the observation deck. "He can't do this, Zak. There's still at least an hour of light left."

Zak tried to think of something else to say, but she was right. They could continue for at least another hour; further even, if they decided to travel through the night. He looked out ahead of them and saw the reason they'd stopped. A broad expanse of featureless terrain awaited them, without so much as a small range of foothills in sight. What distance they might cover in an hour would put them out in the open, exposed on all sides. Where they were now, at least they had some cover. He turned to tell her this, but she was already headed for the hatch.

CHAPTER 16

"We can't just stop here Mark," Brooke said. Her voice was rising as the command mech continued to slow down near a defensible position at the base of a large vertical rock face. "You can't expect me to just sit here and let those monsters keep marching toward my town."

"Brooke, the mechs need time to cool down, and time for routine maintenance." Mark continued the shutdown sequence and sent orders for the mechs to get into their now-familiar defensive campsite formation. "The soldiers piloting the mechs and trucks also need rest and maintenance. We can't just keep going. You of all people should know that these machines need to stop, or we won't make it another day."

"The Harbingers must be stopping too," Brooke said pointing out the front glass. "If we just push on, we could make up a lot of ground. Our mechs can take it, I know they can."

"That's not a risk we can take right now!" Mark was getting frustrated and needed to send out more commands but turned away from his console instead. "I can't have us marching blindly into the night only to get us lit up by forces we can't see."

Brooke looked like she wanted to say more, but instead, she walked to the stairs and headed below deck without another word.

"Take over on deck for me, okay?" Mark looked at Zak, who had been trying his best to look very involved with the holographic map table.

Mark left the Maratus and headed to the medical team to check on their patients, if only to get off the command deck for a while. Barkley was still with the medical team but was doing much better. Payne was only still there because they hadn't figured out anywhere better for him to be. The rebel woman, as defiant as ever, glared at him as he walked past her and approached Barkley's cot.

"You up for a walk?" Mark asked. "Doc tells me you should be moving around a bit anyway."

"Sure," Barkley said. "The company in here isn't exactly great conversation anyway."

Mark helped him out of the medical tent and over to two camp chairs far enough from the rebel prisoner to have an open discussion.

"What do you want to talk about?" Barkley asked as he lowered himself gingerly into a chair.

"I don't really know." Mark took a seat as well, searching for something else to focus on. "I guess I just thought we could compile all our information. See if we can piece anything together."

"Well, I think you know most of it. My squadron mobilized ourselves," Barkley said. "We heard a bunch of confused chatter from all over the place. And I mean all over the place. Nobody knew what was going on or what had the highest priority. Our commander got us in the air and off to the first place she could get any specific intelligence on. I think she got us in the air fearing our base was next. Once we were all up, we were supposed to clear out a small force at Nellis, then head north to deal with the forces attacking Taycher."

Mark nodded for him to continue. He did know most of this already but maybe getting the finer details straight would open up a new line of inquiry.

"We lost contact with our own base before we even made it out to you guys. I suppose Galera was right. When we got out to Nellis, it was already a lost cause. I don't know how they mobilized enough people to do what they did there. We did what we could from the air, but Galera eventually made the call to head for Taycher, in case we could make a bigger difference there.

"Once we got there, it seemed like an easy enough task to take them out. Mechs aren't exactly built for defense against an aerial attack. Your command mechs can do some damage, but we were prepared for that. I don't know what the hell happened next. It was like my guys were hitting a wall we couldn't see. None of my missiles made it through either. I saw everyone in my squadron just disappear from radar. Then I was trying to right my jet when I slammed into it too.

"I'd be dead if your friend hadn't come along when he did. I wish I had more to tell you, but that's all I know."

"That's fine," Mark said, trying to imagine all the scenarios Barkley had described. "Zak got me some information about what you hit out there. He got a glimpse of a research paper about something called the Ston. It uses gravitational waves or something. But that's all we know about it.

"Try to think about it again. You may have seen something useful up there. Do you remember any details about what was coming across the radio before you and your guys went up in the air?"

"Nothing too specific, like I said," Barkley said. "But I suppose I did hear a lot of reports, more than I could keep track of. It seemed like it was happening all over the country. Highly coordinated attacks. And everyone seemed surprised. Every one of the targets was unprepared for what they were facing. Do you even know how these guys can pilot the mechs they stole from Taycher? It's not exactly something they teach in the civilian preselection schools."

"They must have had help from people inside," Mark said. "It feels like the only way something like this could be as successful as it has been. I just don't understand what their endgame is, I can't wrap my head around what they plan to accomplish with all this."

"You've got one of them sitting in your camp you know," Barkley said, jerking a thumb back toward the medical tent. The rebel woman was sitting outside, not far from the tent itself, cuffed and guarded by a soldier that was rotated out periodically. "It'd be worth a shot to see if you can get anything out of her."

"You're right," Mark said, thinking it over. He'd had the guards ask her questions occasionally but hadn't pressed her very hard. "I've never held anyone prisoner before, I guess I just don't know how to handle it."

"Sure," Barkley said. "But you should get someone to try, or why is she even here?"

"I see your point and I'll take it under advisement," Mark said. He stood up and offered Barkley a hand. Together they made their way back to the medical tent so he could get some rest.

~

Zak was still at the map table on the command deck when Kalen came up the stairs.

"Hey, the convoy is all settled." Kalen looked at him with concern. "You look like you could use a break. Is everything okay?"

Zak closed his eyes and tried to think up a lie that would get him to leave, but surprised himself by saying what was actually on his mind. "I shot a little girl's father. Everyone keeps saying it was self-defense. I guess maybe it was, but I don't think he was trying to hurt me. He was just scared."

Kalen joined him at the map table and made an effort to get Zak to look at him. "You did what you had to do. That's all we can do out here."

"The rest of the family we were staying with is dead too," Zak continued. "The Harbingers were everywhere, and it was all we could do just to get out of there. I don't know what I'm even doing here. What good is it, what good are we, if good people get caught in the crossfire like that?" He looked at Kalen, pleading for some justification.

"We are all doing what we have to do," Kalen said slowly. "These people are tearing straight through schools and cities. They might say they care about humanity, but if they cared they wouldn't be trying to tear it all down. You don't hurt people you care about, not if you can help it. Anything we can do to preserve what Stability is left in this world is worth it."

"I'm not so sure that what's left is worth saving anymore," Zak said quietly.

"I understand you're upset, Zak," Kalen said standing up straight. "But if you're going to side with the people who killed Zimmer, I don't think I can have this conversation."

"I'm sorry," Zak said, stepping back from the table. He looked out the front windscreen, admiring the slow progress of clouds drifting by. "I just don't know what to think right now."

"Take your time," Kalen said. "But keep in mind who's got your back."

Kalen turned and left him to think. Zak felt useless as he tried to tie all his emotions back in place. Nothing seemed to be where he left it. He had thought that once he found Mark and Brooke, he'd be able to fit back into the machine of the group. That everything would even out. Instead, he felt like an outsider, like he'd been brought in from some other place. It was a feeling he'd experienced before, back when he was the Ghost Kid.

The clouds outside continued their ambivalent journey. He was beginning to feel a bit like them, pushed along on a current he couldn't see. Perhaps the clouds would coalesce into something more substantial down the line. Maybe they would dissipate completely, leaving nothing but emptiness.

A fire at the center of camp cast flickering shadows out into the night. A light rain had started to fall, but the area beneath the command mech was protected by the broad swathes of canvas they stretched out in between the legs of the mech. The cool air and scent of rain still swirled beneath the machine, reminding Mark of nights outside in better days. He'd spent summers at various athletic camps during his preselection schooling years. His parents were always trying to enrich his unscheduled time with other activities. In reality, they'd just wanted him out of the house.

The camps were all out in the wilderness, a rare luxury given to only those who could afford it. He hadn't known it was a luxury at the time. Back then, he would have rather been back in the city trying to get laid or finding some way to cause trouble. Now, beneath the commend mech, he missed the simple days spent at those camps. His responsibilities had been so small.

Mark sat on a metal case filled with rations and looked around the fire. Most of the camp was in for the night or posted to a watch detail somewhere. Only a few stragglers remained, talking in small groups. Brooke sat close to the fire, idly poking at the burning wood with a branch. Across from her was Zak, laying on his back using his pack as a pillow, staring at the underside of the Maratus.

"Hey guys," Mark said, breaking the silence. "How are you doing?"

Brooke responded by tossing her stick into the fire. An updraft of sparks curled into the chilled air. Mark followed the paths they left, and by the time they'd died out, Brooke had already begun to walk away.

"She's pretty angry about you stopping the convoy," Zak said, not breaking his gaze from the dancing firelight reflections on the mech's armored hull above them.

"I know that." Mark shifted on the case to face Zak. "I'm not a complete idiot. There's no way we'd be in any kind of state to do anything if we caught up to them with no rest. And these mechs need to cool off occasionally. She has to know that."

"Sure, but that doesn't mean she has to be happy about it," Zak said. "She doesn't need to hear all that from her commander; she wants to hear it from you."

"Zak, look at me," Mark said, pivoting the conversation. "You haven't told me what's going on with you."

"I'm not even sure myself." Zak closed his eyes. "I'm still trying to wrap my head around what's going on, what happened at that house. I know you think it wasn't our fault, but it doesn't make the feeling go away."

Mark wasn't sure how to respond. Zak and the others had just done what they had to do to escape. He tried to think of another way to console him, but Zak talked again before he could get the words to form.

"I feel like any minute now, we're going to get orders from someone, anyone really," Zak said. "But after each moment, no one calls to tell us it's over, and we're still out here chasing after these shadows on the horizon. What good can we expect to do even if we catch them? What if there's nothing left to fight for out there? Dammit, who even are these people that they can do all of this so quickly?"

225

Mark paused again to form a response. Then, with a flicker of inspiration, he remembered that the answers to all of Zak's questions were already in their camp.

"Why don't you find out?" Mark asked. "We've got that rebel in camp and we haven't been able to get anything from her. I mean, we haven't tried hard enough. You've got questions, see if you can get some answers."

"Why me?" Zak asked.

"To be honest, you're not doing anything else," Mark said, regretting the implication. He smiled and adjusted his tone accordingly. "I need to make you useful before everyone starts thinking I'm giving you special treatment."

"You'd better get back to Brooke," Zak said. "She's more upset by this than you even know. She's really worried, and you're honestly not showing a lot of urgency. I understand taking a rest, but there must be something more we could be doing."

"Sure, you're probably right," Mark said. He looked and found Brooke standing out away from the camp. She was again staring out in the direction of her hometown, the direction of the enemy path. She was idly fidgeting with the penny necklace around her neck he had given to her before all of this began. It felt like a memory from years before instead of only a few weeks prior. He'd forgotten that, while Brooke was his chief technician on an operation to intercept a dangerous enemy, she was also still his partner. Watching her standing at the edge of the firelight staring into the darkness, he grasped for the first time how hard standing still must be for her at that moment.

Mark finally decided to approach her. As he covered the distance, he could feel the heat of the fire receding. He stood beside her, the chill of the night replacing the warmth of the fire. The cold felt somehow more appropriate. Comfort and safety, he was beginning to realize, were mere illusions now.

Zak had watched as Mark left the fire and approached Brooke. They made a good pair, but the current circumstances were toxic for a relationship. In another time, Brooke would have already graduated and shipped out. Mark would have pined for her, and she would have pined for him. Hell, they might have even been able to work through the distance and time away from each other. Not here, though. With Mark as the leader of their group and the enemy making their way toward Brooke's hometown, it was a wonder they hadn't come to blows yet. Perhaps he was wrong though, Zak thought, as he watched them embrace out in the darkness near the edge of camp.

Zak began to feel uncomfortable the longer he watched them, so he got up and busied himself with extinguishing the fire. His wrist still bothered him a bit, and there was a dull throb in his head whenever he turned too quickly, but he was in remarkably good condition, considering. He shoveled dirt onto the few remaining pieces of wood. When the flames were extinguished, he watched the rippling waves of heat pulse through the embers, threatening to catch the wood again.

Eventually, he looked up to see that Brooke and Mark had disappeared somewhere. Good, he thought. At least someone was happy out here, if only for a moment. As he scanned the camp, he saw Jensen standing guard over their rebel prisoner.

They didn't have a cell to keep her in, so she was still being kept with the sick or wounded. The pilot, Barkley, and a couple of other cadets were in care there. One was in for dehydration, which seemed a bit ridiculous to Zak. But constant fear could make even the best trained soldiers forget even the simplest things. He walked to the tent then, intending to relieve Jensen and get started talking to the prisoner.

"Go get some rest, Jensen," Zak said. "Mark wants me on shift tonight. Gotta start being useful, you know."

While this wasn't entirely true, it kept his motives concealed from the woman for the time being.

"You sure, Zak?" Jensen asked.

"Sure, go get some sleep," Zak reassured him.

The woman seemed to take little notice of their interaction. She continued to busy herself with the apparently engrossing act of sorting pebbles into various piles in front of her. Her knees were drawn up to her chest, and she used her bound hands to move the pebbles from one pile to another in a pattern Zak recognized vaguely. Jensen departed his post with a wave, clearly excited at the prospect of a few extra hours of rest. He was probably even more excited not to be stuck watching over a silent rebel who was probably plotting to kill them all in their sleep.

Zak took up Jensen's position, leaning on the bumper of the truck pulled close to the medical tent. He watched as the woman continued to move her rocks around. Two rows with various amounts were slowly transferred from pile to pile into two larger groups at either end. Zak laughed aloud as he realized it was an improvised mancala board. Zak remembered hours of his youth spent playing the game as a substitute for actual conversation

228

with adults when he was in the care of the state. It was an easy game, involving the transfer of one pile of pieces, in this case rocks, into the next in the sequence until they'd all been moved to one side or another. It was a two-player game but could be played out of boredom by oneself.

"Who's winning?" Zak asked.

He couldn't be sure, but it seemed like the woman smiled. Zak crouched down and looked at her face. There was blood and dirt smeared along her hairline and under her chin. She hadn't let anyone clean her. Probably nobody had offered.

"Can I play?" he asked.

As an answer, the muscles in her jaw tightened. She waved across the improvised board as if to say, 'whatever you want'.

Zak busied himself with resetting the board, putting an equal number of rocks into each of the twelve piles. She must have been playing the game a while, as there were small divots in the hard-packed earth where she'd been scooping and transferring the rocks. When the makeshift board was reset, he made the first move by picking up one pile and dropping a rock along the next few piles until he had to stop and yield play to the rebel woman. They continued to play, settling into more comfortable playing positions as time went by. When about half the rocks had been moved out into their respective piles, Zak ventured another look at the woman's face.

He should have hated this woman. She should have served as a face for him to project all of his confused emotion onto. Finally in front of him was a living, breathing member of the opposition. Someone who not only attacked Mark, but also agreed with the people instrumental in the deaths of his family so many years ago.

At the thought of this, he was finally able to muster up some hate for the woman. What did she know of the pain and suffering she'd caused him and countless others? As he watched her eyebrows come together, contemplating her next move, his hate dissipated again as if it were only a mist in the desert heat. She was just a young woman playing a game of mancala, lost in a world where she had no power or control over her own fate. What pain had she seen to lead her there?

"Who taught you to play?" Zak asked, as she finally made a selection and moved her rocks. He got no response, but he hadn't expected one. "I used to play this all the time when I was a kid." He reached out and made his move. "Come to think of it, my mom taught me how to play."

Without warning, what he said seemed to break something loose in the woman. She tensed up and kicked out both bound feet, sending the rocks and a cloud of dust flying into the air. She let out a sound that was half scream and half pleading cry. Her hands came up and covered her head.

Zak looked up to see Hartley poking her head out from inside the medical tent. He waved her off and stood up, then slowly gathered up the scattered rocks, getting new ones when the correct number couldn't be relocated. He set up the game again and sat in the dirt, waiting for the woman to look back up. She didn't.

"She taught me just before she died, or close enough," Zak said. Whatever he had said had done something, and maybe it would bring something out of her. "Everyone would always ask me what I wanted to do after it happened, and I'd always choose playing mancala or checkers. This one helped more, though. It's more methodical. There's less thinking involved."

When this still failed to rouse her, Zak continued. "We were having breakfast when it happened. Some of your kind, rebels of some sort, were apparently living next door." He waved a hand absently at the canvas wall of the tent, indicating how close they'd apparently been. "And when the government came to shut them down, the rebels just started shooting. It seems like they fired randomly. This line of bullets kind of ripped through our kitchen wall, you know? It went on for forever, or it felt like it did. Eventually, someone came and pulled me out, and I was in the care of the state."

He said all of this calmly, with none of the frantic emotion he expected. Zak wasn't sure why he was telling her, but she seemed to relax as he talked. It was helping him to talk about it too. He hadn't shared this much information with anyone in a long time.

The recent events had stirred these old memories up in his head and talking about them was letting the dust settle over them again. He waited another moment, feeling the chill of the night air as the last vestiges of the day faded in the west.

"So, I was in and out of various foster homes." Zak laughed and picked up a pile of rocks, making an opening move on the reset board. "That's the most cliché thing I say about myself, you know? In and out of various foster homes. It doesn't help anyone understand, but it gives them a place to nod and say they're sorry. Nothing can really sum up a stretch of time where you're plugged in and out of people's lives like a secondhand appliance."

"What makes you think we did it?" the woman asked, as she picked up a pile of rocks and made her move.

"What do you mean?" Zak asked, surprised she'd said anything. "Maybe not your particular brand of rebel, but it was some terrorist organization or other."

"No, you said the rebels just fired randomly into your home," she said. "I'm asking why you think it had to be the rebels."

The question had floated in and out of his mind many times in his life, of course. He wondered which group had fired the bullets that killed his family, but always came to the conclusion that the blame rested on the rebels who had decided to set up shop next door.

"It's what the reports all said when they finished the investigation," Zak said.

"Of course that's what they said," she replied softly.

"At any rate, it doesn't matter," Zak said. "If they hadn't been there, the government wouldn't have shown up. If they hadn't started shooting, no one would have been shot."

"Did you ever think that if the government hadn't shown up, no one would have had to shoot?" she asked.

"No, because that's not an option here." It was his turn in the game, but he was getting frustrated and couldn't concentrate. This wasn't going the way he thought it would. "The rebels were a threat to Stability. It was the government's job to show up and take those guys in."

"No," she said. "It wasn't."

Zak didn't reply. He wanted to argue with her and explain to her how important it was that the government do its job to preserve Stability. That, otherwise, the whole system would succumb to the same things it did before the Decline and come crashing down all around them. He wanted to say all of those things, but didn't. That was precisely the outcome that the rebels wanted. The Harbingers of the Fall openly stated their intent to bring the world as it currently stood to an end.

He also didn't say anything because he wasn't sure he could mean it. Instead, he reached down, selected a pile of rocks, and moved them along the piles until he had to stop and yield play to the rebel woman. Zak made no effort to speak, fearing that she might cut through him again.

~

They'd ended up inside the cab of a truck stowed in the cargo hold of the Maratus. It was tucked away behind a pile of poorly organized crates filled with ammunition, rations, and anything else the group been able to pull from the training mech garage before they left. Brooke and Mark had managed to fog the windows a bit and he was vaguely proud of that. He ran his fingertips along the curve of her forehead, down her cheek, and along her collarbone.

"You're going to put me to sleep if you keep doing that." The corners of Brooke's mouth turned up and she adjusted her position on the narrow bench seat to rest her hand on Mark's chest.

"That's the idea." Mark felt a simultaneous tug of contentment and despair within him. He wanted to fire up the engine of the truck and drive away into the night. Maybe they could find that cabin they always joked about, tucked away in a forest to the north. "You deserve some rest."

Her body tensed, and she brought her eyebrows together in frustration. "We can't rest, Mark. We have a job to do out here."

"I'm sorry," he said. "I've been so focused on all this. I've been focused on trying to lead this whole thing and not get anyone… Not get anyone else killed. I lost track of the reason we're out here, I think. I'll send out a volunteer party first thing tomorrow to catch up with the enemy forces. Just to scout and return intel as we plug along. Nothing heroic. I'm not going to try and stop you from going, but I'm also not going to like it."

"Thank you." Her body relaxed into his once more. "I just hope we can stop them, Mark. I know everything's gone to shit, but I can't just stand here and follow them while they're barreling down on my family. Who else do you think will go?"

"I know for a fact Turner will want to lead the party," Mark said. "You know he's been itching to get ahead of this thing too. He'll also enjoy being in command; doesn't much like my style, you know.

"I've enjoyed not having to say goodbye." Mark lifted the penny on its length of silver ball chain. He turned it over in his fingers a couple of times and then let it rest back on Brooke's skin. "Whatever the circumstances now, I guess we've had that as a result of all this."

"I'm sorry, Mark," Brooke said. "But if anyone's going ahead, I have to go."

"I don't want to lose you," Mark said. "I've already almost lost Zak twice, and now you're going out there. You're one of the only people I've ever been able to trust fully. One of the only people who believes I'm more than a jock with rich parents."

"Is that what you think people see?" Brooke looked up at him with a stern expression. "Mark I'm not the only one who believes in you. Nobody would be out here if they didn't respect you. Even Turner understands that you've got something important that he doesn't. It's not just that people like you on the surface. They trust you."

"But what if I can't do this?" Mark wiped at his eyes in frustration as tears began to form. "What if I can't keep us all safe?"

"It's not your job to keep us safe," Brooke said calmly. "And staying safe isn't our job. We're out here to protect people."

Mark didn't reply. Instead, he lifted her chin and kissed her. Brooke kissed him back, and he could feel tears fall through the stubble on his face. In the morning, they would part, but not until.

CHAPTER 17

As the first hues of the coming day broke over the mountains, the camp began to stir. After managing to stay awake through his watch, Zak was finally relieved by another soldier. He headed toward the command mech to get a couple of hours rest before they moved out. On his way, he saw Mark, who had a look of distracted worry painted across his face.

"What's up, Mark?" Zak asked, falling in step with him. "Might want to look a bit more sure of yourself if you've got something planned."

"Fuck you," Mark said, a little too seriously. He shook his head and took a deep breath. "Sorry. It's nothing, or maybe too much. I'm arranging a scout party, and Brooke's set on volunteering. I don't know how to stop her."

"You can't," Zak said. He stopped and grabbed Mark's arm, forcing him to stop as well. "Her family is out there. Staying this far back with the command mech, and the half-hospital half-prisoner truck must be killing her. It's been hurting a lot of people. This is going to relieve some pressure."

"Where were you headed, by the way?" Mark asked, changing the subject.

"The Maratus." He pointed up at the massive command mech. "I was up all night on watch with the prisoner. Well, not the whole time. She did eventually fall asleep."

"Did she open up about anything?"

"Not much." Zak paused to collect his thoughts, then continued cautiously. "Just standard rebel stuff. The system is broken, it's all going to end. You know, that kind of shit."

"Well, you got her talking at least." Mark smiled. "It's more than anyone else has gotten. Stick with it, see what you can get out of her. Anything you can get, even if it's just a slip, might be useful."

"Sure," Zak said, nervously reaching up to scratch at the stubble beginning to grow on his face. "I'll do what I can."

"If you're going to be working with her, you should review the only other time she's talked. Screamed is more like it." Mark squinted, as if trying to recall the words exactly. "It was when she ambushed me out in the city. I'll get you the event I have from my optics if you want to review it. She rambled a bit about the same kinds of things you mentioned. Blamed us for the death of her family, told me I didn't understand, that kind of stuff. Go ahead and get some rest. I won't let the scout team leave before you're awake."

"Thanks," Zak said. "I'll take a look at the vid later and try to get some more out of her when we stop again tonight." He paused and got a lock on Mark's eyes. "She's going to be okay, alright? Brooke, I mean. It's just a scout party."

Before they became wrapped up in another conversation, Mark clapped Zak on the shoulder, excusing himself. He walked over to where people were gathering for the morning briefing.

Zak watched him approach the group of cadets and noted a distinct change. Mark walked differently now. His normally loose and relaxed gait had stiffened. Zak turned away and headed to the command mech, wondering what changes might be happening to him.

Everyone who wasn't resting or tending to vital tasks had gathered near a truck that had become an unofficial kitchen and mess hall. Mark took a few deep breaths, mentally preparing for the storm of questions that might come with his announcement.

"Good morning, everyone," he said to the assembled group. Their faces were expectant. Some even seemed eager to hear him speak. "I'm sure many of you already know what I'm going to say. After thinking about it, we're going to be sending out a scout team ahead of the main convoy. We're already a small core, and I don't want to leave our main body completely defenseless, so only one mech and a support vehicle will be needed for this. I'm open as to which mech heads out, and I'm looking for volunteers."

Only a brief silence followed, promptly broken by Turner.

"Sir, I'll pilot the Kapu with my crew. We've already been talking about the need for something like this."

"I thought you'd say that Turner," Mark said with a calculated smile. "I'd like you to take point on this. Nothing heroic, you understand. We just need to get a look at what we're chasing. Meet me in the command mech after this, and we can draw up our final strategy." He looked away and looked over the group of expectant faces. "I need a truck and four volunteers to ride along with Turner and his crew."

As he knew she would, Brooke raised her hand. Several others were also quick to volunteer. Too many, in fact, to go along. Mark saw a thin opportunity to keep Brooke from going and jumped at it.

"Turner, you see your volunteers. Please select your crew before we meet." Then, to the group, "Everyone else, get this camp packed in as normal. We'll head out after I meet with Turner."

Mark caught the look Brooke cast at him before he could avert his eyes. Turner would no doubt add her to his scout party though, he would be crazy not to. Mark walked back to the Maratus and began helping to pack away the huge overhead canopy that they spread between each leg whenever they made camp. It was hard work, rolling and storing the large sheets of canvas; hard enough that he could take his mind off everything else. He was reminded of the yearly boating excursions with his father. The feel of the rough canvas reminded him of the sails on the old boat. Mark wondered if it was still afloat, docked on the Pacific coast, waiting for all of this to end.

Mark refocused on the task of rolling the canopy for the Maratus. The straps they used to secure it were taut and thick, and the ratchets made a repetitive noise as they cinched the roll tight. Once they were raising the rolled tubes into their storage compartments in the legs of the command mech, he looked up to see Turner walking away from a small group a few dozen yards away. Turner caught Mark's gaze and gestured up toward the command module.

Mark wasn't sure why he was so worried. It was certainly dangerous, but it was just a scout mission. They would tail the enemy and occasionally radio back a report when there was a safe window. But he'd already lost people. Had almost lost Zak twice. Sending anyone out ahead, especially Brooke, tied his stomach in knots.

"You guys handle the rest of this?" Mark asked the soldiers raising the last two rolls of the canopy. They all nodded or grunted in assent as they continued their work, so Mark made his way to the center ladder. Turner met him and, with a flourish of one hand, gestured to let Mark go up first.

Once inside the center module, they made their way up to the command deck. There they found Zak sleeping soundly in the reclined pilot seat. Evidently, he wanted to be sure he was awake before anyone tried to leave.

"Shit, over here." Mark led Turner up through the roof hatch and onto the viewing platform. Once out in the open air, Mark took a moment to appreciate the view. Spread out below them were the only friendly forces for hundreds of miles. The scent of rain on the wind drifted by him, and he looked out to a distant puff of white behind the mountains on the horizon. The desert seemed to know when things were about to change. Turner walked toward the railing, looking out along the path of the enemy mechs. It headed toward the distant clouds to the north.

"They're not just brown," Mark said, as he admired the landscape.

"What?" Turner asked. "What's not just brown?"

"The mountains. They're all kinds of colors." Mark looked down at the group of people Turner had selected for his scout party.

"I'm taking Brooke with me," Turner said. "She told me you'd try to talk me out of it, but that you'd eventually come around on it."

"I'm not going to talk you out of it," Mark said, watching as Brooke loaded the truck she would be riding in. "It's not like I'd be able to stop her, short of ordering her to stay. If I did, I'd risk a one-woman mutiny. And she's smart, dammit. She knows more about these machines than anyone else here. You might need her out there on your own. I don't want you guys breaking down in that junker mech you're piloting."

"Hey, it's not that bad," Turner said with affection. "The class that built Kapu may have left a bit to the imagination in terms of aesthetics, but it's quick and hasn't broken down yet. I'll do my best to keep us out of trouble."

"I appreciate the sentiment," Mark said. "But I'm not sure there's any way to be completely safe out there. We have no idea what they've got with them. Let's put that aside and talk about what we do know."

Mark pulled out a piece of chalk, and Turner sighed dramatically.

"Again, with that damn chalk. We can just talk this out you know?"

"It helps me think," Mark said. "Just indulge me."

"Sure, whatever gets your rocks off," Turner said and crouched down.

Together they debated and discussed how far to stay from the enemy group and when to try reporting in. They worked out a plan for retreat if they were discovered. After more time than was strictly necessary, Mark relented and stood up.

"Get your crew ready to go," Mark said. "I want you out ahead of us before the rest of camp starts moving," Mark said. "I'll be down in a bit."

Turner nodded, visibly relieved to be done, and headed for the hatch to get his team ready to leave.

The sun was up and burning away the morning chill by the time the camp was completely packed away. The two groups were ready to leave. Mark sized up his assets. The six assorted smaller mechs were piloted and crewed effectively with two to three people in each machine. To think of them as small was, of course, only by comparison to the Maratus, his massive Neith class command mech. He had nine soldiers in the Maratus with him, and three soldiers in each of their three trucks below. Turner and his team were taking one of the mechs and one of the trucks out of the main party.

Mark didn't like the idea of splitting this already thin group, but he'd come to believe it was the best way to relieve tension and gain sorely needed intelligence. He continued to hope that the enemy forces would be taken out by someone else, some team of veteran soldiers sent from command, and that all of this would end. As the days of radio silence continued, however, Mark had begun to worry that he would end up mounting his own attack before anyone arrived to help them.

The morning breeze had turned into a stiff wind, picking up dense sheets of desert dust in periodic waves. The heavy machinery moving around didn't help either. By the time Mark was seeing the scout party off, he could scarcely say a word without gritty earth filling his mouth.

"Reports every six hours," Mark said, then spit, clearing out the dust. It tasted like metal. "More, if necessary, of course. Stay back from the enemy forces. Just follow behind and keep track of where they're going. Stay just within range of your scans. Your small footprint should conceal your position at that distance."

"We've been over this, Mark," Turner said, standing firmly against the increasing wind. "I'm not an idiot, and I know what I'm doing."

"I hope you do," Mark said. "If anything goes wrong, we're right behind you."

"Sure. Again, we've done this dance already. Can we get out of this wind please?" Turner spread his arms out wide.

As an answer, Mark nodded and made a little shooing gesture with his fingertips, like a mother sending her children out to play. They really had talked this plan out more than they needed to.

Turner faced his team, and without opening his mouth, pointed toward the Kapu and their truck. The scout party began to walk away, leaving Brooke and Mark alone to say their goodbyes. Vicious gusts of wind tore at their eyes as they walked toward each other.

"This is exactly the kind of thing they're trying to avoid by forbidding relationships within units," Brooke said. "I love you, Mark."

He told himself it was the sand that was causing him to blink away tears, but he knew that wasn't the truth. The leader of this mixed bag of soldiers was crying at the thought of sending out a simple scouting party.

"I don't care what Turner says," Mark said. "You guys need to be careful out there. We've got no idea what we're even following, what you'll find."

"Exactly. We'll find out, we'll follow, and then we'll get these rebel bastards somehow." Brooke smiled, closed the distance between them, and pulled Mark in close.

He could smell her hair as it whipped around them in the wind, just as he had the first night they kissed, and suddenly he was deep in a forest with her. They were hundreds of miles away, among high mountain pines. They were alone. He imagined a cabin they built together from trees on their own property. It was a fantasy he often returned to; one they had built together in whispered conversations over the last few months. Mark placed his hand on her ballistic vest above her chest and felt the cool metal of the penny necklace beneath his palm. He took it in his hand and tucked it beneath her armor.

"You just make sure and come back to me, okay?" Mark said.

"Why don't you just go ahead and catch me?" Brooke said. She leaned in and kissed him, pressing into him so hard he had to take a step back. The sand between their lips brought Mark back from the forest and into the desert reality. He pulled back and looked at her, not wanting the moment to end.

"Deal," Mark said, and kissed her again. "Now get back to your unit soldier, I'm sure Turner is fuming every moment he's not giving orders and stuff."

They parted and headed for their respective vehicles. Brooke got into the passenger side of the scout party truck, and Mark headed back to the dangling ladder that led up to the central module of the Maratus. As he climbed, he watched the scout party leave. Turner wasn't wasting any time. The Kapu, and the truck carrying Brooke, had disappeared into the dust before Mark even reached the top of the ladder.

CHAPTER 18

The main group maintained their pace as they followed behind Turner. The Maratus just wasn't built for the kind of speed that other mechs were. Mark had asked Barkley to join them on the command deck and take over at the weapons station. Kalen moved to Brooke's now vacant position at the communications station. He filled the post well, but the command deck felt emptier without Brooke there to provide her technical knowledge and assessment. She was also usually good for a tension-breaking snide comment or two.

As they were moving, Mark asked Zak to run some distance calculations at the map table. The enemy still seemed to be headed in the direction of Ember Springs, and with some guesswork, determining how long it should take Turner and his group to intercept the enemy wasn't particularly hard. He overlaid his calculations on the map table and waved Mark over.

"Okay, assuming they take the same amount of rest we do, the earliest our scouts should encounter any forces from the Harbingers is midday tomorrow," Zak said. "But I've been thinking, while we're on the subject. Do you think the enemy is even still moving in a large group? They took enough mechs out of Taycher that they could have sent a faster party out ahead."

"I think I have a theory on this," Barkley said, turning away from his station. "When my squadron came up on them, we wondered the same thing. They were right out in the open, in a tight formation like I told you. Tighter than anything I've seen our forces ever train to maintain. I honestly thought we'd blast them into next week, no problem. We circled them a couple of times at high altitude and they were definitely arranged in that formation on purpose. Then, when we went in for our first run at them, we hit, or were hit with, the Ston device they took from Taycher. So, I'd venture to guess that the device's protection is dependent upon them traveling in close quarters. That doesn't mean they didn't have a similar idea and sent out a small party ahead, but they are just a rebel group. These may be the only mechs they have. I doubt they'd risk any of them leaving whatever safety net they've got."

"I hope you're right," Zak said. "But I also did some calculations based on if they did send out a faster party ahead. And, if they sent out a faster group ahead, they may have gotten to Ember Springs yesterday," Zak said.

The group on the command deck quieted at the thought of it. The destruction they saw in Tonopah was devastating. The group of rebel mechs had torn through the city and left a path of shredded buildings in their wake as they moved through. Ember Springs was a small but densely populated government township. If the rebel forces had gone through it the same way they did in Tonopah, the town may have already been completely destroyed. Mark didn't understand why they would tear up a town like that, but it was possible. Considering that the group called itself the Harbingers of the Fall, it would stand to reason that they didn't exactly place a high value on human life.

"We'll operate on the premise that we can still help Ember Springs. We have to at least hope there's a chance," Mark said. Then, without thinking, he continued. "But I'm still not sure what we're even going to be able to do if we catch up to them."

Airing his uncertainty to the group was a risk, and he hadn't known he was going to say it even as the words were coming out of him. Now, having said it, he felt more at ease with them. The crews in each mech and truck had probably already had similar conversations among themselves. Each crew seemed to have developed a bond, stuck inside the cramped quarters of their units during each day's long trek. No doubt they had talked about the major questions with each other without having to know all the answers. Mark began to feel even more comfortable as he saw the faces around him relax as well.

"We'll figure something out," Zak said. It looked like he wanted to say more, but he let the statement stand.

"While we're on this subject," Kalen spoke up. "Why would they head for Ember Springs? I've been thinking about this for a while, and I think I might have figured it out."

"It's a secluded mountain area with resources. We figured that already," Mark said. "It's as good a place as any to hunker down."

"Sure." Kalen turned his chair around and addressed the whole group. "But if that's all they need, there are a number of other towns they could have used. And they wouldn't have to go as far. So, something must make it special. Worth the risk of being out in the open this long."

Mark was intrigued and motioned for Kalen to continue.

"If you look at the map, there's a pretty big dead zone around the town. There aren't a lot of military installations near it. To be honest, there isn't much of anything around there. It's just a government mining town on the slope of a mountain with a bunch of other ranges around it. But I remembered something Zim told me once. He was always a big fan of pre-Decline history. The whole area around Ember Springs was called The Hollows."

"Yeah, I remember Brooke mentioning something about that," Mark said. "A bunch of old mines that were closed off because the cost to get the ore out became too much to justify. She's got a couple of good ghost stories that talk about the mines around her town."

"There's a lot more conspiracy theory stuff worked into it than that," Kalen said. "According to Zim, some people believe there were some bunkers built into the ranges around Ember Springs when things started to go south before the Decline. The theory goes that the government and corporate elite rode out a lot of the violence of the Decline in bunker complexes across the country. The mining that went on in the ranges isn't a secret, of course, but if there's really something more substantial left there, it might explain why they'd target that area."

"I know for a fact that the military does operate a few complexes like that for members of the government to this day," Barkley said. "We used to run red-flag scenarios and we'd cover the airspace over three that I can remember. The Hollows, or whatever, wasn't one of them, but it could be abandoned."

"So, it's not only Ember Springs we're worried about," Mark said. "If we follow this thread, we're dealing with an underground rebel stronghold inside pre-Decline bunkers, armed with mechs and something that can take out an entire squadron of fighters mid-air."

"That or they're bearing down on a secret bunker containing the last leaders of the United Entities," Kalen said.

"Well," Mark said. "That's bad."

After six hours of tense waiting, a crackle finally came through the radio. Mark let out a startled shout. Then, more calmly, he tuned the radio to filter static as best as he could. The frequency pattern they were using skipped along at a predetermined rate and was virtually impossible to decrypt without the key. The radio bursts themselves could still be detected, of course, so they had to play with direction and intensity to mitigate those risks. They were careful to speak as briefly as possible, especially in the direction aimed back toward Turner and his group.

"Read you," Mark said. "What's your progress?"

"Moving well." Turner's voice came through clearly, with only an occasional fuzzy intrusion as the radio skipped along, picking up the static on different frequencies. "At the last ridge, we saw them moving in the predicted direction."

"Any sign they also saw you?" Mark asked.

"None so far," Turner said. "They appear to be setting up camp for the night. We couldn't get a clear view of the whole core, but we're pressing forward to make up some lost time."

"Careful to power down any exterior lights as the sun sets, we don't want you shining in the night," Mark said.

"Yes sir," Turner said, and if he was annoyed by the reminder, he didn't let it come through in his voice. "They're still too far out to get an accurate scan so that's all we have to report for now. We'll update you when necessary."

"We actually have an update for you," Mark said. "Kalen and Barkley believe there may be a system of bunkers ahead, near Ember Springs. We think that might be the actual destination, if it exists. Confer with Brooke. She's a local and may have heard something."

"Will do," Turner said. "Hold on."

Minutes went by and Mark began to think they wouldn't be back. He was about to give up when Turner came back on.

"Brooke says that was a popular rumor when she was a kid too," Turner said. "She and her friends never found anything but abandoned mineshafts though. We're going dark again. Talk during the next window."

The radio crackled loudly. After the static hissed for a few moments and no further voices came through, Mark turned it back down.

Through the front windshield, the desert landscape was broad and bright. A seemingly endless sea of sagebrush and Joshua trees stretched into the distance. At the fringes of the horizon ahead, storm clouds sat like white pillars beneath the sky. The dark shadow below flickered with lightning and began to curl over the mountains there. Turner and his team were halfway to the storm by now, with the enemy ahead soon to be shrouded within it. From here it was a daunting sight, and Mark could only imagine the constant state of tension the scout team must be under.

Zak walked up behind Mark and shared the view for a minute before either of them spoke.

"If that storm gets bad enough, we might lose contact," Mark said, worry hanging at the edges of his voice.

"I thought of that too," Zak said. "Let's hope it clears up or disperses. But I'm less worried about our communication and more concerned their sensors won't work as well as they should. Without the advanced sensor systems of the command mech, they'll be essentially blind if the storm is charged enough."

"If Turner is smart, he'll bed down for the night and wait for it to pass," Mark said as he pulled up a sensor sweep. He looked for any sign of Turner and the truck. "I can't see them anymore. They must already be out of our range."

"Turner won't stop for the night, you know," Zak said, rubbing the back of his neck. He raised his hand and pointed out the window at the storm. "That storm will give him just as much cover as it does the rebels. He was going to have trouble staying out of sensor range of them anyway. Now would be a perfect time for him to get close and get a solid look at them. If I know Turner at all, he's not going to waste an opportunity like that."

"Are you sure that's a good idea, Zak?" Mark pulled up another sensor sweep and nervously searched the resulting image.

"Absolutely not. It's risky and ill advised," Zak reached over and swept away Mark's scan. "But they're probably going as dark as they can to reduce their sensor footprint. You're not going to find them. It's also probably why he ended his transmission so quickly. If I had to guess, I'd say he's made better time than we thought. I think they're headed into that storm right now."

"God dammit," Mark said, pulling the scan back up. "Why the hell wouldn't he say anything to us?"

"Why do you think?" Zak asked. "It's pretty clear; if he said something, you would have told him to wait."

"Goddamn right I would," Mark said. "I don't want them charging into things blind. I should send them a direct order to back off."

"Not a good idea," Zak said. "If they're near The Harbingers, you'd be sending a clear signal, however brief. You'd alert the rebels there's someone close. From what we've seen so far, these guys are smarter than we've ever been briefed on. They're piloting mechs, they took out those jets somehow, and they've kept ahead of us this whole time. They've got some advanced training, some of them do at least. And the *first* thing we learned was field communication. It's safe to assume they've got that, too."

"I'm just worried." Mark paused. "What about that rebel woman? She has to know something. How much have you been able to get out of her?"

"Nothing more than what happened that first night," Zak said. "She spouted some anti-government stuff. Basically said, it's not our place, not the government's job, to take out The Harbingers."

"What does she expect us to do?" Mark asked. "Just let them plow their way through cities and on to whatever doomsday quest they've got planned for the rest of us?"

"Listen, I don't know. That's just what she said," Zak said. "Anyway, I haven't had a chance to talk to her again. I'll press harder next time and see what I can get out of her."

"She's our only link to these rebels, and they're bearing down on another town as we speak." Mark looked at Zak and shook his head. "They're within earshot of Brooke and the others."

"I know," Zak said, holding up his hands. "I just think the woman has been through a lot. I was giving her some time."

"Fuck her, Zak." Mark turned away from the screen and faced him. "Her kind are attacking places all over the country, hell, maybe even the world right now. And we don't know what the hell is going on or why they're doing this. She knows something, and you need to get it out of her or we're leaving her in the desert the next time we leave off."

Mark hadn't known this anger was brewing, but now that it had manifested, he couldn't pull it back in.

"Either she produces something of value, or we're done with her. Make that clear when we set up camp," Mark said.

"Sure, Mark." Zak was clearly holding back any further thoughts. "I can do that."

Mark turned back to his display and pulled up a third sensor sweep. He glanced at it only momentarily before angrily swiping it off the screen and pulling up another one in a different spectrum.

CHAPTER 19

Zak watched Mark as he continued to look at the empty scans of the horizon. He was right, the rebel woman had information they could use. He walked to the back of the deck to collect his thoughts and sat on a metal bench that jutted out of the wall. Mark, Kalen, and Barkley worked through various scans and delivered orders to maintain the constantly shifting formation as they moved forward. He felt useless as he watched.

He pulled up a screen of his own with his optics. He noticed a message from Mark he hadn't read yet and remembered it was the video of the encounter Mark had with the rebel woman before she became their prisoner. Zak pulled the file out and began playing it in front of him. It was a first-person video taken directly from Mark's optic implants, and it began the way Mark had described it.

Zak watched the video as Mark worked to remove ammunition canisters from the wreckage, then the viewpoint suddenly shifted. A figure stood over him. This must have been the rebel woman. There was a scuffle and then Mark was running for cover. Very shortly after, the two of them were facing each other with their guns drawn. The look on the woman's face was familiar to Zak. She'd lost something or someone close to her, and recently. Zak had missed a few moments, a few words, but almost as confirmation, the rebel woman began yelling.

"You don't understand! You've had it all! The care, the money, all the shit you could ever want was *yours*. But us? No. No, we haven't earned our place among the elite."

Zak was entranced as sadness and confusion transitioned fluidly into rage on the woman's face.

"You murdered my family, and I'm supposed to understand?" The rebel woman said in the grainy footage. The blood ran out of Zak's face. Momentarily he was left without breath. He took in no sound from the video at all, as panic rose in his throat.

"You think I care!" The woman yelled, cutting through Zak's haze. "You do, don't you? That's a *fucking* mistake."

As she reached up to angrily wipe tears from her eyes, Zak could feel the warm sensation of tears on his own face. The camera dipped suddenly, and Zak knew what happened next. The woman would be tackled by Mark, knocked nearly unconscious, and then taken into custody. Zak swiped the video away. As he did, he realized he had forgotten to breathe. When he tried to correct this, his breath came in with the potential to explode out as a sob. He couldn't do that on the command deck. The suppression of the outburst sent him into an uneven pattern of halting breaths. He could feel a panic seeping in around him as he connected points in his mind that did not want to click into place. With effort, he closed the circuit in his brain, and the thought finally rang clear.

"I killed them," Zak said softly. "I killed her family."

He was there. The family at the farmhouse. The man he shot when coming around the truck. The little girl and her mother who must have been torn apart as the windows of the house exploded into serrated dust as he, Lund, and Manner fled into the darkness.

His breathing and tremors made it hard, but Zak managed to grab hold of the metal ladder at the back of the room. With effort, he was able to make it up and outside into the open air.

Once outside, where he should have been able to breathe and calm himself, he was blasted by wind and grit. Disjointed visions came to him, connected by a burning through-line. He saw the kitchen wall in his family home when he was just a child, its plaster cracked where the bullets came through. Then, the same cracked wall but in the house in the clearing, with the same line of dark holes punched through it. A silhouetted child in a doorway. The figure of the rebel woman wiping away stubborn tears from eyes the color of honey. A searing white flash, then, pain.

He gasped and reached for the back of his head and found it wet with sweat, too much sweat. He was lying on the cool metal hull of the observation deck. He must have fallen. Zak wondered how he had sweat this much in just the last few minutes. When he pulled his hand around in front of his eyes, it was coated in blood, not sweat. He took a quick breath, then another. He began to feel cold, and then everything went dark.

—

Zak opened his eyes and saw a swath of dark brown canvas as it fluttered in the wind above him. His head hurt, like a hangover

257

but with a sharp center near the back of his skull. He reached back and found a bandage wrapped around his head. This was the camp's makeshift medical tent and prisoner quarters. The rebel woman would be around somewhere. Of course, he had ended up here, he thought. Hartley, sitting at a card table organizing medical supplies, noticed that Zak was awake and hurried over.

"Zak are you okay?" she asked as she approached his cot. She knelt down to get closer to him.

"Yeah, I'm fine," Zak said. He looked at Hartley and saw a question forming. "I must have slipped up there. There was a lot more wind than I was expecting."

This seemed to be enough for her, and she began busying herself with removing the bandage from his head.

"You lost a lot of blood when you fell," she said. "If we hadn't stopped to make camp when we did, you might not have made it, you know. Now that we've got the bleeding stopped you won't need this. Fresh air should help it close up. Just don't scratch at it or I'll have to sew you back up again."

Once Hartley finished removing the bandage, she handed Zak a painkiller and some water. She promised to be back later with some food, and headed outside, presumably to alert Mark that he was awake.

He was alone in the tent now, useless again. The canvas continued to rustle softly in the wind, and after just a few moments spent listening to it, he was asleep again.

When Zak opened his eyes next, Mark was poking him in the face.

"What the hell, man?" Zak asked, reaching up to swat his hand away.

"You were asleep, and I was starting to get bored," Mark said, dropping his leadership persona for a moment. "Anyway, I brought you some food. How are you feeling?"

"I feel like someone smacked me over the head with a hammer," Zak said. "Who found me?"

"Kalen did," Mark said. "Made quick work of getting you down and out here to the medical truck. You went upstairs and didn't come back down for a while, and when we decided to stop for the night, he went to check on you. You hit the deck pretty hard, based on how much blood you lost."

"So I've heard," Zak said. "Have we gotten any word from Turner and the scout party?"

"No, they didn't check in at the last scheduled comm time," Mark said, his eyes growing momentarily distant. "Kalen says it's probably because they're close to the enemy and don't want to give away their location. Or it could be the storm. We figure if they're smart, they'll hold back a bit, get some distance from the enemy, and contact us with whatever intel they've gathered."

"That would be my hope, too," Zak said. He took a moment to collect his thoughts through the fog in his mind. "If they're close enough, their time is much better spent gathering information than checking in with us. And Kalen's right, it's not safe to send messages if they are that close. Brooke knows better than any of us how all the sensor arrays work. She would have turned most of them off completely, to be honest. In case you tried the broad spectrum to contact them directly."

"I'm not sure if that makes me feel better, you know," Mark said, producing a weak smile. "What good are you if you can't make me feel better?"

"Hey, who's the one with extreme blood loss and a concussion here?" Zak asked.

"Point taken," Mark said lightly, and then brought his tone down. "What happened up there, Zak? One minute I saw you reviewing the video I sent you, and the next time I turned around, you were gone. Probably bleeding out on the roof."

Zak hesitated, unsure of what to say next. He was surprised Mark hadn't put it together himself yet. The rebel woman practically told him what had happened during their confrontation in the video. It should have been an easy thing to say, that they killed her family, but he couldn't seem to form the words.

"I'm just glad you're okay," Mark said when Zak remained quiet. "You've been pretty distant since all that stuff back at the house. And I get it, I don't know that I'd be any better than you if it had happened to me. I just want you to know that if you ever need to talk, I'm here."

"Thank you," Zak said, his eyes glossing with tears as he was involuntarily pulled into the events again.

"You're important to me," Mark said. "I've almost lost you too many times. I won't lose you again."

"We can't know that," Zak said. "None of this is up to us. Everything out here is just so much bigger than us. The

Harbingers, Stability, everything. I feel like a broken cog spinning uselessly in a machine pushing forward. I'm a ghost."

"Only if you want to be," Mark said. "We need you; I need you. Listen, I'm going to head back to the Maratus and wait for a message from the scout party."

"Let me know if you get one," Zak said.

"Sure," Mark said. "Just eat and get better. We'll need you back on the command deck as soon as you're able. You're a valuable part of all of this. Everything happening might be bigger than us, but together we are a force for good, and that's not nothing."

Mark headed for the exit and lifted the canvas flap of the tent, for a moment revealing the storm cell in the distance. It was much closer now, towering into the sky. As he stood in the doorway looking at Zak, the sweet but vaguely acidic smell of wet creosote blew into the tent on a cool wind. The clouds were filled with the darkness of night, and a jittering strobe of lightning pulsed from within. Then Mark was gone, and the flap fell back down. Zak was alone again, watching the canvas above him as it fluttered in the increasing wind. For a while, he was able to tune out his thoughts by watching the ripples move along the canvas.

Rain began lightly tapping the tent on all sides. He heard movement outside, as people began relocating into tents to get out of the rain. After a few minutes, the rain progressed into a steady static hiss against the outside of the tent. Zak was not sure how long he allowed the hum of the rain to hold him, but his trance was broken when he heard a noise outside.

"Move, get inside," a voice just outside the tent said sharply. "I'm tired of standing out here in the rain."

The flap lifted and the rebel woman, soaked and shaking, entered the tent. Jensen nudged her forward and motioned for her to sit on the ground near the entrance. She complied with a flat, defiant look on her face. Once on the floor, she busied herself by picking at the dirt floor with her bound, shaking hands. Jensen, with a quick nod at Zak, sat on the ground as well with his back against a box of supplies.

The rain outside picked up its intensity and began to drown out all other sound. Zak had managed to keep his composure since the woman entered the tent by focusing intently on this sound. By closing his eyes and listening to the rain, he could almost pretend he wasn't even out in the desert. He imagined he was thousands of miles away on a simple boat, far from land. He had tried this tactic many times before. One time in ten, he was able to use this method to avoid the onset of his flashbacks and the ensuing panic.

His breath came in, short and sharp, and a growing pain beneath his sternum seemed to radiate like a fire through his whole chest. He refocused on the vision in his mind, focusing on how the wind made the boat rock gently, the wood flexing slightly. All at once, he was faced with an image of the tree at the farmhouse. The wooden bench, tied to one branch, creaking in the night. And the man, Jack, sat there with a shotgun across his lap. He remembered the panic he'd felt when he realized the house was surrounded. He had done everything he could to save himself and his fellow soldiers. The image in his mind spun forward, and he neared the point in his memory where he came around the truck. He was face to face with a man he'd just that day saved from a rooftop. He fired and looked up toward the house. Eva stood in the doorway, and Zak forced open his eyes.

The tent was somehow smaller than he had expected. Zak had been so lost in his mind that the solidity of everything around him was reassuring. Jensen was asleep on watch, and the rebel woman was staring at Zak. Her hands were bound, but at any point she could have taken Jensen's rifle and killed at least the two of them. But instead, she was still sitting on the floor. Her defiant glare was replaced now with confusion, or even something approaching concern. She didn't say a word, but Zak felt an obligation to speak.

"I'm fine," he said. "Just dealing with the pain."

In response, she raised her eyebrows and stared at him intently. Zak looked away then, a jolt of pain pulsing through him. He had seen that the rebel woman's eyes were the same shade of honey brown as Eva's. After a few moments, he turned back. She was still watching him, and he looked from her to Jensen.

"Why didn't you run away while you had the chance?" he managed to ask.

The woman shrugged, opened her mouth to speak, and then changed her mind. She continued looking at Zak as he pushed himself up into a sitting position on the cot.

"Did they give you dinner?" he asked.

She clenched her jaw tightly, but still refused to speak. The rain at least had cleaned some of the blood and dirt from her face. He turned to the food Mark brought for him. It was cold but still good. He swung his legs onto the floor, grabbed the plate, and started to stand up. He quickly found that the effects of his blood loss and concussion hadn't dissipated in the least and had to sit back down. Instead, he set the plate on the floor in front of him, then nudged it closer to the woman with his foot.

"I'm still pretty nauseous from my fall." He reached up and felt the even lines of the stitches at the back of his head. He looked at the sticky blood on his fingers and wiped it off on the cot. "I'm not going to eat it, if you want it."

His adventure in sitting up was drawing to a close, as he found it hard to keep his balance even sitting. He laid back down and turned his head back to the woman. She eyed him suspiciously, but also fidgeted with her hands in a way that said she wanted to reach out and take the offered food. Zak fumbled on the table next to him for the silverware Mark also brought and separated the knife from the fork. He tossed the fork the short distance to the plate. It landed next to a piece of rehydrated chicken with a sharp clang. They both looked quickly at Jensen, who didn't stir.

The woman decided the food was worth a risk and scooted herself across the floor to the plate. Zak turned away and looked up at the canvas roof as she approached, not wanting to see those eyes again. He heard the sounds of her eating, carefully and slowly. After a while, he heard the plate slide back onto the low table next to him. Zak turned to look at the woman then. She was close, and his sudden movement startled her. For a moment they stared at one another. Her eyes seemed to ask him what was wrong. He felt a measure of concern for him in her eyes, and his guilt threatened to destroy him.

"I was there," Zak said, the words tumbling out before he could think to stop them.

The woman, her hand still on the plate, tensed up as if struck by something. Her expression transitioned through a rioting mix of emotions. He could see anger, fear, and pain whipped into a potent fury in her eyes. He expected her to hit him with something, the plate perhaps.

She didn't. Instead, she stared at Zak, her eyes rapidly scanning his face. Zak wondered what this moment must look like from her perspective. Three simple words, but they had been enough to convey his full confession.

Zak willed his face to tell her how sorry he was, that he hadn't had a choice. He wanted to say that the rebels shot first, but he wasn't certain that was true. He wondered if he did have a choice.

CHAPTER 20

Mark heard a familiar crackle over the radio and jumped up from his seat. He sprinted the few steps to the communications console and looked at the numbers on the screen. It was them.

Reaching past Kalen, he flipped the receiving switch and listened as silence came through the speaker. At first, he was sure the signal was already gone, but then he detected traces of a voice in the noise. The signal must have been weakened now that they were all underneath the storm.

"...under heavy fire," was the first thing Mark was able to parse from the static. The voice was female. Had it been Brooke? He couldn't be sure. "Repeat we have retreated under heavy fire and we need assistance."

Mark inhaled sharply, briefly forgetting that he needed to respond. Mark took a deep breath and concentrated. He held the button down and spoke. "We read you. We've got you. Where are you?"

"What's going on?" Barkley asked, noticing the look of panic on Mark's face. As an answer, Mark held up one hand to quiet him.

"Come in," Mark pleaded. "We need a location, or we won't know where we're going." He clicked off and waited for a reply.

The static hiss of radio interference filled the speaker, and then a response. "Twenty miles southeast of Ember Springs. Mark, is that you?"

It was Brooke.

"No. Oh, no," Mark said. Then into the radio, "I mean yes, it's me. Hold on, we're on our way. Go dark, and we should be able to get to you by…"

He stopped and looked at Kalen, who had his eyes closed in concentration. Then he quickly mouthed the word five.

"Five hours," Mark said. "Oh god, five hours. Just hold on, we're on our way."

There was no response from Brooke on the radio, as continued radio static asserted itself once more. After a few moments spent listening to it, Kalen spoke up.

"If we're going to get there, we need to leave now."

"Get out there and get everyone up," Mark said staring at the radio receiver. "I'll get this mech running."

Kalen left, taking the ladder to the ground as fast as he could. Through the front windshield, Mark saw him sprint through the rain toward the closest mech and its campsite. Barkley headed for the ladder as well. He was healing quickly but wasn't able to keep up with Kalen. Mark fired up the systems on the command mech. He worked quickly through the engine startup protocols, then remembered the canvas flaps currently spread out between each of the eight legs. He swore and keyed himself out of the controls at the pilot seat. There were emergency release switches on each of the legs that would take care of the canvas problem.

Mark rushed down the ladder and when he was nearly eight feet from the ground, jumped. Barkley and two others must have already reached the same conclusion, because just as he hit the ground, one of the huge pieces of canvas detached from one of the legs and began flapping wildly in the storm. As this happened, the rain the canopy had been holding back cut through to the ground. Barkley hit the switch on the next leg, releasing the flap fully and sent it flying away violently into the night. Mark wiped stinging drops of rain from his face and saw the mechs around him coming to life. Lightning flashed intermittently, throwing the massive machines around him into sharp silhouettes.

He looked toward their trucks as Zak emerged from a tent with the rebel woman. Jensen was leading them both to the back of the medical truck. The camp was in chaos as everything was haphazardly broken down and stored. The rain was so dense that he couldn't even see the whole camp anymore. Wind struggled against the canvas flaps above, pulling them viciously.

He remembered the pull of the wind, the day he and his father had fought ahead of a storm to get back to shore. His father had remained calm, even as Mark started to panic. He hadn't known what to do as their small boat was tossed in ever increasing waves.

"Just focus on the task at hand," his father had said. "If you get too far ahead of yourself, you'll forget something. Just keep moving forward."

They'd continued to adjust the sail as the storm overtook them. Rain poured from the sky like a dam had burst in the clouds above them. It was all he could do to keep from drowning while standing. Eventually, they'd managed to get the boat back to the dock.

Another of the huge triangles of the canopy detached from the command mech's legs, bringing with it even more rain. This brought Mark back to the task, and he sprinted to one of the legs that hadn't been freed yet.

Once all the legs were cleared of the canopy, Mark dashed back to the central ladder and climbed up to the command deck. He scrambled back into the pilot seat and keyed himself back into the controls. Mark radioed to each of the mechs to make sure they were fired up and see what their departure status was. It was the same situation for all of them: their mech was nearly ready to go, but there were some things still being loaded and packed away. It had only been ten minutes, but it felt to Mark like they had been idling for hours. He couldn't stand to wait any longer.

"The Maratus is ready to go," Mark said in a message to everyone. "I'm leaving now. We all know this damn thing can't move as fast as the rest of you. When you've finished, catch up. If anyone sees Kalen and Barkley, tell them to get their asses back here."

Kalen entered from the stairwell immediately after this message and took his seat at the sensors panel. He began pulling up scans of the area ahead of them. Mark busied himself with the last few steps of getting the mech ready to move when Barkley arrived, breathing heavily. He limped to his seat at the weapons controls. All of them were dripping wet and breathing hard as Mark began to pilot the mech forward.

"Mark, we should be able to get to the scout party in a little under four hours if we push the Maratus to the absolute limit of its capability," Kalen said, still working on multiple screens. "Punch it."

From the ground, each step the command mech made was a tremor. Zak sat with his back against haphazardly loaded supplies in the cargo area of the medical truck. The rebel woman was curled up at the other end of the enclosed truck bed, near the back of the cargo space. Zak had only a faint understanding of what was going on. Something had happened with the scout party.

"Here, Zak," Jensen said from outside the truck. "Take this. You're on watch while we get the rest of this crap packed up. Turner and his crew are four hours out and under fire."

Jensen dropped a pistol into Zak's hand and disappeared quickly back out into the deluge. Zak looked at the gun uncomfortably, stowed it between two water jugs, and looked up at the rebel woman.

"You should get out of here, now," Zak said, surprising himself. "It's the only time. I'm so sorry. Please, you have to go."

He scooted to one side and dropped the tailgate of the enclosed cargo area. Outside, the Maratus continued lumbering heavily on its eight legs out of the camp and into the storm. Each movement shook the truck, inspiring a renewed awe at the engineering that had gone into each of these machines.

He looked back at the woman, who remained curled at the back of the space.

"Where do you think I would go?" she asked coldly.

The question struck him as odd, until he thought about it. They were miles from the nearest sign of civilization. If she left, she'd have no choice but to wander in the direction they were headed or out into the empty desert. It was raining but at any time the storm would pass, leaving her without water, food, or even shelter. Her restraints, he realized, weren't meant to keep her from fleeing. Their purpose was to make sure she didn't hurt anyone or break anything important. Mark's threat to send her off into the desert came back to him then.

"Listen, I don't even know your name," Zak said. "I think they're going to kill you or send you out there unless you start giving us information. I don't need a lot, but I need something. Please let me do something."

"Why would I…" she stopped herself and turned her eyes on him. "You killed my entire family you son of a bitch. What makes you think that threatening me will get you anything? I have nothing left to lose."

"It seems like that now." His voice sounded like the counselors and psychologists he'd learned to hate as a child. "But I swear it fades. Eventually, it does. It will."

"Does it really?" she asked. In her voice, he heard malice and grief joined into something black and cold.

The question was simple enough, but each word had barbs that sank deep into him. The wounds of his own past ached and threatened to burst open. He wondered whether or not they would actually close over someday. His silence seemed enough of an answer for the woman. She lowered her head and curled into herself, becoming a nondescript shape in the gloom.

271

The truck's engine eventually rumbled to life, and Zak was jolted as the tires dug into the desert hardpan, thrusting the truck out into the unknown. He pulled the tailgate back up and watched through the open back window as they left a path of ripped earth on their way toward their stranded friends.

Zak lifted himself up and out of the back window, with his legs inside the truck. The rain was a shock to his system. The cool drops stung his face, each one sending a tiny jolt of pain through him. The sensation was somehow calming. He closed his eyes and let the desert rain wash over him in waves.

The trucks were pouring on as much speed as possible to keep pace with the mechs, who did not have to worry about every rock and hill beneath them. He was reminded of the drive, before all of this began, to a party in the desert near Tonopah. They'd talked around the fire about what the future held for each of them. No one could have known then what they would be facing.

When he opened his eyes, there was frenetic movement all around him. The trucks were speeding along the desert together, making progress however they could. As they crested the smaller hills, they bounced and slid in the loose desert sand and mud. Each truck took a path forward that made sense to only the drivers.

The mechs themselves pumped their legs in an Olympic sprint across the desert. They were traveling in a loose circle around the trucks, pounding the ground and tearing up large swaths of grit with each step.

The Icarus and Iris, built like birds, or more accurately like massive theropod dinosaurs, took long graceful strides as they cut through the downpour. They seemed to glide with each step, occasionally using thrusters to propel themselves up and over larger sand dunes. Lightning, mostly hidden behind the cloud layer above, occasionally threw sharp highlights onto the rain-slick surfaces of the mechs. Zak could see the Cronus behind the truck moving through the rain like a mythic giant. It plowed forward in a similarly graceful manner, but its steps were more improvised. It ran like a trained trail runner, deftly choosing where the next foothold would be and pushing off from there. Occasionally it would stumble and correct with another split-second plant of one massive leg. All of this happened as they approached the Maratus, which was still a few miles off in the distance.

Mark's mech scurried across the landscape, from this distance looking so much like a massive tarantula that Zak couldn't shake the image. The sheer scale of the command mech was camou-flaged by how fast it was moving. Mark must have been pushing the structural integrity of the Maratus to its absolute limits. He wouldn't doubt that a few safety protocols had been completely overridden. The rain and airborne debris began stinging his eyes, and he was forced to retreat back into the truck.

He rubbed the palms of his hands into his eyes in an attempt to dislodge the accumulated grit there. Once free of most of the dirt, he allowed his eyes to stay shut, as a way to avoid seeing the woman in the truck with him. Without meaning to, he fell asleep, aided by the painkiller and his head wound, no doubt.

Zak woke with a start as a beam of sunlight poured in through the back window of the truck. At first, he was confused, because the rain continued to pour down outside the truck. The sun had risen above the horizon beneath the storm, painting the frenzied clouds around them with broad strokes of red and gold. He blinked the sleep from his eyes and began to wonder how much time had passed when the truck crested a large sand dune. He and the contents of the truck became momentarily weightless. When the truck landed on the other side, Zak landed hard on his tailbone.

"Shit, ouch. Are you all right?" He looked up at the woman.

He only had a moment to react as she crouched, ready to leap at him. He reached for the pistol he had stowed between the water jugs and found the spot was empty. Then she was on him. Her arms were still bound, as they had been for all but her most intimate moments. Even as restricted as she was, she was still able to catch him off guard and do some damage. She struck him over the head, and the symptoms of his fall came back strong. Zak was dizzy. His vision blurred immediately. He reached up to protect his head, but the woman wasn't going for his head any longer. Instead, she reached for the tailgate release and fumbled for the handle there.

When she pulled it, the tailgate dropped with a heavy thud. They both nearly spilled out into the dust cloud being pulled up behind their advancing force. Zak's throbbing head dangled out over the edge of the flattened tailgate. The woman pushed against him, trying to get free of his grasp. She didn't have much trouble and managed to kick herself away from him just as the truck crested another hill. She got back into a crouching position and waited.

She leaped from the tailgate just as the truck was coasting through the air and landed on the downward slope of a sand dune. He watched as she rolled down the dune with her arms pulled in tightly to protect her face and neck. Zak managed to do the same he slid off of the tailgate along with a number of the boxes of supplies in the back of the truck. He rolled down the dune, hoping for the movement to stop and for his head to remain intact. Eventually, he slid to a stop facing the ground. He was remarkably unhurt. He could feel places that would bruise, but no pain felt sharp enough to imply he'd broken anything.

Zak pushed up from the sand and looked around for the mechs or the other trucks. He noticed a number of the supply boxes scattered around him, but no one had stopped. Higher up on the dune, he saw the small shape of the rebel woman. He couldn't tell if she was breathing or not. The truck they'd fallen from was still tearing forward into the storm, unaware of what had just happened.

Suddenly, one of the Aves class mechs came over the dune using its thrusters to clear it. The blue light of the jets matched the flickering lightning. It mech landed only a few yards from him, sending an explosion of earth in his direction. Zak shielded himself from the debris as the mech continued forward in formation with the rest of their advancing forces. He shot up into a standing position, yelling and waving his arms frantically. But he knew there was no way anyone would see him. They were moving too quickly, and no one was looking in the rear-view mirror in their mad sprint forward.

After yelling for a few more moments, he gave up and watched as they moved into the distance. Rain had already soaked him completely, and he wiped it from his face. Zak turned and walked up the steep grade toward the rebel woman, not knowing what he was going to do next. As he got nearer to her, he saw that she was still breathing and couldn't decide if that was good or bad. He put his hands up in a half defensive, half soothing gesture as if he were approaching a wounded animal. She was still facing away from him, so he stood his ground and waited for her to move. She rolled onto her back, and in her still-bound hands, she held the pistol. The woman didn't aim it at him, but the threat was implied.

A deep rumble of thunder shook the ground. When Zak turned involuntarily to look, he saw that it wasn't thunder. In the distance, a plume of black smoke was rising. The mechs couldn't be more than a mile away. The woman must have heard when they would reach their destination and waited for just this chance. A flash of golden light, so much like the light from the sun, bloomed in the distance. Seconds later, another deep rumble washed over them, as the sounds of a battle began to rise.

CHAPTER 21

"What the hell was that?" Mark yelled. "Oh god dammit, is everyone all right?"

"Everyone's still accounted for," Kalen said. "I think they're just firing on us without a lock or we'd have been hit."

Mark looked out at his mechs around him, recognizing the danger of their current formation. He opened his short-range communications. "Spread out, fast. Spread out and go dark!"

The group didn't need to be told twice. They scattered like insects from a flame and disappeared from his scans. He knew that the command mech was in the most danger, as it gave off the largest signature of anything in the desert. His mech would take a few more seconds to disappear from the enemy scans and go dark, so he took this extra moment to gather all the information he could.

"Run a wide spectrum scan," Mark said. "I know we'll light up like a beacon on their screens but it's our only shot. I can get us moved in time."

While Kalen prepped the scan, Mark got the mech ready to move as soon as it was complete.

"Scan complete in ten seconds," Kalen said. "Five. Four."

Mark's hands hovered over the controls. He felt like he could feel the enemy rounds soaring through the air, coming toward them.

"Three, two, go!" Kalen shouted and gripped his chair.

Mark jerked the controls, and the Maratus lurched sideways into a spin. The mech pitched, and its legs curled in, creating a ball shape for them to roll on. Inside the command module, things didn't look quite as graceful. It felt like they'd been dropped from the edge of a cliff, and anything not tied down became a projectile.

Moments later, a concentrated burst of explosive rounds crashed from the sky and blasted the ground they had been scanning from. For an instant, the rain stopped, either pushed away or vaporized by the blast. The rain returned, and everything was dark. The only light came from the flashes of lightning that flickered in through the front windshield and the faint glow of the sunrise.

For a while, the three of them sat in silence. Mark hoped anyone below the command deck had the foresight to have strapped in when the first shells impacted around their mech. Kalen leaned back in his seat and unbuckled his harness. Barkley remained harnessed. The way they had landed, the entire mech was tilted, and his harness was the only thing keeping him from sliding across the floor and into the opposite bulkhead. Mark also remained in his harness, but only because he was straining to look through the gloom for anything, anyone moving in the distance. Another series of explosions erupted near the spot they had scanned from, this one with a slightly wider spread.

"That's probably the last they'll volley without new information," Kalen said. "I'm sure they don't have ammunition to waste, either. Those first few were just to get us to stop and give away our exact location."

"I had to get a look at what we're facing," Mark said. "We need to know what's out there."

"I know," Barkley said. "We did all right. If they knew our position now, we'd be hit already. A hit wouldn't be the end of the world for us, right? This thing looks like it can take a beating."

"They can," Kalen said. "The Neith class is one of the most heavily armored vehicles ever created. You don't want to go taking direct hits all the time, but they're designed to take a few."

"My jet was designed to take hits too," Barkley said. "And you saw what happened to us."

"When can we pull up the scan?" Mark asked. "Would it show where Brooke is, where our scout team is?"

"It might, but I don't think we should fire up any systems yet," Kalen said. "They've already got a fix on the general area we're in."

"That also means they could be headed our way, right?" Barkley asked, looking out the front windshield. Rainwater streamed down the glass, and lightning continued to occasionally light up the horizon, but there was no discernible movement otherwise.

"They might be, yes," Mark said. "But Kalen was right. They don't have ammunition to waste, and they certainly don't have mechs to waste coming at us blind either."

"I don't know how you groundhogs do this," Barkley said. "I feel like we're a target on a shooting range, asking to be shot."

"I know we can't stay here forever," Mark said. "We need to find Turner and his team and either make a stand or back the hell off until we can get reinforcements or another plan."

"You know reinforcements aren't coming," Barkley said, surprising Mark. "Anyone left is in the same situation we are, without clear orders and desperately outmanned. We're alone and you know it."

Mark let these words rest in the silence, then he spoke.

"If that's the case, it's even more important that we get this situation resolved as fast as possible. We'll wait for our core temperature to drop and then we'll fire up auxiliary power to review the scans and level the mech out."

Barkley and Kalen nodded at this, though Mark was acutely aware he hadn't proposed an actual solution. The three of them listened to the sounds that penetrated through the hull of the mech. A deep rumble of thunder came and went beneath a constant layer of rain noise. After a few minutes, Kalen flipped a few switches, giving the mech emergency power. Mark used most of the reserve power to slowly level the mech out so they could move on the deck freely. Then he powered down the legs so that the command module rested evenly on the ground, making their mech look like a tarantula curled in, defending itself.

Mark and Barkley headed over to Kalen's station where he pulled up their final scan. On the screen, they saw an agonizingly small set of information. Almost directly north, about a mile out, they saw what appeared to be only three or four man-made objects giving off a strong signal. It was always possible with a scan like this that there may have been more behind what was shown.

"I don't see the scout team on there anywhere," Mark said. "Am I missing something?"

"I'm not sure," Kalen said as he squinted at the scan, periodically zooming in and out of spots on the screen. "Why would the rebel mechs be here if our scout team isn't…"

Kalen stopped talking suddenly and zoomed into a section about a half-mile out and to the northeast.

"What is it?" Mark asked. He didn't see anything on the screen but noise, like a fine grain of random color. As Kalen continued to examine it closely, Mark asked, "Sam, what is it?"

"I can't be sure, but this must be them." He pointed to one of the many splotches on the screen. "They've been here a while, so they wouldn't be giving off a lot of signal. Almost none by this point really."

"Get to the point. Is it them? Are they alive?" Mark asked.

"I can't tell you if they're alive, but yes, this has to be them," Kalen said. "The more I look at it, the clearer it is. Sometimes you need to look into the signal noise. Everything gives off at least some kind of signal, and a lot of times it's within the noise range so you wouldn't even notice it. Rocks and trees, you know. But this spot here, it's all got a uniform level of noise, like it's made of the same stuff and connected as a whole. It's got to be a mech. I can't tell if it's still functional, but it's them."

"It's better than nothing," Barkley said. "Any plan for what to do next?"

"Everyone's probably got auxiliary power up now, too," Kalen said. "We can talk in short bursts if we keep the signal low and everyone talks fast. A half dozen radio transmissions spread out between our mechs might be enough that the enemy won't be able to get a specific fix on any one of us. That doesn't help with a plan, but it does let us talk to the others when we do."

"I'm not sure there's much we can do tactically," Mark said. "We got here late to the party. They know the layout of the terrain, and they have the upper hand with us powered down and in the dark."

"I only counted three mechs out there," Barkley said. "This looks like just a few units trailing behind their main party. I think we've got to take our chances, power these big things up, get out to your scout party, and retreat to higher ground."

"You're right," Mark said. "Who knows if there's anything we missed, but it did look like we have them outgunned. And when we're powered up and we have scans going continuously, we'll get a clearer picture."

Kalen didn't seem to have anything to add and began preparing the sensors to come online as soon as the mech was up and moving. Mark returned to the pilot seat while Barkley strapped into his seat at the back of the room to control the large gun on top of the mech.

Mark keyed himself back into the mech and prepared to power up. His heart was racing and he could feel adrenaline beginning to flood his nervous system.

"Sound off, team, let me know you're awake," he said into his radio, with the intensity dialed as low as it would go.

A flurry of radio messages came in confirming that everyone was online and awaiting orders.

"Prepare to power up. We're headed to the scout team. Radio back immediately," Mark said quickly.

The radio responses were fast, but he wasn't sure if they would be enough to confuse any scans directed at them.

"Scout team is half a mile northeast," Mark said. "Enemy one a mile to the north. Radio back immediately for radio cover."

The responses this time came a bit faster.

"Twenty seconds to power," Mark said.

A flurry of responses.

"Ten seconds to power."

Another group of responses came then, incoherent but universally frenzied and tense. A heat spread through him as his hands prepared to work the controls. A new sensation took hold of him, something that Phillips told them they would someday understand. He'd called it battle fever.

"Let's go get our team back," Mark said, so calmly that he was momentarily afraid his team would mistake his resolve for apprehension.

The responses that came through the radio, however, joined into a simultaneous battle cry, resonating through the inside of the command deck. Mark powered up his mech. The sudden movement was disorienting as the center module rose from the ground. The legs fanned out around them. Kalen must have already begun scanning, because he started to call out the locations of the team around them.

"Evasive maneuvers and head southeast," Mark called through the radio. "Stand by for coordinates."

Mark nodded at Kalen, who transmitted the freshest scans he had to the other mechs around them. Included with these scans were the coordinates for what they believed was the scout team, and the last known locations of the enemy units.

An explosion jolted the command module from above as Mark moved the mech quickly in the direction of the scout team, toward Brooke.

"Damage report?" Mark called out to his small crew.

"No damage, sir," Barkley said. In another setting, Barkley calling him sir would have felt wrong, but it felt right in that moment. "That was our gun up top. I had a clear shot."

"Did we hit anything?" Mark asked, continuing to push the mech forward.

"Unclear," Kalen said. He was struggling to keep up with the volume of information coming in through the scanning array. "It looks like we might have hit one of them. Actually, affirmative! It also looks like we've got..." he paused. "Six enemy mechs, sir."

"Six?" Mark asked, a panicked edge working its way into his tone. "Fire at will, Barkley. Try to keep them back. We need to keep them from advancing on us if we can."

"We've got enough information for visual scan overlay, Mark!" Kalen shouted over.

Mark looked out through his windshield and could clearly make out two of his squad's mechs against the sky during the brief flash of a lightning strike. Suddenly, as he peered through the glass, it lit up with a broad range of information. He could see where his mechs were with blue triangles. Red triangles showed up in the spots where confirmed enemy targets were. The horizon, elevation, and even geographic features became outlined to aid navigation.

The gun on top of the mech fired once again, making his teeth chatter, and he scanned the terrain ahead. The enemy mechs were making slow progress toward them.

"This doesn't look good." Mark selected two of his units and sent orders to fan out, so they didn't interfere with each other. "They're advancing on us. We would be better off if we could take cover and fire from a distance. Kalen, get the foothills to the east tagged as our retreat rendezvous point."

"Yes, sir. Just a bit farther to the scout team," Kalen said. "We should be coming up on them any second."

~

For a long time, Zak and the rebel woman stayed exactly where they were. She continued to lie in the wet sand with the gun clasped in her bound hands. She didn't make any attempt to get up or to aim it at him. He stood still, not wanting to push her into action. The entire time, the rain continued to drench their clothes. Then, he heard another explosion from behind him and turned to look. He had to know what was happening. He could barely make out the shape of the Maratus as the gun on top fired. He saw the explosion in the distance as the round connected with an enemy mech.

The sound of movement from behind him made him turn back to the woman. Now she did have the gun aimed at him, but she seemed to be watching the scene in the distance as well. Her eyes widened, and Zak decided it was safe to turn back. He did, just in time to see the tail end of another explosion, the yellow and orange flames breaking against the hull of the command mech. It stumbled from the force of the impact but continued along its course.

Other friendly mechs became visible then, illuminated only briefly as they fired their weapons at targets somewhere in the distance. Zak looked out to where the enemy should be and saw their weapons firing as well. They were moving in, and Zak watched, unable to move, unable to help. He turned again, reluctantly, away from the scene to face the woman once more.

She took her eyes away from the battle, focused them on Zak, and tightened her grip on the gun. She began to stand, then winced and cried out in pain. She must have injured herself when she jumped from the truck. Realizing she wouldn't be able to stand, a look of fury enveloped her. She seemed to also realize that if she was going to survive, Zak could be her only chance. The woman lowered the gun. She looked down at the cold metal, speckled with rain, and then cast it out into the wet sand.

Zak walked to where it landed, crouched down to pick it up, and wiped the sand from it. The reddening clouds above were reflected in the metal of the gun, giving it the appearance of being coated in blood.

He turned to look at the woman and considered the choice he needed to make. It was one he was not completely comfortable making. He could leave her there or take her with him as he attempted to make his way back to the group.

There was also a third option, he realized. The cold metal heft of the weapon in his hand was momentarily magnified by the thought of using it. No one would have faulted him. They may have even seen it as something done out of mercy. No one would even have to know. From his place on the high dune, the fighting below became little more than a backdrop for his own personal conflict. He stood and began to walk back toward the woman lying in the sand.

~

Another explosion rocked the Maratus, cracking the front windshield but not yet penetrating onto the command deck. Mark couldn't believe he had mistaken Barkley firing the gun up top for an actual hit. The jolts from the gun had become a rhythmic drumbeat to move forward by. Mark launched their secondary weapons in time with it, all while moving toward their goal. When an enemy barrage struck their mech, it was like the world was weightless for a moment as they were blasted to the side.

"Damage report?" he yelled out.

"We've got significant structural damage to one... no, two starboard legs." Kalen paused. "And we've still got hull integrity, but I have no idea how long that's going to last if we keep getting hit like this."

Mark looked ahead and finally saw the scout team behind one of the larger dunes. Turner's mech stood in front of them, clearly leaning to one side, compensating for a badly damaged leg. Their support truck was below, intact, and running. Out beyond them, the enemy mechs stood firm in their relentless assault.

"Everyone, get into a defensive position around the scout team," Mark called out over the radio. "We've got to hold this position."

"Sir, reporting for duty," Brooke's voice came through the radio. Mark was momentarily lightheaded at the sound of her voice. "Before you ask, everyone is alive. Turner is down in the truck with the others. He took a major hit while piloting the mech. It's pretty banged up, but it can move, and all of its weapons are still functional."

"Brooke." Mark switched to a private channel. "It's good to hear your voice."

"Sure, it's good to hear yours too," Brooke said. "But can we do this later? I'm not sure we have a lot of time."

"Sure, you're right." He switched back to the team channel. "Is everyone ready to move out? We'll cover you."

"Yes, sir," Brooke said. "Like I said, this mech can't move at any real speed, but it can move."

"All right, we're moving out team. Continue to fire at will when you have clear shots. Retreat out of the range of their guns and we'll regroup once we're clear. Keep your guns hot and—" An explosion rocked the mech and cut him off.

"Mark, they're advancing on us," Kalen said. "I have no idea why. It doesn't make any sense."

"What the hell do we do?" Mark asked within the command deck. "I can't lose anyone. I can't..."

"You have to give a command, Mark," Barkley said, while still trying to get a lock on an approaching mech. "These people are counting on you to do something. They need direction or this whole thing is going to come apart."

Mark turned to his screen and examined the enemy forces. The six mechs were now only five, but they were all fully armed and quickly making their way toward them. His team was also firing, peppering the advancing mechs and the ground around them with rounds. The explosions and the frequent lightning created a series of strobing images on his retinas. He remembered a lesson from one of his courses, and the image of a wave came to him.

"We have to concentrate our fire and hold this ground," Mark said to those on the command deck. "We need to take these mechs down before they can reach this hill, or they'll pick us off as we try to retreat."

He opened the radio channel to give his orders.

"Everyone focus on the two mechs furthest from the center of their formation. We'll force them to come together." He checked his screen and marked the units. "Keep covered as much as possible, but we have to pour everything we've got into these guys."

His command was understood, and everyone fluidly shifted focus to the mechs he had tagged. The advancing mechs were newer and better equipped than theirs. After all, their mechs were just training mechs, pieced together from the rusting heaps of other machines. But perhaps the pieces, forged together by their class, and the ones before them, would hold together long enough to maintain their position.

The gun on the top of his mech fired at a rapid pace. Mark armed the other weapons systems and launched his own volley of rounds at the targets.

He was just about to launch another barrage when one of the tagged enemy mechs stumbled forward. It had lost one of its legs completely, and the momentum it was carrying caused it to pitch forward violently into the earth. In a last effort, the pilot

of the mech engaged the jump thrusters, but this only acceler-
ated its descent. The plan was working. The remaining enemy
mechs involuntarily began drifting closer together.

"Next!" Mark called out to his team. He tagged a lumbering
Jotun class mech.

They shifted focus and were able to bring it down quickly. It
burst open, its core erupting with white-hot flames, momentarily blinding him. The force of the explosion caused another
advancing mech to stumble. Mark's team was able to bring that
one down before it could regain its footing. The two remaining
mechs attempted to break off in new directions. One made a
break for open desert, and the other attempted to take cover behind a dune.

"Focus fire on the one behind the dune," Mark shouted
through the radio.

The concentrated fire on the stationary location was too
much for the dune to be much help, and another blinding white
flash proved the mech was gone. The one that broke off turned
suddenly and engaged its jump thrusters, taking to the sky. It
took this opportunity to fire down on Mark and his team, unhindered by terrain. When it came back down, it was only a few
hundred yards away. Mark realized that his team was also too
close together, too easy for the enemy to target up this close. If
any one of their mechs was hit and its core was compromised,
the whole group could be destroyed.

"Break formation. Get some distance between us," Mark ordered. "We're almost done, just keep it up."

The team broke from what little cover they'd had, and the
scattering mechs were too much for the enemy to handle. It

didn't seem to know where to shoot and began firing randomly as it turned and ran.

Mark's team advanced, firing short, concentrated bursts at the enemy mech. It sprayed the landscape as it attempted to retreat. Its shots came close sometimes, but only the occasional round connected. Mark felt the gun on top fire. Moments later, the fleeing mech erupted in flames, scattering parts over a wide area.

The cheers that came through the radio were almost instant. Mark breathed heavily and let his arms relax at his sides. His fingers were freezing from the frenzied activity. They'd done it. Out in the distance, flames dotted the landscape, the remnants of the destroyed mechs.

As he looked over the battlefield, he noticed some movement on the far ridge, and his body went as cold as his fingertips. He asked Kalen to run a scan but already knew what it was. Another group of mechs appeared on his screen with red triangles. He didn't have time to count them, but knew it was too many for his team to face right now. The enemy's main force must have turned back for support. He'd led his team into an ambush. The flashes he saw on the horizon then weren't lightning. His team was being fired at by an overwhelming tide of mechs, and they stood no chance out in the open.

"Run," Mark said over the radio. His voice was quiet. "Get out of here as fast as you can. We have to go."

His team was far enough out that they might make it to the foothills to mount a defense if the enemy pursued. Mark saw his units on his display begin to fade back as they retreated toward the rocky point to the east. He turned his mech to retreat with them, and then remembered that Brooke was still trapped inside her damaged mech. As the others fled, Mark brought his hands back up to the controls of his mech. He turned back and began to fire at the horizon with everything he had. He could feel the gun up top begin it's steady rhythm and knew that Barkley was still working his station.

An incoming wave of rounds slipped through the sky and raced toward them. The rockets left bright trails that looked like the tentacles of some ancient beast as they raced toward him. Then, all at once, the rounds began landing with the rain all around them. Brooke was unleashing everything she had at the units on the ridge even as small rounds ricocheted off her mech.

"Go," Brooke said over the radio on a private channel. She sounded sure and calm. "There is no way I'm going to keep up. I'll try to draw their fire for as long as I can. I love you, Mark."

She had already begun a slow advance on the ridge before Mark could stop her.

"No," Mark said. "I'm not leaving you. I'm not going to let this happen."

But it already was. Mark watched as one of the enemy command mechs on the ridge fired a round from its powerful gun on top. He dialed up the power to the legs of his mech with a reflexive movement and engaged the limited jump jets. His mech surged toward the incoming round with a sickening lurch, attempting to block the round.

Then a joint in one of the damaged legs, he didn't know which, was overstrained. A sharp metallic pop rang through the entire frame of the mech, signaling a major mechanical failure. His unit buckled and fell to the ground, throwing up chunks of earth outside his windshield. Through the glass, he saw the round slice through the rain and connect with Brooke's mech, square in its center mass. It was jolted backward from the impact. The round must have been impact delayed because nothing happened for an agonizing moment. Then, just as Mark placed his hand on the cracked front windshield of his mech, the landscape was painted with searing white light.

The force of the explosion rocked Mark's crumpled mech, pushing him back into his seat. He fumbled for his radio and gripped it in his fist as he waited for the burning afterimage to clear from his vision.

"No!" he screamed through his radio, his final link to her. "No, no. Brooke!"

His throat began to burn from the cries he pumped through the air. Maybe she could hear him if he screamed loudly enough. Then Kalen was pulling at him, trying to get him free from the harness of the pilot seat.

"We have to get out of here!" Kalen yelled, trying to get through to him. "They're coming, Mark! We need to go."

Kalen and Barkley continued to pull at him, and Mark threw his arms out. He punched at them until they backed away, and then began working to bring the mech back up. Kalen and Barkley watched as Mark fumbled with the controls. They were knocked to the ground when another round impacted the top of the command module. Barkley turned and grabbed his radio transmitter ordered the rest of the crew to evacuate the Maratus. The two trucks were still with them and could fit them all if they were packed in tightly.

"Mark, we have to leave," Kalen said calmly.

"Go then," Mark said.

Kalen and Barkley retreated to an emergency hatch set into the bulkhead. It fell away heavily, leaving an opening out into the driving rain. They attempted one last desperate plea for him to leave, but Mark could hear none of the words. They climbed through the hole and dropped out into the storm outside.

Mark was finally able to wrangle the systems of the mech and forced it to begin rising back up. Without one of its legs, and badly damaged from the continued barrage, Mark only managed to get the unit into a lurching crawl. He pushed it toward the enemy forces on the horizon, firing everything that would still function. Without systems helping to stabilize the command module, he felt every step the mech took for the massive impact that it was. The deck rattled and jolted as he fired every gun that still had ammunition. Alarms went off, and he let them scream; perhaps by the end, they would match the intensity of his own.

As he continued to advance, the forces on the horizon seemed to be getting further away. They must not have thought it worth their time to continue a fight with what was left of Mark's forces.

"Get back here you sons of bitches!" He screamed over a high-frequency open channel. Anyone for hundreds of miles could hear him. "I'm right here!"

An explosion sent burning shrapnel arcing through the sky in front of him. He pushed through the smoke, firing the gun on top blindly into the distance. His mech took one more step and then suddenly gave up on him. Alarms inside the cockpit reached a crescendo as he watched the ground come up to meet him. The lights on his display became a twisted smear of colors as tears obscured his vision. His mech crashed into the ground and everything went dark.

He sat inside the darkened command deck, still strapped into the pilot's chair. Rain streamed down the front glass, and the rumbling of natural thunder again filled his ears. On the horizon, he could see the last enemy mech as it turned and disappeared back over the ridge.

CHAPTER 22

Mark quietly unbuckled himself from his seat and stood on the command deck. A persistent ringing in Mark's ears punctuated the silence around him, a holdover from the explosions that had blasted the mech. He tried to control his breathing as he tried to decide what to do next. The wind blew rain in from the hatch Barkley and Kalen had used to exit. Flashes of lightning continued to paint the landscape in brief moments of light, throwing his shadow against the far bulkhead.

Mark walked to the open hatch and looked out into the storm. Across the desert, he could see the destruction left behind following the brief battle. At least two of his team's mechs had been taken apart in the barrage. Their hulking masses were still engulfed in flames. Further out were the scattered remains of the mechs Mark's team had managed to destroy.

He descended to the ground using metal rungs on the outside of the hull and slowly walked in the rain back toward the wreckage of Brooke's mech. He left behind the massive remains of the Maratus, now a crumpled tangle of legs and debris. How he had managed to make it out alive was a small miracle, one he hoped was possible for the mech Brooke was in as well. As he got closer, he could see that these hopes were misplaced. The Kapu had been reduced to little more than a pile of shattered parts. Water poured from the clouds above, and his hot tears mixed with the cool rain on his face. He took great heaving breaths as he tried to force his way through the ruined mech, searching for any sign of Brooke.

Flickering orange light from flames illuminated the area, punctuated by the occasional flash from the storm. He reached a large section of the hull and saw a long, clean weld. It had been laid down with dedicated precision and care. He reached out and pulled hard against the piece of the hull, trying to work his way further in. Fire had heated it enough that his hands came away burned.

Mark screamed, more in emotional than physical pain, and pulled on it again. His hands slipped away from it, and he sank to his knees in front of the mech. He clenched his hands against his uniform, soaked through with rainwater, to soothe them. He lowered his head and slowly swayed back and forth.

"I love you too," he whispered.

When he opened his eyes, he saw a glint in the firelight. Something on a short length of broken chain was half buried in the sand. On his hands and knees, Mark crawled to it and pulled it out. In his burned hands, he held the necklace he had given Brooke as a graduation gift.

He laid down in the sand on his side, facing the wreckage for the heat, and clutched the penny close to his chest. Then, bringing the coin to his lips, he pressed them to the smooth surface and tried to remember her as clearly as he could. He was with her in a forest, a place they'd never been able to go. A place they would never be able to go. She was above him, her long brown hair flowing down. Her fierce green eyes were mirrored by the dense canopy of leaves above her. Mark reached out to her but felt only the coarse sand of the desert.

He thought about getting up and trying to catch up with the others. He thought about standing up to search for anyone else that may have been lost in the attack. He thought about these things, but he couldn't force himself to get up. Not yet.

~

It all happened so quickly. At first, it looked like Mark and the others had won. Zak watched as the last two enemy mechs were brought down with concentrated fire. Then it all went wrong. Before Zak even knew where it was coming from, explosions had begun tearing into their mechs, into his friends.

The overwhelming enemy force on the horizon had been gone for over an hour now. The remnants of Zak's team, what was left of them, had headed off in the direction of a range of short rocky foothills. He was still holding the pistol, and the woman was lying a few yards away, occasionally letting out a low moan of pain.

Zak broke his gaze from the wreckage below and looked down at the pistol in his hand. He should kill her and move on, he thought. The people she had aligned herself with were responsible for hat had just happened. She was responsible, at least in some small way, for whoever was dead now.

He turned his gaze from the gun to the woman. She was lying on her side, and she had one leg drawn close to her body, as if the pressure would somehow heal her injury. He looked at her and tried to project the pain and anger he was feeling onto her. He should have been able to kill her. He could have simply fired a bullet into her head and that could have relieved the pressure building up inside him. He looked at her, and, against his will, his feelings softened to pity. The anger, sorrow, and intense pain flowed away from her and, with nowhere else to go, seeped back into him.

"Fuck!" he screamed in her direction. "Why? I don't know—"

He brought both of his hands up and pounded at the sides of his skull. The gun in his right hand struck his head, sending jolts of pain through him. He shouted again, this time a wordless shriek. He breathed heavily and stared down at the woman, trying again to bring his anger to a focal point on her. When this failed again, he turned away instead.

"I needed to see if she's still there." The woman said it so quietly he wasn't sure she'd said anything. "Even if there's nothing left. I have to go back. I have to go back."

Zak didn't turn back around, and instead walked to one of the crates that came with them as they tumbled from the truck. Its contents were spread out. Zak shoved the pistol into the holster on his thigh and gathered anything that looked useful. He walked over to the woman, who tensed up as he approached, and tossed a packet of pills in front of her. From what he could tell, it was enough painkiller to help her with the pain and get her moving.

"Take these," he said. "I'm leaving in an hour, with or without you."

Zak left again and returned with a pack of supplies. Most of them were medical, but there were a few rations in the crates that he was able to salvage. He crouched down and cut along her pant leg to expose the injury. The leg looked straight, which was a good sign. He pressed in a few places to see if he got a reaction that might indicate a break and she remained silent. When he worked her knee joint, however, she let out a short gasp of pain. He nodded and pulled out a loose tube from the pack.

"This is going to…" He started to warn her. "Well, you'll see."

When it was positioned correctly, he activated a switch at one end of the tube. The tube contracted and inflated, immobilizing the joint and applying pressure. The woman cried out in pain, but she cut off her scream and glared up at Zak. She took one of the painkillers and swallowed it.

"From what I can see, nothing is broken," Zak said. "You might have ligament tears or something, but I'm not a doctor. This should be enough to let you move. If we're going to make it down, we have to move now. I'll do what I can to keep you alive. But, if you don't do what I say, I'll leave you here."

"Why?" the woman asked. She looked down at the wreckage, where fires continued to burn. "Why are you doing this?"

"I don't know," Zak said.

"I need to get back." She wore a look of desperation he hadn't expected. "I need to see if she's alive. I have to go back. Please."

"They're gone." Zak didn't want to think back on it, but it seemed he had no choice. "I saw it all. There was no one left."

"You don't know that." Her voice was strained, as she struggled against the pain in her leg. "Please, I need to know."

She looked at him, as if searching his face for some clue as to what he might be thinking. He looked away and reached a hand

300

down toward her. She took it, and Zak helped her into a standing position. Zak watched as she struggled not to fall back down. She tried to take a step forward and her hand found a place on Zak's shoulder. He flinched at her touch but allowed her to stabilize herself. After another step, her knees buckled, and Zak caught her. He placed her arm roughly around his shoulders and one of his arms around her waist. Together they walked slowly down the dune, toward the wreckage below.

Mark stayed lying in the fetal position for a long time. He couldn't tell how long, but he knew he had fallen asleep at least once, because the storm had subsided a bit when he looked up. The lightning was more distant now. He sat up and forced his hand to open and reveal the penny he still held. His hand was stiff, and the burns were painful. Thankfully he hadn't made another attempt to move the metal hull, or he'd likely have injured himself severely. As it was, the burns hurt, but didn't make it impossible for him to use his hands. Mark stood and walked around the wreckage, now dark and smoking. He made no attempt now to get at the inside of Brooke's mech. Another mech, fallen and blackened by flames, lay close by. In between them, he saw what was left of a blasted truck.

Mark walked toward it, knowing already what he would find. A couple of crates lay open near the back of the truck. He looked at what remained inside one of them. Bandages and other medical supplies, once neatly organized, were haphazardly strewn in the sand. This was Zak's truck. Mark waited for tears to force their way out again. He waited for his knees to give out and for his lungs to begin another alternating war of sobbing against breathing. Nothing came. He stared blankly at the open container of medical supplies, and he was surprised by emptiness. He felt as if his ribcage had been hollowed out, left bare. He stood for a long time before turning and walking back to the looming wreckage of the Maratus. He still clutched the penny in one hand, its length of chain swaying with each step.

Mark gathered what he could to start a small fire, and once he was able to get it started, he stared silently into the dancing orange flames. The heat and the persistent crackling reminded him of the battle, but also of the bonfire party that happened what felt like inside someone else's life. He remembered the way the firelight had danced along her face, highlighting curves and features he had never taken enough time to fully admire. He remembered the orange sparks flying as she welded armor onto a mech just like the one she died in. And he remembered the brilliant sunset, back at the Academy, where she focused so intently on their game of chess that she didn't notice him staring at her.

As he stared into the flames, the light around him increased for some reason. He looked up, confused, to see that the sun had begun to kiss the tips of a distant mountain range. On the underside of the retreating storm, brilliant pink light fanned out from the direction of the sunset, filling the sky completely. Gold and orange hues mixed, and a final shaft of unhindered sunlight bathed the area. Mark stared as the sun slowly moved behind the mountains in the distance. His eyes strained from looking at it directly, but Mark watched until the final brilliant pinpricks of light disappeared, casting a cold shadow over him. The brilliant hues continued their slow transitions in the sky above him, even while he sat below in darkness.

The colors lost their vibrance, giving way to the grey of the coming night. Then, as the final pink strands of the day left the clouds, he heard shuffling footsteps from behind him. Turning slowly, he put his hand down near his sidearm holster out of instinct. He was just about to draw his weapon when he saw Zak stumble from behind the smoking remnants of a downed mech. Then, as Zak came more clearly into view, Mark could see that he was helping the rebel woman walk.

Any rational thought was burned away by the sight of Zak's arms around the rebel woman. Mark drew his weapon, and with a trembling hand, he aimed it at the two figures in front of him.

~

For a brief moment, Zak saw confusion flit across Mark's face. Then it transformed into a grief driven rage. With tears streaming down his face, Mark pointed his pistol at both of them.

"Why is she here?" Mark asked in a quiet scream. "Zak, why the *fuck* is she here?"

Zak didn't know what to say. His emotions were still sorting themselves, but he knew that something seismic had begun to shift inside him. Grief and anger told him to throw the woman at Mark's feet, to allow some form of justice to be served for the ambush he'd just witnessed. Guilt and his growing self-loathing demanded that he protect her with his life. These two conflicting urges manifested as a complete lack of action.

"I don't know," was all Zak was able to say. "I don't know, Mark."

"Brooke is dead," an answer to an unasked question.

Moments passed, and something changed in the air between them. Zak made the decision to stay with the rebel woman, to get her back to whatever was left of her family home. He could no longer pursue the broken path that had led him there.

"She lost everything, Mark. Everything," Zak said, trying to explain himself. "If there is even a chance that someone is left alive back at that house, I need to go. Just let us go. I have to make it right."

"Make it right," Mark laughed. An ugly, unsettling sound. "Sure, go off and play hero."

"That's not—" Zak started to say.

"Go now," Mark whispered, aiming the gun squarely at Zak now. "Go, before I kill both of you."

The smoking hulk of the command mech loomed behind him like a fallen god. Its eight massive legs were like the collapsed buttresses of an ancient cathedral. Zak didn't know where Mark's path would lead, but he knew that it could only be to more ruin. Zak had chosen to follow along that path himself for too long, it was time to face what was behind him.

"I'm so sorry," Zak said, and began to back away.

Mark screamed, a deeply troubling, wordless cry. His eyes were dark, and there was no reason in them. With each hacking breath Mark took, his aim wavered. Zak was afraid that he would shoot, even as they continued to retreat. He turned and pulled the woman along, leaving Mark alone. His screams echoed among the twisted, burned ruins of massive war machines, like the pleading voices of the dead.

EPILOGUE

Alison woke early in the morning and headed for the kitchen. She wanted to exist in the house for a few minutes before the general fuss about her departure in the next few days became unavoidable. The night before, she'd spent time on the porch with her father. They'd sat in the semicircle of warm light cast by the bulb mounted above the door. Invariably, when they got to reminiscing out in the backyard, he'd eventually tell her stories about the Decline and how he'd had to abandon the house for a few years. The house was old and had been in their family for generations.

The evacuations started when her father was a small child, no older than Eva was now, he'd told her. His family left the home with nearly all their possessions still inside it. They'd retreated with the thousands of others in the area to the fortified government encampments. He'd often interject with some quip about his parents never knowing when to stop trusting authority.

The government had touted the Protection Sites as areas of safety. In reality, they were a measure put in place to keep civilian populations under control while they handled any rogue elements. If families were locked inside the Protection Sites, they weren't a threat. So, the family had ridden out the worst of the decline under so called government protection. Only when Alison had been born, her father would always look at her as he recounted this part, only after that did he think about returning to the house.

He only vaguely alluded to the pain of the decline. How his own parents had been conscripted into the civil defense forces and fed into the war effort like bullets in an extended magazine. He only made passing mention of the countless deaths from otherwise treatable illnesses that swept through the protected zones.

No, what he always ended up focusing on as he wound the story down was the house. How he'd slipped away from his duties on the farms and worked on it to get it back in a livable condition. He brought in others who worked on the other homes in the area, and they'd built a community again.

The sun came over the tree line outside, casting its dappled glow through the broad windows on the eastern side of the house. The whole house seemed to radiate with golden light, and Alison hopped up and sat on the counter next to the sink. The old laminate creaked beneath her weight, but she trusted that it would hold her. The house was the only home she knew. Others still lived in the government housing tracts, but she was lucky to live out here. It was illegal of course, but her parents and the others in the community had long since worked out some arrangement with the government patrols.

Something crashed to the ground in Eva's room down the hall and Alison smiled. She was probably up to something in there, waiting for the call to breakfast. This was what Alison missed when she was away on her courier routes. This was what she was fighting for; what she'd given up in order to preserve.

Her next assignment would be a long one. She was headed to the north. Luckily, after that, she was coming back down to make a quick trip out to Taycher Mechanized Armor Base. She would go gather some intel from a repeat informant. If she was quick enough, she would be able to spend few days at the house again before another assignment came through.

"Allie," a soft voice came from the hall. "Come look what I made."

Alison smiled and looked toward Eva's door. It was open just a sliver, but she could see a pair of honey-colored eyes peeking out. She pushed off the counter and walked to Eva's room. The door opened, revealing an admittedly impressive sight inside. Eva had managed to construct a small structure with all of the furniture and bedding in her room.

"It's my secret base," Eva said as she lifted one of the sheets aside. "Only super-secret agents allowed inside."

"Are you sure I can be trusted with this kind of responsibility?" Alison asked.

"Uh huh," Eva ducked into the fort without another word.

Alison lifted the flap and crawled inside. It was cramped, but Eva had made sure to leave a spot big enough for her to sit down. She sat and looked at Eva expectantly. Eva looked up at her with the same expression.

"What's the mission?" Eva asked.

"You're in charge here," Alison laughed. "You invited me, remember?"

"Please, Allie?" Eva sounded a bit whiny, but not quite to a level that was annoying. "You said you'd play with me before you left."

Had she said that? Alison wasn't sure, but it seemed like the kind of thing she might promise and forget about in the rush to get herself packed up.

"Okay," Alison put on a gruff voice, one that made Eva smile. "Your mission, should you choose to accept it, is to stop the evil Robot King from smashing the Fairy Kingdom."

"Oh no!" Eva looked genuinely distraught, leaning into the story. "What about the Rainbow Warriors?"

"Oh, they're all here too," Alison searched her brain for any memory of the organization. Had she told a story about Rainbow Warriors before, or was this some new emergent group Eva had just created? "How many do you think you'll need Agent E?"

"Just two," Eva said with authority. "Agent E and Agent A can take care of it."

They played for a while. So long that, by the end, the story had developed many layers and Alison had begun to lose track of the plot. The Robot King and his villainous crew of stomping bad guys had already been vanquished and returned half a dozen times. Alison's mother called from the kitchen and Eva stopped to listen. She held a stick in one hand that she'd been pretending was a sword.

"I don't want you to go," Eva said. "I like when you're here."

"I like when I'm here too," Alison said, pulling off a blanket that had become her robe during their play. "But you know I have to leave."

"Why can't you just stay here and stay with us?" Eva tossed her stick on the floor of the room. It was littered with the remnants of the fort she'd built.

309

"Because someone has to fight the real Robot King." This was as far as Alison felt comfortable going with the conversation. Eva knew better than to talk about Alison with anyone outside the family. But it was still important to make sure she didn't hold too much vital information in her young brain.

"I'll tell you what," Alison took both of Eva's hands in hers and looked her in the eyes. "What if I tell you a big secret?"

Eva's face lit up with a broad smile and she nodded vigorously.

"Okay, so there is another secret base that you can tell no one else about." She tried to remember the details and found them locked away behind layers of adolescent grief. "There's a super-duper secret base just to the west of the house, through the trees. I built it when I was little, just like you, and it's still there. It'll be like a secret place for just you and me."

In truth, her father certainly knew about the little hut she'd made in the trees when she was a child. It was only a few hundred yards from the house, but to her small self, it had felt like a world away. Eva was big enough now that the hut could serve a similar function for her.

"Do you know which way is west?" Alison asked.

"That way," Eva pointed without having to think too hard about it.

"Yep, that's right. If you go that way for a ways, you'll find it. That's Rainbow Warrior Base One. It's the central base and you're the agent I'm leaving in charge."

Her mother called again from the kitchen and Alison let go of Eva's hands.

"You keep the base safe and I'll be back before you know it," Alison stood and opened the bedroom door. "Let's go get some breakfast before Mom discovers the mess we made in here."

They both left the room and went to eat at the small wooden table in the kitchen. Her mother and father were already sitting down, smiling at the sight of them coming from Eva's room. Alison felt uncomfortable under their gaze, like she'd somehow stepped into a role they secretly wished she'd fill out full-time. But her place was out in the desert. Her network of courier routes connected cells across the western United Entities. Sure, if she stopped showing up, they'd find someone else, but that would take time. If they were ever going to bring down the United Entities, they needed every piece of the organization to be working at full efficiency. It would take a machine of superior precision to dismantle what had already been constructed around them. That machine couldn't have pieces falling out whenever the warmth of home got too alluring.

If Eva were to stand a chance of having any sense of freedom, Alison and the rest of the Harbingers of the Fall would have to do their part flawlessly. She would have to leave and make her rendezvous in the north. Information traffic in the region had been picking up lately. Something was happening, and she needed to be ready.

Alison looked over the table at her family. Her father, broad and strong, had managed to forge this safe bubble in the world of uncertain horror that existed all around them. But at any moment it could collapse. Her mother, quiet but never wavering, was focused on bringing up Eva to be the best person she could be. And then there was Eva herself, a pure and elegant representation of everything Alison was fighting for. But maybe Eva wouldn't want that title. After all, she was just a child. There was really nothing particularly emblematic or noteworthy about her. She liked to swing, read, and do somersaults in the tall grass. She wasn't some mythological construct, just a kid.

But Alison saw a symbol all the same. She'd given up all of this in order to protect it. She'd managed to find some small way to push back against the tide of malice that threatened every child just like Eva. She would leave soon and continue her small contribution to the Fall by ferrying information further than she'd ever been before. She was headed to a small mountain town called Ember Springs. But first, she would eat her eggs and smile as her father told bad jokes in the glow of the morning sun.

ACKNOWLEDGEMENTS

I've been working on the From Rust series for over ten years. A lot happens in ten years. I could list every important life event here, but I'm not writing an autobiography. What I'm trying to say, I suppose, is that I have a lot of people to thank.

First of all, thank you to my partner Deanna. You put up with my erratic sleep schedule that often had me writing feverishly at 3 a.m. and beyond. You somehow understand not only how to provide the space in our life for me to create, but also how to reel me back in when I drift too far offshore. We tackle the big waves together.

My kiddos, James and Carlene, you guys don't know how much you've helped me grow. The story I started ten years ago has been indelibly shaped by the experience of being your dad. I am so lucky.

Kaleigh. On an obscure message board created by a musician we both enjoy, you took a chance on an internet stranger and agreed to read and work through my manuscripts. While your insights weren't only limited to grammar of course, it cannot be understated that without your help, every single comma in this book would be in the wrong place.

To my team at Vulpine Press. David, thank you for responding to my email and taking a chance on a debut as ambitious as mine. I wrote three books and you saw that as an opportunity, where others saw risk. Lisa, your guidance through this process and incisive suggestions have turned this story into something I feel confident in releasing to the world.

And my friends and family who have, to varying degrees of intensity, put up with my rambling on this project for more than ten years. Thank you. I won't be stopping any time soon. I have more stories to tell.

Finally, I'd like to acknowledge the countless minds that have shaped my understanding of storytelling. Fiction, I know, rarely forms in a vacuum. I owe much to the stories that have shaped me, and I hope that this one can someday shape someone else.

Daniel James Clark was born on a U.S. Navy base in Naples, Italy, and after a number of brief stops across the world early in life, settled in Henderson, Nevada, a suburb of Las Vegas. He began writing early but didn't begin seeking publication until 2019. His first short story, *A Sky Made Black*, was published in the Bell Press anthology *Futures* in November of 2021 and received a nomination for a Pushcart Prize. His first major publication is the *From Rust* trilogy of military science fiction mech novels from Vulpine Press. When not writing, he divides his time between professional photojournalism, nonprofit website management and design, and homemaking for his wife and two children.